How in the blazes had a simple kiss turned so wrenching?

Fletcher knew what Eirene would say. They were meant for one another, their futures bound by a dream or whatever hocus-pocus controlled people's futures.

But it was going to take more than one remarkable, quite poignant kiss to convince him that was true.

Two kisses perhaps? Four or seven? No, nothing would be proved by kissing her seven times. If he did that, it would be because he was in love with her.

A love resulting in the logical progression of their relationship, not destiny.

The greatest mystery in this situation was that he was giving the idea of being in love any thought at all.

CAROL ARENS

Meeting Her Promised Viscount

Recycling programs for this product may not exist in your area.

ISBN-13: 978-1-335-72375-8

Meeting Her Promised Viscount

Copyright © 2023 by Carol Arens

For questions and comments about the quality of this book, please contact us at CustomerService@Harlequin.com.

Harlequin Enterprises ULC
22 Adelaide St. West, 41st Floor
Toronto, Ontario M5H 4E3, Canada
www.Harlequin.com

Printed in U.S.A.

Carol Arens delights in tossing fictional characters into hot water, watching them steam and then giving them a happily-ever-after. When she is not writing, she enjoys spending time with her family, beach camping or lounging about a mountain cabin. At home, she enjoys playing with her grandchildren and gardening. During rare spare moments, you will find her snuggled up with a good book. Carol enjoys hearing from readers at carolarens@yahoo.com or on Facebook.

Books by Carol Arens

Harlequin Historical

The Cowboy's Cinderella
Western Christmas Brides
"A Kiss from the Cowboy"
The Rancher's Inconvenient Bride
A Ranch to Call Home
A Texas Christmas Reunion
The Earl's American Heiress
Rescued by the Viscount's Ring
The Making of Baron Haversmere
The Viscount's Yuletide Bride
To Wed a Wallflower
A Victorian Family Christmas
"A Kiss Under the Mistletoe"
The Viscount's Christmas Proposal
Meeting Her Promised Viscount

The Rivenhall Weddings

Inherited as the Gentleman's Bride
In Search of a Viscountess
A Family for the Reclusive Baron

Visit the Author Profile page
at Harlequin.com for more titles.

Dedicated to the memory of Bobbi Pearson.
We will always cherish your bright and happy spirit.

Chapter One

Warrenstoke Estate—June 1875

'Mother, I do not know why you like such dreadful stories.' Eirene closed the cover of the book with a snap. It was not as easy to close her mind on the dark, mysterious raven in the tale.

'Why, I suppose it is because at my age, it is the only adventure I have. Mr Poe does keep one perched at the edge of her chair.'

'Running out of the library, more like it.'

Her mother smiled as brightly as if they had been reading a merry tale about Father Christmas. 'Oh, my dear…you do know that *The Raven* was inspired by one of the stories of our very own Charles Dickens?'

'Then tomorrow we shall read something by him.' Eirene stood, setting the book aside.

Her mother lifted her cheek for a kiss. Mother's cheek was sunken, her skin lined with ill health.

The physician believed that living in the fresh country air would do her a great deal of good. It might be true. During the year they had been living at Warrenstoke her mental attitude had improved and she could take several steps without becoming too winded. In spite of her mother's admiration of Edgar Allen Poe's dark works, she seemed happy. Far more spirited than she had been in London.

'Run along, my sweet girl, and enjoy the rest of your day.'

A walk on the manor grounds was just what she needed.

Coming outside, she stood on the back terrace, took a deep breath of summer air and smiled.

It was a day among days with sunshine making the sky bright blue and birds singing like happy little spirits in the trees. Not a raven in sight.

Eirene wanted to twirl down the steps. Since there was no good reason not to, she caught her skirt in her hands and did just that.

Once on the garden path, she walked along, singing. She was far from being an accomplished chanteuse, but she enjoyed it anyway.

'Remember yourself, Eirene. Who you are.' Percy! Drat, she had not noticed him lounging on a terrace chair. 'And do look your best for tea. I have invited guests.'

It grated on her the way he acted as if he were already Viscount Warrenstoke. As if she was already his wife and could tell her how to act.

The only claim he had on Warrenstoke was as heir presumptive. A title he was likely to gain since the late Viscount's eldest son, born of his first wife, had passed away a year ago and his second son had disappeared along with his mother many years before, never to be heard of again. But there was a search going on for him and until possession of the title was determined one way or another, she was not going to wed anyone.

Father was the one who dealt with Percy most of the time. The Larkin cousin had arrived at Warrenstoke soon after Henry's death and was quite unprepared to act as Viscount.

Assuming he would be one day, Father had been training him in what was required of the title.

'Of course, Percy,' she said pleasantly because he was easier to deal with when things went as he wished them to. 'I will see you at teatime.'

Until then she had hours to spend rambling about the estate she had visited and loved since she was a baby.

Father and Viscount Warrenstoke had been the greatest of friends from the time they were boys right up until the night, a few years ago, when Warrenstoke died in Father's arms.

Grass and flowers brushed her skirt while she strolled across the meadow. The mingled fragrances floated up. She breathed in so deeply that she could nearly taste summer.

Being at Warrenstoke at this time of year was as close to heaven as one could get, in her opinion. Her parents' opinion as well, which was one of the reasons they had left London and visited the estate so often. Their home in that vast city was as elegant as any in town, but not nearly as wonderful as it was here. Her own family had had a country estate at one time, but the Viscount a couple of generations back had been forced to sell it for reasons now forgotten.

No one minded, not with Warrenstoke seeming more like home than London did.

There was far more to it than love of the countryside. Father, Mother and James grew up like family. They enjoyed one another's company too much to be apart for long.

Once she wed the Warrenstoke heir, they would never have to leave here again. And now with her mother's health to be considered, Eirene was glad not to have to go back to the city.

Since the day of her birth it had been the plan for this to be their home. She was grateful for it.

Eirene climbed the gentle rise of a grassy hill. She sat down at the crest, leaning back against the trunk of a great tree whose shade spread far and wide. Speckles of sunshine and shade made patterns on her skirt when leaves shifted in the breeze.

This was her favourite spot on the estate. She had spent a great deal of time here with her friend, Henry.

Gazing down at the meadows and hills, she could nearly see him, his blond hair glinting in sunshine while he dashed about with his friends and she tagging along behind them. Although he had been several years older than she was, he patiently tolerated her presence. Henry was a kind and gentle person. She had always been happy that their marriage would unite their families and their fortunes.

She missed Henry…and now there was Percy to take his place.

It might be unkind to think it, but Percy was not much fun.

But it did not matter so much. Not as long as she and her parents would be able to call Warrenstoke home.

None of that would happen until the search for the heir apparent was exhausted. On the one hand she hoped it would be soon. On the other hand…well, Percy.

Never mind. She would enjoy this moment as fully as she knew how. Which was quite fully.

She gave a great yawn and did not bother to politely cover her mouth. Yawns were ever so much more expressive that way.

Lying back on the grass, she closed her eyes.

Standing on a dock, the ocean swirling darkly about the pilings, Eirene gazed at ship coming into the harbour, its full sails white and billowing. There must be a breeze, but she did not feel it. Did not hear it either.

She was dreaming, she knew she was, yet this was not a typical naptime dream. It was a seeing dream—some people would call it a prophetic one. That was what she would call it and she was the one dreaming it. This was not her first dream of the kind so she knew it meant to show her something.

But a ship in the fog? What could it be? Without moving her feet, she somehow ended up at the edge of the pier. Silently, the ship came alongside. It did not stop and she glided beside it, looking up.

A man walked along the rail, keeping pace with her and gazing down. His hair was long, blond and wild looking. It rippled back from his face in the breeze that could not be felt. His eyes were quite blue, intensely so. The way he looked at her gave her heart the oddest quiver. It was as if he saw her soul.

His face was rough with beard stubble. She did not believe he was a gentleman of polite society. Then all at once he smiled down at her and laughed, but she did not hear the sound. He had a pair of dimples which in no way made him appear soft…no, rather he looked a rascal to the bone. To accentuate his rough image, a smear of blood welled on his bottom lip.

No, not a gentleman. But he was something to her. Someone important.

In the second she knew who, he pantomimed a kiss across the rail and the dream dissolved.

She sat up with a start, her heart pounding and her blood racing.

The man was her husband!

And he was as far from Percy as a man could be.

One day she was going to meet this dream man, recognise him at first glance.

She stood up, shaking the loose grass from her skirt. She would need to hurry if she did not wish to be late for tea.

All the way back to the manor she tried to convince herself she was mistaken about the dream because… really? Why would she wed such a man? She preferred mannerly men, kind and gentle men. Men like Henry had been.

Even Percy, who could be exacting at times, seemed more refined than the sailor.

She was meant to wed Viscount Warrenstoke, not a coarse sailor.

Very clearly, this one time the dream had been wrong.

Fletcher Holloway stood by the ship's rail while the *Morning Star* entered the Port of London.

'I have the oddest sense someone is watching me,' he told his uncle, Hal Holloway, who stood beside him, keeping a practised eye on the ships coming out of the port.

It was not that the man whom his uncle had hired to

pilot the ship when Fletcher was not at the helm wasn't competent, but long habit made him watchful. It was what came of owning the *Morning Star* for longer than dirt was old. This ship, while sound, was not up to modern standards. Loved though. No ship was better cared for, steam or wind powered.

'Different than the itch you feel every time we make port?' His uncle's heavy, white moustache twitched.

'I suppose not.' He shrugged away the shiver which he did not normally get when he felt watched. 'Just never got it aboard the *Star*.'

'It's my fault. I should have raised you on land. Too much time at sea has got you on edge.'

His uncle did not believe a word of what he said. If anything, Hal Holloway believed living on land put a man on edge. Fletcher agreed. The sea did have its dangers, but not as many as a fellow faced on land.

In cities was where he felt eyes on his back most often. He'd never caught anyone outright staring at him. Heaven help them if he did. The only reason anyone would have for looking at him would be that they were thieves who wished to lighten him of his funds.

He needed every penny he could earn, both from the cargo and what he gained with his fists, in order to purchase his uncle and the crew a newer ship.

'You're feeling jittery over tonight's match, my boy. One of these times you are going to get seriously hurt. I wish you would not take the risk. What we make off our cargo suits us fine.'

'Wool, whisky and textiles will not get us a new ship.' It was steady income, but slow. Which would be fine if Uncle Hal was twenty years younger. 'Fighting will earn it more quickly.'

His uncle sighed, shaking his head. 'You always were stubborn as a stone. But you will use those padded gloves? No bare-knuckle business?'

'Bare knuckle is illegal.'

'Don't give me that grin, you young rascal. I don't want a new ship if it means you end up lame. I won't be your nursemaid.'

He had been, though, when Fletcher was small. Uncle Hal had been the one to raise him from the time he was five years old. His mother had been a passenger aboard the *Morning Star*. The vessel was primarily a cargo ship, but on occasion it did carry a passenger or two. According to his uncle, his mother had quickly become like a daughter to him. When she died it was only natural to take Fletcher in and raise him aboard ship.

No boy had had a better upbringing than Fletcher James Holloway.

Now it was time for him to take care of his uncle. To that end he competed in boxing matches when they made port. More times than not he made a pretty purse. He was even gaining a reputation. People wagered on him.

'I'll send Harley to watch your back tonight. I don't like London. Too many thugs and thieves.'

Harley was big and mean looking, but gentle as a guppy.

'Don't want to have to watch out for me and Harley both.'

'He's big, people will leave you alone.'

It was true that Fletcher was not a giant, but not a minnow either. Which was an advantage because his opponents in the ring underestimated him. The first time they faced off. Not after that.

* * *

Two days after the dream, Eirene managed to convince herself that it could not possibly have been that sort of dream.

She and Mother were enjoying a sit on the terrace enjoying a spot of sunshine. It had all been quite pleasant until Percy strode past and spotted them.

'Good morning, ladies,' he said, then took off his coat and proceeded to hop about on the balls of his feet, jabbing at a post on the terrace steps as if sparing with it.

He glanced up at them now and again. She guessed it was because he wanted to be sure they were watching, admiring his skill.

After a few moments and probably a splinter or two, he blew on his knuckles, grinning.

'I used to compete in boxing matches, you know.' He made a muscle of his large bicep, flexing and clearly anticipating their admiration. 'No one was better than I was.'

'Yes, Percy,' Mother said, giving him a polite smile. Mother was a lady and would never give any other kind. 'You may have mentioned it.'

In the moment, Father came out of the house, frowning.

'You are late for your instruction, Percy. I have been in the office for more than an hour, waiting for you.'

Percy shrugged on his coat. 'I do apologise, Lord Habershom. I had a guest last night. We took a morning ride before he departed. But here I am now, ever eager to learn.'

Seeing him come up the terrace steps, his expression resigned, Eirene thought he was not at all eager.

Percy was a man who liked being admired. He was

more suited to a ballroom than an office. In her opinion he would rather do anything other than prepare for the responsibilities of running Warrenstoke.

'It is a lucky thing your father will be here to make sure the estate does not fail,' Mother said. 'The late Viscount—both James and Henry, I mean—would be concerned if they knew Percy was in charge.'

As long as Eirene carried though with the long-held arrangement and wed the heir, Father would be here to guide Percy. More, Mother would be here to gain strength and live her best life.

Not that there was any doubt Eirene would wed within the Larkin family. It had been arranged…also she had dreamed it.

How old had she been when she had the 'knowing' dream? Just out of plaits, as she recalled.

In the dream she saw that she would wed the heir to Warrenstoke. It had not been revealed who it would be wearing the title. It was assumed to be Henry. Everyone was thrilled with that first dream since it was what they arranged the day she was born.

Of course everyone loved Henry. She would have enjoyed living here with her friend. But Percy? She would tolerate him. Try and think of him in the kindest light she could.

'Has Father heard any news about the search for the second son?'

'Only that the hunt goes on. I wonder what became of him after all this time? Anything could have befallen him. Your father and I remember him as a child. Joseph was such a lively little boy. It was sweet how he followed Henry about wherever he went.'

'I did that, too.'

'Yes… I've always thought Henry allowed it because you were like a little sister to replace the brother he lost.'

'It must have been so hard for the Larkins to go through such an awful thing.'

'It broke them both for a time. But you helped, Eirene. Having you toddling about and demanding they love you—well, it did help them go on.'

'Has Father made a decision on closing up the house in London after I wed?'

'Oh, I think he will not. We will need to travel to town upon occasion and then there is the staff to be considered. Your father would never put them out of their jobs.' Her mother gave her a look, the one a mother used to see past words and into her child's heart. 'But there is something troubling you. It is not the London house.'

'It is nothing really. A dream which I am having some trouble letting go of.'

'That certain kind of dream, Eirene?'

'I do not think so.'

'It is puzzling that you're not sure. That time when Aunt Izzy came to live with us, you had been certain of it even though at the time she lived in Paris with… well, that is better forgotten, but the very next day there she was at the front door, bags in hand.'

'I loved Aunt Izzy.'

'As did we all. And there was that time when you were very small and you dreamed we would get a dog having one white ear and one black ear and missing its hind leg. We insisted there would be no dog. You were adamant that there would be.'

Eirene smiled at the memory. When a week later said pup wandered up the steps and into the house…well she had got her puppy.

'This was not one of those dreams.'

'And yet you are troubled.'

'It is only that I wonder how much longer I will need to wait to discover who I will marry.'

'Six weeks, your father says. The time allotted to find our missing Warrenstoke will have run out. It cannot go on for ever, after all. You will be free to wed Percy after that.'

She nodded. Perhaps she would wed Percy, but there was the recent dream, for all that she tried to dismiss what sort it really was.

It was all too confusing. In the first dream she had wed a viscount. In the second she had wed a sailor. Only one dream could be right.

'My sweet girl.' He mother reached across the space between their chairs, stroking Eirene's hair. 'If you do not wish to wed Percy, simply say the word and we will return to London. We all love Warrenstoke but not at the cost of your happiness. Your father and I would never see you tied to a man you dislike.'

They might not be willing to do it, but she would do it anyway. Mother's health depended upon remaining here. And Father had dreamed of living here since... for ever.

It was not as if she disliked Percy, exactly. Surely once they were wed he would grow on her.

Chapter Two

'Where are we going?' Eirene asked when the carriage turned off the main road. 'This is not the way to Margate.'

'Just a brief stop before we go to dinner, my dear,' Percy said with a grin.

Wherever they were going, he seemed eager to get there. He tapped the ceiling of the carriage to signal the driver to go faster.

'Father?' She slid a sidelong glance at him where he sat beside her on the seat. Interesting that his grin was as wide as Percy's.

'We are making a short stop at a farm. You and Percy will make your first public appearance together afterwards in Margate, just as we planned.'

Showing her off was what it came down to, she thought. Having the daughter of a viscount on his arm would make Percy feel important. Percy did have that need to feel accepted and admired.

'Why are we going to a farm?'

'To see a fellow.' Father's answer was evasive. He avoided looking at her but grinned at Percy. 'Ah, but here we are!'

'What fellow?' she asked, gazing out the window to see a large crowd of people gathered.

The coachman opened the carriage door, helped them down the steps.

Father hurried away and joined the crowd.

'There will be a few of them, but it is a Mr Gladfalcon we have come to watch.' Percy punched one closed fist into his open palm. Slap, slap, slap…the sound of him punching himself was unnerving. As far as she knew he had not raised that fist in violence against another person, however she did not know all that much about him. It was not all that difficult to imagine he would.

'What are we watching him do?' She thought she did not need to ask the question since it was becoming clear that they were attending a country boxing match.

Leave it to her father to bring her to such a place. Perhaps it was because at Warrenstoke society and its rules seemed less important. That and she was all but engaged…to someone.

'We are watching him make me money.' Percy grinned. 'It is said that Gladfalcon never loses a match.'

'I will wait in the carriage.'

'Nonsense.' He caught her hand and tucked it into the crook of his elbow. 'It is not as if this is some tawdry event in London. Even your father is eager for it. Look about, you are not the only woman in attendance.'

Well, no, she was not. But she might be the only one got here by trickery…or, if not that, by being kept in ignorance of the plan.

But here she was and there was nothing for it but to put on a good face. If it got to be too much, she could close her eyes.

Father and Percy seemed to be enjoying themselves and who was she to dampen their fun?

Fletcher Holloway stood at the corner of the barn watching the match before his. He took the time to mentally prepare to face his opponent. Gladfalcon was his name...not the name he was born with probably, but one to give his boxing reputation flare.

A reputation which went before him. It was said that Gladfalcon had never lost a fight. Given the man's girth and height, Fletcher figured it might be true.

People would be betting heavily on Gladfalcon to win. Good, then. When he lost, Fletcher would get the winner's prize and a portion of the wagering.

Fletcher needed this money. Uncle Hal could not wait for ever for his new ship.

The boxing ring was surrounded closely by low hills on three sides and a barn on the fourth. A great, cheering crowd stood on the hill slopes in order to get the best view.

Uncle Hal stood steps from the ring, his hair glinting white in the sunshine. Even from here Fletcher could see how worried he was.

Uncle Hal feared for him and for good reason. His opponent was bigger and more experienced. But then his uncle worried every time Fletcher fought.

So far he had not suffered any serious injuries. But Uncle Hal was not wrong to be concerned. Every time he went into the ring he took a risk. He had seen men go in hale and whole, only to come out maimed and never the same.

But what was he to do? He knew of no other way to earn what boxing paid. If he meant to see his uncle secure and happy in his old age, he must continue on.

The match he was watching ended with neither man too badly hurt, just a little blood and some bruises.

Fletcher approached the fighting arena, then stepped into the ring. So did Gladfalcon. Fletcher had to look up to return his opponent's nod.

Even if he beat the man, and he did intend to, there was still the off chance he might have to fend off an angry bettor. No one expected the smaller man to do anything but get knocked out. Money would be heavily upon Gladfalcon.

Fletcher had never been knocked out cold and would not be today, either.

Eirene tried to watch, truly she did, though she was the only person in attendance purposefully standing behind someone so she did not have a good view of men pummelling one another.

This match, the third she had viewed by peeking out from behind her father's back, was between a large man and a smaller one.

She barely gave them a glance, not wanting to see the certain outcome of the large man battering the smaller one. Not that covering her eyes did a great deal of good. She still heard hard fists pounding soft flesh.

To her this hardly seemed a fair fight.

People cheered, they groaned and gasped.

Some cursed, Percy among the loudest of them. That got her curious enough to take a clearer look. She knew he had bet a great deal of money on the fighter named Gladfalcon. Father had wagered on the smaller man.

Peeking around her father's arm, she saw the small man give Gladfalcon a swift punch in the chin, then the side.

They backed apart, warily eyeing one another, probably deciding where to deliver the next blow.

The smaller man circled, giving her a clearer view of his gloved fists slowly moving, his gaze sharp on the other fighter...of the cold determination in his smile.

Eirene's breath caught, leaving her in a rush.

Everything went fuzzy for a moment. Cheering grew muffled, light came to her in flashes. She feared she might be sick.

She tugged on her father's sleeve. 'I need air.'

Without taking his gaze off the match, her father stepped aside to give her room to wend her way up the slope and though the crowd. At the top of the hill she paused, jerking her gaze back at the boxing ring.

Gladfalcon seemed to be taking the worst of the beating.

His opponent grinned as if being hit was no more than being tickled.

She had tried to deny this moment would come and yet here it was upon her.

She knew this man.

The man of her second dream, her future husband was not a sailor...but a brawler. Very clearly not a viscount.

The last thing she wanted was to stand by and watch him be maimed...or maim someone else.

She fled down the far side of the hill. At the foot was a copse of trees and a wide stream. On the far side of the stream there was a watermill. It made enough noise to cover the sounds of the fight and the agitated crowd.

It was peaceful here in the woods. She sat down beside the stream, cupped water in her hands, then dashed her face with it. Cold and brisk, it settled her some. She took a deep breath. But even a duck with a line of comical ducklings swimming past could not make her smile.

What kind of turn had her life just taken?

Watching the wheel catch a scoop of water, carry it up and then dump it was soothing. The regularity of the process, the gentle splashing noise was calming. She began to feel somewhat herself again.

But only somewhat…because she was stunned in a way she never had been. If there was one thing she knew, it was that her special dreams always came true. How could it be that she'd had two which conflicted with one another?

Was she to wed a viscount or a brawler?

If it was not Viscount Warrenstoke, whoever he turned out to be, what would become of her family's long-held dream of uniting Habershom and Warrenstoke?

Now what was she supposed to do? Tell Father? Confide in Mother? If she did, what could they do about it…about Percy?

Informing Percy she had a dream and in it she discovered that she would wed someone else would do nothing but make him laugh at her…or make him cross. What it would not do was make him give up Warrenstoke. Only the discovery of the true heir could make him do that.

So far there had been no word of success in that.

Was he even alive? If he was, what would he look like? Lithe and tall? Would he be gentle natured like Henry?

The boxer, in the brief glance she had of him, was nothing like her late friend Henry. Henry was tall. The boxer was not tall, but not short either. He was built as if he were one great, walking muscle…rough and…well, to put a fine finger on it…masculine in every look and gesture. He wore a short beard, the same as he had in the dream.

One of the ducklings separated from the rest, circled around and came back to inspect the ruffle of her hem which dipped close to the water.

'What do you think I should do?'

The duckling cheeped.

'That's what I think, too.' She dribbled another scoop of water on her face. 'There is nothing to be done.'

With a flick of its small tail it swam back to its mother.

'I would rather be a duck,' she called after it, but the fluffy creature did not seem to care.

The noise from the other side of the hill became louder. The fight must have ended because a great cheer went up…so did shouts of anger.

Well, people had won money and people had lost it. But what had become of her dream man…the man in her dream? she meant. He was far from being her dream man in the sense that young ladies longed for a romantic suitor.

Fletcher Holloway—that was what she thought his name had been announced as—was not her idea of a romantic suitor. Not that she had ever expected to have one. Even Henry, as much as she had liked him, would not have been that.

She heard another noise…someone scrambling down the hillside, it sounded.

Turning, she saw Mr Holloway running fast down the slope, his arms pummelling and his feet nearly slipping out from under him. His blond hair flew out behind him, just as she recalled it doing in the dream.

His attention was on the water wheel and the small

structure attached to it. He would have stumbled over her had he not looked down at the last moment.

She was struck by how blue his eyes were, no different than she recalled. Similar to Henry's, she thought, but not by common ancestry. Many people had blue eyes.

His quick grin set his dimples flashing and she forgot about the colour of his eyes.

The pocket of his coat bulged. Perhaps he had won the fight and his winnings were in the pocket.

Lifting one finger to his lips, he made a silent plea for her not to give him away. The corner of his mouth was bloodied but he did not seem to notice.

It was nearly all she noticed because she had seen it bleeding once before.

Then he dashed across the stream and into the waterwheel structure.

Of all the bad luck! Fletcher had not expected to encounter a lady sitting beside the stream. A lovely lady at that. The bigger surprise was that he noticed how pretty she was in the moment.

Even now while he hid inside the watermill being pursued by some angry loser, he could not quite get her out of his mind.

Her hair was the unique shade of honey with a strawberry or two thrown in. She'd given him the oddest look…it was almost as if she recognised him. Which she could not possibly have done. Had he ever seen those clear, sky-blue eyes before he would recall the event.

Giving himself a shake, he listened for the man coming after him. Better he spend his time planning an escape from here in the event the lady gave him away.

And why wouldn't she? She had no reason to protect a stranger crossing her path.

For all she knew he might be a convict on the run.

Strangely enough, she began to sing. Her voice was not polished, but her joy in singing shone through and made it one of the nicest sounds he had heard in quite some time.

He thought this while glancing about for an escape from the watermill.

Damn it! There was not one. Even going under the water would not hide him, being as clear as it was.

Heavy footsteps crashed, stomping down the hill. His only hope of escape lay in what the woman would or would not say.

He could see her through a gap in the wall slats.

Glancing over her shoulder, she looked up and spotted his pursuer who was now halfway down the slope. Casually, she fluffed her skirt, then leaned back on her arms and continued to sing, her voice a little louder now.

Was she trying to cover any inadvertent noise he might make? He did not dare to think so.

Through the crack he saw the man stop. He gazed down at the lady, breathing hard.

'Why, hello, Johnson. What are you doing out here? Has Mr Larkin dismissed you from attending the coach?'

'Someone robbed him of his money. He sent me to get it back.'

The fellow might be a coachman, but that was not all he was. Fletcher knew a thug when he spotted one. This one made the hairs of his arms stand at attention.

The lady was alone out here. She could easily be taken advantage of.

She was not alone though, she only looked alone.

His heart beat so hard it felt like it might come out his throat.

'Oh, dear! How dreadful.' The lady rose to her feet, wringing her hands in front of her waist. 'A man did run by. I wonder if he was your thief. His pocket seemed rather full, if you ask me.'

'Which way did he go?'

'That way, into the woods.' She lifted her arm, pointing wide of the watermill. 'Over the hill.'

Footsteps splashed across the stream. Boots crunched brush and twigs in the man's supposed pursuit of him.

Relieved, he bowed his head for a second, letting out the breath he had been holding. Unbelievably he was safe. So was the lady.

For the moment anyway...until the man discovered Fletcher had not run over the hill and she had deceived him.

'Good luck, Mr Johnson!' she called, waving at the coachman thug's back.

It would be wise to wait moment before he emerged from hiding in case Johnson doubled back right away. But the sooner the woman got back to whomever she had attended the fight with, the safer she would be. If the coachman thought she had tricked him, who knew what he might do?

Flinging the wheelhouse door open, he dashed back across the stream.

'You should get back to the farmhouse before he finds that you tricked him.'

He could not say what came over him in the moment, but something made him lean down and kiss her cheek. Gratitude, he guessed.

Although he had never been quite that grateful to anyone before. But if it were not for her, he might not be leaving here with his fairly earned winnings. Not without another fight and he was done in by the one in the ring as it was.

If not for her, whoever she was, things might be a great deal different in the moment.

He wished there was a way to repay this lady who looked steadily at him with eyes so pretty it made his breath hitch.

'I do not know why you did not give me away, Miss, but I'm grateful beyond words.'

She made a shooing motion with her fingers.

He lifted her hand, kissed that, too, and then he dashed off.

She mumbled something which he must have misheard in his rush to be gone.

What it sounded like was… 'Oh, you will.'

Hurrying up the rise of the hill, he glanced back several times to make sure she was safely coming up behind him. Only when he was assured she was safe among her company would he gather his uncle and get back to the ship.

If Eirene had any doubt that her dream had been wrong, she no longer did. Seeing Fletcher Holloway with her own eyes put any question of it to rest. The dream had been accurate down to the dot of blood on his lip.

It was nearly funny—in an odd, not funny way—that they had shared their first kiss and he did not even know it. Something of a kiss, at any rate. He had no idea what they meant to one another, or would, if it was this dream and not the other which turned out to be true.

There was no way both of them could be.

In the moment, while she considered the mysteries

of dreams and reality, he appeared to have nothing on his mind but collecting his prize and getting back to wherever he came from.

That and making sure she got back to the safety of company.

He had been right about her being in possible peril. Johnson would not be amused to find he had been led astray. Not that he could say anything about it without giving away that he was robbing someone.

Even so, she stood beside her father, her hand tucked into the crook of his arm.

Nearly half an hour later Johnson returned, breathing hard and sweat dripping down his face. He hurried to Percy who was watching another match. He was not likely to react well to learning that the coachman failed to steal his money back.

In the event Johnson accused her, Percy could not say anything about it either, not without admitting that he meant to rob the fighter.

Not in public, anyway. She was not sure what he would have to say once they were in private. Since they lived in the same house they were bound to be alone at some point.

Seeing him today, his greed and lack of scruples, well, it gave her a shiver. She dearly hoped she did not meet him in a hallway one dark night. In the past she thought him a bit domineering, impatient and vain, but after seeing him this afternoon, she wondered if he could be violent when provoked.

Which, she thought, looking at the coachman gesturing and glancing at her, he was being.

Percy said something to the coachman, cursed at him, probably.

Truly, she did not wish to spend her life with Percy Larkin.

Not that she knew much about Fletcher Holloway, but what she did know was that rather than immediately escape with his money, he had waited and watched to be sure she was safely beside her father before he went into the barn.

She sensed in her soul that she had nothing to fear from the fighter.

All along she had been resigned to marrying Percy, hoping that once they were wed he would somehow grow upon her, that she could overlook what she disliked about him and go on with her life.

Those moments at the stream had changed everything. She understood now who he was at heart. A cheat and a thief. A title and marriage would not change him. Warrenstoke would not be safe with Percy in charge of it.

Her best hope was that the missing heir would be found. That she would marry him and that dreams of the Warrenstokes and the Habershoms would come true.

And yet…she had been in love in her second dream. That had not been the case in the first dream. In that one she had not seen a face, not felt her heart stretch in a peculiar yearning.

Standing beside her father, she felt her cheek become warm in a curious, fluttery manner. Almost as if the boxer were still kissing it. Percy had never made her feel fluttery. Only nervous.

She really must stop touching her cheek or Father was going to ask—

'Is there something amiss with your cheek, Eirene? You keep rubbing it. Have you been stung by an insect?'

Perhaps she'd been stung. But not by an insect.

Percy came back at that point, giving her an odd, sharp look.

'Let's go to Margate, I'm hungry,' was all he said.

Just because Percy did not mention what had happened in front of Father did not mean Johnson had not accused her.

'Can you still afford dinner, Percy, with all the money you lost?' Her father laughed good-naturedly because that was who he was.

'Those things will happen,' Percy replied with a tight smile.

For all that Percy strove to appear in a light mood, the tick in his jaw gave him away.

Eirene wondered if Father noticed.

'That's all right, my boy. I won enough to pay our bill.'

Wasn't that the worst thing he might have said to a man as vain as Percy was? The meal would be uncomfortable if Percy took offence. The man could be charming when in the mood to be, but stone-faced when he was not.

When Percy was unhappy, he spread the mood to everyone he encountered.

She watched the tic in his jaw, thinking that he was chewing on some sort of violent thought. There was every chance it was directed towards her.

Chapter Three

The next day, Eirene spent her morning as she usually did, reading to her mother. For all that she was head over heels in confusion about her conflicting dreams, the normalcy of reading to her mother was grounding.

However, the tale was not. 'The Pit and the Pendulum'… 'Truly Mother, this is the grimmest story I have ever read.'

'Tell me about dinner last night.'

While not as awful as the story, it was not a happy time, either. Percy's frustration at losing his money was directed towards the restaurant staff.

She had not been sparkling company either, her mind in a whirl after meeting Fletcher Holloway.

It was still in a whirl.

She wanted to confide in her mother that she that she might not wed a viscount, but somehow she could not. Not until she understood it all, herself. Did the second dream cancel the first?

That made little sense because, if it did, why would she have dreamed the first at all?

Not that anything she might or might not understand would change what was to be.

Her reluctance to tell her mother had much to do with Percy. She could hardly talk about meeting her boxer without revealing the ugly side of Percy's character she had seen.

Her mother would never let her wed him if she knew. If she did not wed Percy, then she could not ensure that her mother would remain here to continue healing. Not only that, Father would not be here to make sure Percy did not run the estate to ruin. All of them loved Warrenstoke far too much to allow that to happen.

She could not refuse to wed Percy. Nor could she wed Fletcher Holloway even though her dream decreed it.

Besides, the likelihood of her ever seeing the dream man again was remote. Her one and only hope of a satisfactory solution was to hope the younger Larkin was found.

After all this time it was a bit much to hope for. In only weeks her betrothal to Percy would be announced. If that time came and Henry's half-brother was not found, what was she to do? Proceed with the announcement and hope it all came out right?

Refuse? Who knew how Percy would react to that? He already considered himself Viscount and her his… his acquisition whose behaviour was his to direct. It still rankled that he thought he needed to tell her how to dress for company, as if she had not been trained for a position in society.

She had known she would be Viscountess Warrenstoke all her life. The possibility of him being Viscount had only come about since Henry died.

If only she could be a normal person who was not troubled by 'seeing' dreams, or other dreams like the one she had last night. She had never had one quite like

it. Not foretelling, but interesting…absorbing and tanta-
lising. Fantasies of Fletcher Holloway had popped into
her dreams, made her toss and turn on her mattress.

She was still trying to figure out whether or not she
was pleased to feel such yearning towards a man she
had met all of a few moments. As far as she could tell
she was pleased and distressed at the same time. What
an interesting state to be in.

'My girl.' Mother reached across the distance between them to stroke her hair. Mother often did this to
express her affection. 'I believe Mr Poe is too much for
you. Tomorrow we shall read Dickens, or perhaps Jane
Austen. Why don't you go along now and take one of
those walks you enjoy?'

That sounded wonderful! She would sit upon her hill
and try to put everything out of her mind for a while.
What was going to happen was going to happen, which
she hoped would be the return of the rightful heir and
that he would be as kind and gentle a spirit as Henry
had been.

She was only halfway along the meadow path leading to the hill when she heard footsteps running after
her.

'Wait up, my dear!'

Hearing Percy's voice, she would rather run than
turn, but he would only catch up. The last thing she
wanted was to be put on the spot. He would demand to
know why she was so anxious to get away from him.

She could hardly admit that he scared her in a way
he had not before. If he was willing to do harm to a
man he believed had robbed him of a small purse, what
would he do to her if she turned him down? A great

deal of money would come with her into the marriage and she had no doubt he already knew how to spend every penny.

Turning, she smiled, her teeth gritted for whatever mood he presented. Percy well knew she had sent his man in the wrong direction. How would he react now that they were alone?

'Percy, what a surprise.'

'Not a bad one, I hope.' He smiled.

Good then, a charming mood, but probably a false one. From one breath to the next, those straight white teeth might clack, then turn into a snarl.

'I only want to apologise for last night. I'm afraid that I was in a dour mood during dinner.' The restaurant staff would heartily agree. 'I will do better once we are wed. I promise.'

'Think nothing of it, Percy.' She must make him think that, although she knew what had happened, she did not condemn him for it.

Tricky business, that.

'I understand that gentlemen's pursuits do not always have the results one hopes for. Perhaps things will go your way next time.'

'I have every confidence of it. I only hope you do not think you will be wed to a cranky fellow.'

'Oh, I do not think I will be.' As long as the true heir was found in the short time there was left. A few more weeks was all there was.

'I'm glad we have that settled. I will leave you to your outing.'

Percy Larkin had a dark spirit which lingered behind even after she had walked one way and he another. It took several minutes to recapture her composure.

What would she do when the day came she could not walk away?

Please, please, oh, please, let Joseph Larkin be found.

Fletcher stood by the rail of the *Morning Star*, gazing at ships bobbing in the Port of London. It felt like a storm was coming. Night hid rain clouds creeping towards shore, but he felt a change in the pitch and sway of the waves. In the moan of the wind whistling about the hull.

By the light of torches along the dock, he watched men scrambling to secure their ships.

Two men were not hustling, but standing a hundred or so feet from the *Morning Star* and staring at it. They looked out of place. Not sailors, these men wore dapper-looking coats and fashionable hats.

Footsteps tapped across the deck. He turned to see Uncle Hal coming towards him seeming weary.

No wonder. They and the crew had spent the better part of last night and today getting ready to sail for New York.

His uncle's age was beginning to show and it cut Fletcher to the heart. Hal Josiah Holloway had been his strength since he was a young child. His arms had always been steady, reliable.

Now Fletcher meant to be those strong reliable arms for Uncle Hal.

'It looks like we will not leave for New York in the morning after all, Uncle. It will be safer to remain where we are.'

'I don't mind. We shall take rooms at an inn where the rocking won't bother our sleep.'

Bother their sleep? Fletcher had always been lulled to sleep that way. He never knew his uncle feel otherwise.

'Are you well? I don't know that it has ever bothered you before.'

'I am as fit as a fiddle, young man, it's only my joints are not as young as they once were. Lately rough seas tend to make them ache. Nothing to worry about.'

Naturally he would worry. No one meant more to him than this crusty old man. He only wished prize fighting would earn him money faster than it was doing. His reputation was growing in villages and towns along the coast. Still, he was not earning what he needed to in order to buy his uncle a new ship.

The two men who had been watching the ship began to walk towards it.

'You recognise them?' he asked.

'No, not by torchlight.' His uncle bent towards the rail, looking hard through his spectacles. 'Maybe they are going to the *Sea Shepherd* docked down the way.'

The men stopped, waved, then started up the gangplank.

'They don't look as if they are seeking work.'

Uncle Hal shook his head, uttering something under his breath. A curse was it?

Why in blazes would he curse at a pair of men coming aboard? The timing of their arrival seemed odd, but they did not seem ill intended.

A great wind caught the mast, making the ship sway to and fro. The gangplank lurched. The visitors dashed the rest of the way to the deck.

Rigging clanked and rattled. The air smelled damper, saltier and charged with the coming storm.

'Good evening, gentlemen.' The taller of the men looked at him rather than his uncle, even though his uncle was wearing the Captain's uniform. 'Do I have the pleasure of addressing Joseph Larkin…or Holloway as it may be?'

Uncle Hal cursed again, not under his breath this time.

'I think we ought to go to my cabin,' his uncle suggested. 'This is going to be a whale of a storm.'

Single file they made their way through the narrow passageway to the Captain's quarters. Luckily loose items were secured or the entire contents of the cabin would be sliding about.

'Would any one like coffee?' Uncle Hal asked. 'Bourbon?'

'Who is Joseph Larkin?' Fletcher asked the obvious question.

'You must be Hal Holloway?' The shorter of the men addressed his uncle. 'If so, it is a pleasure to meet you at last.'

Although no one had asked for it, Uncle Hal passed about glasses and then poured bourbon.

'I believe we should sit, gentlemen,' his uncle said, his voice resigned-sounding. 'I have been expecting you.'

'You have?' Fletcher had never heard his uncle mention it. 'How long have you been expecting these men and who are they?'

'Oh, for years.' Uncle Hal swallowed his bourbon in a gulp, then poured himself another. His uncle was not much of a drinker. 'I do not know exactly who they are, only why they are here.'

'I am George Williamson,' the smaller of the two said.

'And I am his partner, Mitchel Lindley.'

Partner in what, he wanted to know, but not as much as he wanted to know why they were calling him Joseph

Larkin. And why had his uncle been expecting them... for a long time, was it?

'Who,' he asked again with a ripple of unease creeping up his spine because there was something about hearing the name Larkin that tickled a dark, forgotten... something...not a memory, but a shadow of one, 'is Joseph Larkin?'

Both of the visitors grinned. He had a canny feeling that these two were responsible for his recent sensation of being watched.

Not that there was any reason for them to be watching him unless they were sizing him up for a bet. No, that would be extreme and would not explain why they called him by a name which was not his.

'You are Joseph Larkin,' his uncle said, his voice as resigned as his posture when he slunk on to a chair. He indicated that they should all sit down.

'Viscount Warrenstoke, sir,' Lindley greeted him with a broad smile.

'It is our great pleasure to finally meet you.' Williamson stood, made an odd gesture which was something between a nod and a bow. A greeting which commoners such as him gave to their betters.

He, Fletcher Holloway, was as common as they came.

'I reckon I ought to explain. To you, my boy, and to you two fellows.' Uncle Hal tipped his glass, drained the bourbon, then thumped it on the table. Fletcher caught the glass in time to keep it from sliding when the ship listed. 'You were named Joseph Fletcher when you were born. Your mother called you Fletcher and so I carried on with it. I hope you men will understand why I hid him from your colleagues when he was a boy.'

Fletcher's head spun as if he had drained the bourbon snifter and then reached for the whisky.

'According to our records, the search they made was thorough. We are interested to see how you managed it,' Williamson said, sitting down again.

Oddly, his uncle uttered a throaty laugh. 'Aye, well I was more thorough. Raising the boy aboard ship did complicate things for you, I imagine.'

Fletcher wanted to stomp out of the cabin, go topside and stand in the rain which he heard lashing at the portholes. He had the unsettling feeling his life was about to make a turn which he could not come back from.

Larkin. No longer a tickle, the named scratched at his memory. Joseph did not.

Damn it, there would be no running away from this. He needed to sit where he was and discover who Larkin was.

'Tell me what you recall about your mother, Fletcher,' his uncle said.

'Not much. She smelled nice, it felt good when she hugged me... I remember that she loved me.'

'No mother loved her boy more and that is the truth you must keep in mind when I tell you the rest. These gentlemen will already know the facts, not the heart of why it happened.'

The ship rocked. He heard waves slapping the hull, while silence inside the cabin stretched tight.

'Your mother was an American, sent to wed Viscount Warrenstoke, your father, when she was much too young,' Uncle Hal said. 'Barely eighteen. It was all for financial gain. A wedding of your mother's wealth and your father's position. Your parents did not meet before they found themselves at the altar. But I met your mother later when she booked passage on my ship which was bound for America. I did not know, then, that the poor child was running away from her husband and the life of a viscountess which she was ill prepared for. Running from her own father, too.

'She confided all this to me after we were out to sea. She was homesick, poor girl, and yet she could not go home because her father would only send the two of you back. In his eyes she was a disgrace to the family name.'

Uncle Hal paused for a moment as if seeing images of the time in his memory.

'Well then, your mother was in a fix. She could not go to her father, not unless she wished to be returned to England. Once we reached New York, she stayed aboard the ship. By the time we reached the next port she was sick. I did call for a doctor who said she would not die of it, not at once. It was some wasting illness which she fought for a year, right here aboard the *Morning Star*.'

'How old?' he asked. 'When my mother took me away, how old was I?'

Uncle Hal was silent, staring at his hands gripped around the glass of bourbon.

'Five years old,' Williamson said.

'You were but six when she died,' his uncle added without looking up.

Six? How was it that he could not remember his life before the *Morning Star*? He had been told his father died. He did remember that, but vaguely. He had been raised Holloway and that was who he was.

Mr Williamson dabbed at his eye. The detective called Lindley sniffed.

'But she did die and before she did she made me promise to raise you. She was like my own daughter by then... I'd never had one and so...well...' Uncle Hal cleared his throat. 'She was dear to me and I was determined to raise you as she wished.'

'Viscount Warrenstoke was devastated when you were taken from him,' Williamson said, giving Fletcher a direct look. 'You should know that. We saw as much in the old records.'

'I assume you are here to return me to him after all these years?'

'I regret to inform you that he died a few years ago.' Mitchel Lindley looked as if he did regret saying so. More than Fletcher regretted hearing it. The man they spoke of was as much a stranger to him as the Queen of England was. 'Our condolences.'

He nodded because it seemed the thing to do. It also felt the thing to do, to run up to the deck, try to forget what Uncle Hal revealed.

'I am afraid there is more.' Mr Williamson's lips pressed thin. 'It is your older brother...'

Brother? The image of a boyish grin flashed across his mind, there and gone too quickly to bring into focus. An impression of friendly blue eyes echoed in his heart more than his mind.

Given the detective's grim expression, if he'd had a brother he no longer did. The thought made him sad in a way it had not done with his father.

'We do regret to inform you, sir... Henry Larkin passed away a year ago.'

'Ah, my boy...' Uncle Henry slapped his palm on the table, his voice more a croak than words. 'I wronged you in keeping this a secret. You ought to have known your brother.'

Perhaps, yet he did not regret his life at sea for a second.

'How old was my brother…and what of my mother's family?' Sitting on the chairs, the men appeared to be swaying with the rock of the ship. He and Uncle Hal were used to it but the detectives might be feeling green in the gills. 'Are they living?'

'Your brother was eleven when your mother took you,' his uncle said.

'Your grandmother and an aunt are alive and doing well, last we had word of them. Still living in New York.'

According to what had just been revealed, Fletcher had never met either one of them. They might not grieve him being lost to them, but they would have grieved his mother. Maybe felt guilty for sending her away to a heartbreaking fate. Although, the decision to do it might not have been theirs. More often than not in high society a woman's fate was determined by a man.

He looked at his uncle, grey head bowed in apparent guilt.

'I do not recall my mother weeping,' was all he could think of to say.'

His brain and his heart must be in some stupefied state.

'She did cry. I used to hear her in the night. It broke my crusty old heart right down the middle.'

'I wonder if my father wept when I was taken? I suppose I will never know.'

'We cannot speak as to the state of the Viscount's emotions, directly,' Williamson said, 'only that he engaged the services of the company we work for, for many years looking for you. It would indicate he grieved a great deal for your loss. It was your father's lifelong friend who engaged us again after your brother's passing.'

'And here you are, the truth revealed at last.' Fletcher stood, swayed a bit. Due to his life at sea he was in no danger of losing his balance. The visitors might be. 'I thank you for your due diligence in locating me. And now my uncle and I will escort you off the ship before the storm makes it impossible.'

He had much to think over, too much. He could not do it while they remained aboard.

'May we inform Viscount Habershom that you will return and assume your title?'

What was that he said? A title? As in British nobility? He might have been born in England, but he was raised aboard a ship and knew nothing of what went on in that society. Dukes and barons were all the same to him.

'You may assume that I will stay with my ship.'

'But, sir, a title is not something you can cast off,' Lindley said. 'With your brother's death it falls to you to take over the estate.'

'Viscount Warrenstoke, you are a very wealthy man. There are people who depend upon you.' Williamson arched his brows, looking as if he were confused that Fletcher was not pleased to be rich and...

Damn it!

'The crew of this ship depends upon me.'

'Gentlemen.' His uncle was the last to stand. When he did he was slow, careful, as if the effort caused him pain. 'This has all been a shock to the Viscount. Come back tomorrow and we shall speak more of it.'

'If you call me that again, Uncle, I'll jump overboard.'

He would not, but he felt like doing it. The sea was not particular in who it drowned. It accepted seaman and gentlemen alike.

After seeing the men ashore, Fletcher and his uncle remained on deck, silently getting wet.

'Come inside, my boy. It is the dickens out here.'

'Not now. I have things to think over.'

'I'm sure you do, lad. Just do it inside.'

The masthead was where he liked to do his thinking. Up so high there were fewer distractions, the world and its troubles seemed further away.

Dickens of a storm or not, he would climb to the crow's nest, attempt to sort out his newly scrambled life.

'I cannot beg your forgiveness out here.'

'Do not attempt to, Uncle. You owe me no apology. I will not hear one.' He raised his voice to be heard over rain slapping the deck.

With a grunt and a shake of his head, Uncle Hal went below decks. Fletcher climbed the mast. It was slippery business, but he had done it often enough that it was not overly hazardous.

Once in the crow's nest he drew a tarp over himself, settled into the comforting, if erratic, sway of the mast.

He was a sailor, not a viscount. No one could tell him he was something he did not wish to be. His life was the sea, not the land…but then, quite suddenly he was hit with a memory.

In it he saw acres of grass and rolling hills. He ran up one side of a hill, then down another. No…that was not quite it…he rolled down the hill laughing because it was what he saw the older boy doing.

Henry, his brother. His late brother who was only five years his senior. Recalling, now, how he had adored

Henry, he wept. His shoulders shook as the memories came one upon another. He had loved Henry. He did not remember his father as well, but he did recall a man smiling at him, being bounced upon his knee. He remembered feeling as tall as a tree when the man carried him about on his shoulders.

What the men told him…what his uncle confessed… it could only be true that he was who they said he was, Joseph Fletcher Larkin. Even his own memories, shaken suddenly loose, confirmed it.

What remained to be seen was if he would give up being Fletcher Holloway, man of the sea, to become Joseph Fletcher Larkin… Viscount Warrenstoke, was it?

He was who he was and could not simply become someone else because he was informed that he was.

One other thing he had been informed of was that he was a wealthy man.

That gave him pause because as Viscount he could purchase Uncle Hal a gem of a ship which he would not have to wait for.

Also, Fletcher would not need to risk his safety every time he entered a boxing ring. If something were to happen to him—and it could, he was not so naive to think it could not—then who would his uncle have to care for him?

There would be no one. There was more to consider than he had first thought.

For a time he listened to rigging creak and groan, to rain slapping the tarp. In the distance he heard thunder roll across the sky.

This was a signal to go below deck.

Once inside, he took a moment to peek into Uncle

Hal's cabin and wish him goodnight before going down the passageway to his own cabin.

Uncle Hal was a snoring heap under his blankets which meant he must not be overwrought by the events of the evening.

Walking further down the hallway, he came to his own cabin. Once inside he shed his wet clothes, went directly to his bunk and lay down, whereupon he proceeded to stare at wood knots on the overhead.

Surely in the morning the storm would be gone and he would know what to do about his life.

If nothing else, he could rest assured there would be no other revelations. What more could possibly be revealed?

Chapter Four

These days, Eirene spent more and time on the hill.

It was where she was now, looking down at the manor house and the grounds surrounding it, at the pretty stream lined with trees which split the property nearly in the middle.

Further out she saw the road which lead through the village and then to Warrenstoke where it ended at their drive.

She remembered how as a child she used to burst from the carriage before the driver helped her down. Within moments of arrival she would be dashing about with Henry. It did not matter that he was much older than she was, he always paid attention to her. It was Henry who had taught her the joy of rolling downhill.

Perhaps she should do it now, feel as carefree as she had then.

But, no, she was not carefree and if she did roll on the grass her gown would be stained green.

Memories would have to do.

In the moment, looking back was preferable to looking forward.

It was only one more week until the search for Joseph Larkin would be abandoned and Percy would be announced as heir and she as his betrothed.

Quite a coup for a mere cousin to get a title, a viscount's daughter and a great deal of money along with her. No wonder he had not sought a bride of his own choosing.

One more boon to wedding her was that he got her father, who would see to the day-to-day running of the estate and leave Percy free to his social pursuits.

To Father, running Warrenstoke would be an act of love, to the land and to his late friend. To Percy it would be a burden. Hopefully Percy would go happily about his pursuits and leave her at the periphery of his life.

Ever since the prize fight and witnessing his ruthlessness, his greed, she had seen him in an honest and unflattering light. This afternoon Percy was away from the estate and she could only admit it was a great relief. When she thought about sharing marital intimacy with him, her mind went quite blank.

She stared at the road. *Where, where, oh, where are you, Joseph Larkin?* Whoever he turned out to be, he was bound to be a better husband and Viscount than his cousin.

For that matter, where was Fletcher Holloway? Even though she had spent no more than a minute or two with him, she had no trouble whatsoever imagining what sharing a marital bed with him might be like.

Perhaps because he was the man she was supposed to share one with? Were they fated somehow, even though her dreams conflicted?

Fate, she had heard, was a fickle thing. She could not figure it out.

And dream or not, if the second son did somehow

come riding up the drive, what was to say he would be willing to marry her?

Well, her first dream had said so, but there had been the second and they could not both be true.

She buried her face in yards of cotton skirt covering her bent knees, took a deep sniff of whatever soap the laundress used.

Rose petals, how nice. She would think of flowers instead of the future.

Hearing a dog bark, she looked up. There was a carriage turning from the road on to the drive. Business associates of Father coming by was a common occurrence.

Many carriages had come and gone since the day of the fight. For all she hoped one brought the new Viscount, it never had.

Fletcher gripped the door handle with more than half a mind to jump out of the coach and flee.

His uncle snatched his hand, yanking it back.

When he had assumed no further revelation would be possible he had been wrong. The words that had come out of Mr Williamson's mouth might be the most stunning of them yet.

'A bride? The estate comes with a bride?' He could not have heard that right.

'Yes, sir. That is correct.' Mr Williamson had had the audacity to smile. 'The arrangement was made on the day the Eirene Smythe was born. She is to wed the Warrenstoke heir.'

'It was meant to be Henry,' Mitchel Lindley added as if that would make the situation acceptable. 'But then after your brother's passing it appeared that it would be

Percy Larkin...the cousin we told you about. Luckily you are here now. All will be well.'

'Indeed,' Williamson said. 'Everything has worked out as it should, the true heir taking his rightful place.'

A view of his rightful place slid past the carriage window. It was immense. How many windows looked out over the drive? Countless, it seemed. The *Morning Star* would fit within its walls...twice, maybe three times.

When the carriage stopped in front of the place, a man dressed in finely tailored clothing came out. He spoke for a moment with the driver.

Moments later, people dressed in servants' garb came outside. They formed a line along a walkway leading towards the front steps of the house.

'What are they doing?'

'They have assembled to greet you.' Williamson said. 'They would have been prepared and not come rushing out haphazardly, but we were in such haste to get here we did not inform anyone of our arrival.'

'We also wanted to be certain, I mean...' Lindley sputtered over his words, looked as if he wished to recall them. 'Well, you see, to be honest, we wanted to be sure you would not bolt along the way.'

Which would explain why they had waited until now to tell him about the bride.

Bolting sounded like a fine idea. It was what he would do as soon as someone opened the door. He would not be gone for ever, but he did need a few moments.

All this belonged to him? All these people depended upon him? He would rather deliver his ship's crew through a hurricane than run the gauntlet of greeters set before him.

To say he was overwhelmed would be understated. If he was made admiral of the Queen's navy, he would be more prepared than he was for this.

The coachman opened the door. Fletcher stepped down.

Glancing over his shoulder at the men inside the coach, he nodded. 'I need a moment.'

That said, he strode quickly along a path which crossed in front of the house. From the corner of his eye he spotted a man rush out of the home's grand entrance. His hair was as grey as Uncle Hal's was. A great smile split his face.

He imagined the fellow must be someone important to Warrenstoke and he ought to greet him straight away. He simply could not do it until he took a few moments to gather himself. That last revelation had been a hummer.

A wife? His life had dissolved into madness.

The path led around the back of the house, past a terrace and then away towards a meadow.

The view resembled an ocean of rolling green, foreign and yet slightly familiar all at once.

For all that he might wish to, he was not running away. Not from the moment and not from the sea, not for ever from the sea. He had promised his crew he would return to the *Morning Star*. Perhaps by the time the acting Captain brought the ship back from America, Fletcher would have matters settled at Warrenstoke.

How he was going to do that, he could not imagine.

Especially now that he had been told there was a woman here who expected him to marry her. Had, in fact, counted on it all her life.

Bilge water was what it was. No one became betrothed on the day of her birth.

As he understood it, as Viscount he was in charge of everything that went on here. Surely given his exalted position, he could refuse to wed.

His mother had wed for duty, had it forced upon her, and look how that ended. With him being separated from his family, not knowing his father or his brother. Not knowing his mother, for that matter, since she caught some dreaded thing that killed her.

There had been one constant person in his life: Uncle Hal, who stood by him even now, leaving the sea to accompany him to the place of his birth.

A dozen times or more his uncle begged Fletcher to forgive him for not bringing him back to his family after his mother died. Two dozen times or more he'd assured Uncle Hal he was damned glad he had not.

He could not have chosen a better life than the one he had. Than the one he was going to take them back to, but in a new and better ship.

Thinking he heard a boy laughing, he turned towards the sound. Nothing but grass, trees and hills surrounded him. No children. An echo of the past was what it was.

What he actually heard was water. A brook or a stream was nearby.

Whoever the visitor was, he must be a guest of some importance. Father had not mentioned a house guest, but he did not tell her everything. With the servants lined up for the welcome, she thought she ought to be there, too.

The last thing she was going to do was hold out hope that perhaps this time it was the lost Viscount coming home. She had been disappointed several times already watching for the one person who did not come.

She hurried down the hill, then followed the stream because it was the most pleasant way to return to the house.

If she meant to meet the guest, she ought to hurry. Oh, but what was more inviting than rippling water. She was tempted to linger.

It would not delay her all that much to take off her shoes and walk along the streambed. It was not as if anyone had informed her there was to be a house guest. What if she had not been watching the road? She would never have known.

The guest might even be weary of greetings by the time Eirene got to the house. Probably grateful not to have be polite to one more person.

Very well, then. She took off her shoes and stockings, then gathered up her petticoats and skirts. She secured everything within the crooks of her arms.

She had managed the manoeuvre many times before with wonderful success.

Cool, flat stones skimmed her heels, slid against her toes.

Babbling water soothed her mind. This was bliss, a great relief from her worry over her future and Warrenstoke's.

But wait! What was that?

Someone was singing.

A man. She stopped walking, cocked her hear to get a better listen.

His voice was smooth and masculine. The quick, lively cadence of the song indicated it was a sea shanty.

Now that was odd. Perhaps the singer was a former

sailor who was in the employ of the important person who had come calling? Or maybe he simply enjoyed lively shanty tunes.

'Oh, Penny, oh, Penny, oh, where did she go? She left this old port to find a new home.'

His voice grew louder. She still could not see the singer because of a bend in the stream. What she ought to do was dash up the stream bank and go back to the house. But then how would she know if Penny found her new home?

'She wandered for weeks, then she wandered some more, but poor buxom Penny just—'

The man rounded the corner, stopped singing, clearly startled to come upon her wading in the stream, her legs bare and dripping.

If he was startled to see her, she was utterly stunned to see him.

Fletcher Holloway! Here in her stream! What could this mean?

One thing it meant was that her knees were trembling and she felt like sinking down in the water.

Was she relieved to see him or horrified?

'Hello, Mr Holloway, how lovely it is to see you again,' she said because it was actually and what else was there to say?

His pant legs were rolled to his knees, water dripping down his calves. She noticed this discreetly, out of the corner of her eye, since it was improper to be looking at all.

Also improper to be standing here with her wet calves exposed. A sight which he might be giving a sidelong glance at.

She ought to drop her skirt, but she would rather not

have to explain why it was soaked. Especially if Fletcher dropped his pant legs and they became soaked, too.

But as it was, he was not staring at her legs, but at her face.

It seemed to take him a moment to get over the surprise of seeing her, but, when he did, he offered a teasing grin.

'We meet again. I wonder if we are fated to encounter one another in streams.'

'Fated, yes, so it seems.' He was here, was he not? Against all reason they stood face to face, a rush of cool water gurgling between them.

She started up the bank, but the grass was slippery and she nearly lost her balance, would have had Fletcher Holloway not rushed forward to take her arm and steady her.

In the process he grasped the lacy hem of her petticoat tucked between her shoe and her elbow. Coarse blond hair dusted his fingers, which were tan and rugged looking pillowed in her intimate apparel.

Fletcher did not have the hands of a gentleman. While it was true that she preferred gentleman to brawlers, she did have to admit that callused fingers were more interesting than manicured fingernails.

'Thank you.' Even his eyes had a rugged look and something else. A twinkle…a teasing twinkle was what it was.

And his smile? She would guess that he had never learned to tame or refine it.

'It was nothing. I owe you far more than I can repay.' He bent, then, grinning up at her, rolled his pant legs down. 'For the day of the fight. I've been thinking about you ever since.'

That made two of them, then.

He straightened, nodding. A ray of sunshine caught the stubble of his short beard, made it glimmer. 'Couldn't quit wondering why you did what you did.'

She did not dare tell him. He would think her insane.

For a moment they stood, bare toes in fresh grass, staring at one another.

Was he here to claim her as his bride even though he did not know it? Maybe she was insane.

All he knew of her was that she was the one who had pointed his pursuer in the wrong direction.

'It was clear that our coachman meant you no good. I thought that Johnson meant to rob you.'

'You've good instincts, Miss. That is exactly what he meant. If he caused you trouble after, just say so and I will set it right.'

'He never spoke of it to me.' To Percy, surely, but nothing had come of it.

Fletcher Holloway glanced over his shoulder at the manor house. 'I guess I should get back there.'

Why? Was he employed by the visitor, perhaps?

'So should I.' She nodded towards a shady spot where a fallen log served as a bench. 'In a little while. There is plenty of room on the log for two people.'

She would have had to have been wearing blinders not to notice the relief crossing his expression, have her fingers plugged in her ears not to hear the grateful sigh when he sat down on the log.

Clearly, he did not wish to go back any more than she did.

'What became of buxom Penny?' she asked as a distraction while she sat down, put on her shoes and then stuffed her stockings into her skirt pocket.

Where were Fletcher's shoes? she wondered. He sat beside her flexing and curling his toes in the grass without a hint of embarrassment.

'Ah, she found a place, but can't decide if she wants to stay or return to the seaport.'

'There must be a man involved somehow. Is there a lost love, I wonder?'

'There is, but it's a few verses on.'

'I hope they reunite.'

'Are you a romantic, Miss—but I don't know your name?'

'Eirene Smythe.' His eyes widened for an instant. He opened his mouth as if he had something to say and then closed it. His lips quirked in the oddest blend of humour and surprise. Her name was not unusual. She could not imagine what had caused his odd reaction to it. 'And I do not know if I am a romantic or not. Are you?'

'Not unless I'm thinking of the sea. Might get poetic over ocean waves and whales.'

She had thought him handsome on their first, brief meeting, but now? While he was not the sort of handsome she was used to, he was perhaps, more. Looking at his suntanned face made her nerves flutter.

In her circle of peers, handsome meant well groomed, neat and finely dressed. Handsome meant refined manners and conversation which was not too stimulating for a lady's sensibilities.

Fletcher Holloway was not refined. He wore a suit, but not of expensive cloth. As far as manners went? The man sat beside her, not at all distressed that his feet were bare.

Clearly, no valet had groomed his hair this morning. It looked as wild as she had seen it after the boxing match.

And mostly, there was his grin. It seemed to declare he was who he was and glad of it.

Fletcher Holloway was not at all the type of man she expected to wed. Truly, wouldn't she be more comfortable with a genteel fellow? One who recited sonnets, not shanties? One who would never use the word buxom in front of a lady? But to be fair, he had used it before he saw her.

In the end, here she was. And here he was.

'Do you spend time by the sea when you are not in a boxing ring?' It seemed that a bit of conversation was needed in the instant and she did want to know more about him.

'It's the other way around, pretty lady—'

'Eirene.'

His dimples flashed. 'Pretty Eirene, then. I'm a sailor first, a boxer second…and apparently one other thing.'

Of course he was a sailor, she well knew it already. Spending days working on the deck of a ship would account for the golden streaks in his hair, his tanned complexion and his strong build…why, even his feet looked muscular.

'And now I am here, the only water in sight is this brook.'

'And may I ask why you are here at Warrenstoke?'

Other than that fate had brought him. It was unlikely he knew it.

He nodded, then shrugged. 'You'd never believe it. But trust me when I tell you, seeing you wading in the stream is the best thing to happen to me in days. Even made me forget all about the legendary Penny.'

'And her being so buxom.' She laughed. It occurred to her that laughing was something she never did with Percy.

In general she did not care for rough men like Fletcher. However, in particular, she did like him.

At least for the brief time they had known one another, she did. After further acquaintance, she might change her mind. But this moment was interesting, in the nicest way. How odd. She had never taken to a stranger in quite this way before.

However, because of her dream he was not quite a stranger. In it she knew him well. In her dream she was in love with him.

Naturally the emotion faded a few moments after she woke as dream feelings tended to do. Still, her mind remembered how her heart had felt in that moment.

'You want to know why I am here?'

It was what she had asked, so, yes, she did want to know…needed desperately to know. Her future was apparently bound with his.

Did his presence at Warrenstoke mean she would not wed the Viscount?

Waiting for his answer, she could hardly put together a logical thought, not with those handsome yet rugged-looking dimples winking at her.

'Did you know Henry Larkin?' he asked.

That counter-question stunned her. Did Fletcher somehow know of her dear friend?

'Of course I did. Warrenstoke has been a second home to me ever since I was a child.' He had been watching water lap at the bank while she spoke, but now he looked up. He held her gaze. 'Henry was one of the best people I ever met.'

His fingers clenched in his palms. 'I am Henry's brother.'

'Joseph?' She did not know how she muttered that one word—very well, gasped it. Dreams collided, became one so suddenly she felt unbalanced, as if she might slip off the log. 'Larkin?'

'I reckon so. I don't remember ever being called anything but Fletcher Holloway.'

And she could not recall ever being so relieved. Her dreams did not conflict after all. They merged in the man sitting beside her who was sailor, fighter and Viscount all in one.

Mostly, she felt a great weight lift off her at not having to wed Percy.

'Joseph Fletcher Larkin, Warrenstoke has been waiting for your return for a very long time.'

And so had she.

'And we are expected to wed? I assume you have been informed of it.'

In more ways than he would ever know. She was in no way ready to admit she had dreamed of him.

'I have known I would wed Warrenstoke since I was a child. I can only imagine the shock it was for you to discover it.'

'Shock upon shock. I only learned of our supposed betrothal half an hour ago.' His lips were narrowed, set and grim.

Naturally, he would be distraught. Half an hour was not nearly enough time to come to terms with the change his life had taken.

How long had he known his true identity?

If she, who had known her fate all her life was knocked off kilter, what must Fletcher be feeling?

Dumbfounded…overwhelmed, flummoxed for certain.

'Rest assured I do not hold you to it. You and I have a say in the matter.'

Let him think so for now. Telling him otherwise would not be well met.

'Do you remember anything about your life here? Did you mother tell you about it?'

He shook his head. A sliver of sun-streaked hair fell across his brow. He stroked it back into place with tanned, work-worn fingers.

'No. My mother took me from here when I was five. She died a year later. My uncle kept her secrets.'

'Perhaps I can help you regain some memories.'

'If you remember more than grass and an older boy—my brother, probably—you know more about my past than I do.'

How very sad it was that she recalled things about Henry that Fletcher, his own kin, could not.

'I did not realise it when we first met, but I think you share some of his looks. They come across different in you, though. Henry was a gentle soul, always kind and...'

Apparently the comment caught him. His breath hitched, his eyes widening for an instant.

'Patient? Do I remember that right?' he asked after a moment.

'Unfailingly so. Even to a pestering little girl.'

'Was it your father, then, who hired the detectives to find me?'

'The second time, yes. Our fathers were great friends. They felt like brothers more than some do who are born to each other.'

He glanced away, staring at a large rock in the stream and the swirls of water pooling around it. She wished she could unsay the words. It must be a great sorrow for Fletcher to have had a brother and not known him.

'The detectives said something about me being rich, too,' he said, looking back at her.

'Oh, yes, quite wealthy.'

He was not smiling at the news as most men would have been. If eyes could actually see into another person's soul, she felt his probing hers. The sensation was not as unsettling as she would have guessed.

'Has anyone ever told you that you are remarkably easy to speak with?' he asked.

'It must be because I feel I have known you for ever. I was eight years old when I learned about you.' She reached over and squeezed his hand because, in her eyes, it seemed the thing to do. 'I am so very sorry for all you lost.'

'I never knew I had lost anything until those men boarded the *Morning Star.*'

'Is that the ship you were on, the *Morning Star*?'

'It is my uncle's ship. It is where I was raised.'

'It sounds adventurous. I grew up here and in London, but mostly here. Our fathers and my mother—'

A wide palm clamped suddenly hard on her shoulder.

'Percy! You are back early.'

She gulped down a gasp when his fingers dug painfully into her collarbone.

Percy. This was the cousin who had stood to inherit the title and the estate if Fletcher had not been located.

Being tall and heavyset, Fletcher wondered how he managed to creep up upon them. Sneaky fellow, probably.

Eirene shook her shoulder free of the grip on her shoulder. Good for her.

'Not early enough, I'll wager.' Fletcher did not need

to hear more in order to know he did not care for man. The sneer in Cousin Percy's voice gave away his character all too clearly.

In an instant he noted the man was possessive of Eirene. In less time than that he sensed the lady was wary of the hulking lout.

Too bad his only relative was a shifty shark.

'What are you doing out here, Eirene, alone with—?' His cousin cast a haughty glance at Fletcher's bare feet. 'Him.'

Deliberately, he wriggled his toes in the grass. Clearly his relative was an opponent. Fletcher needed to know who, exactly, he was up against.

'Someone important has come and you must be at the house to greet him. Remember who you are, Eirene, and do not make me look bad.'

Who she was? Smart, kind, brave? That was who Fletcher saw her as.

What she was not was a reflection of Percy Larkin.

'Seems to me you are doing that all on your own,' he said, presenting an insincere smile. 'Making yourself look bad, I mean.'

'Mind your own business.' Percy gave him a hard look. 'You seem familiar.'

'I have that kind of face.'

Percy's fat fist reached for Eirene's arm. Fletcher caught the fist and flung it hard away from her.

A flush crept up from his cousin's collar, turning his face the shade of a cut-open beet.

'Get to the house,' Percy snarled. 'You are keeping our guest waiting.'

Eirene slid closer to him on the bench. She must sense he would protect her. Which he would.

'I have already met our guest, Percy. May I introduce Joseph Fletcher Larkin?'

Had he been a fish gasping on a hook, Cousin Percy would not look more stunned.

'You may call me Warrenstoke.'

It would take a better man than Fletcher was not to take satisfaction at seeing the stunned expression on Cousin Percy's wide face, watching him stomp heavy footed down the slope.

'Do you see those sparks coming off his shoes?' he asked.

'Outright flames is what they are. I only hope the hillside does not catch fire.'

He liked Eirene Smythe. She was a lady with a quick sense of humour.

If anyone had to be betrothed to him since she was in the cradle, he did not mind it being her.

At least he would not if he did not have a niggling feeling under his skin that she would not be easy to walk away from when the time came.

'Do not suppose you know a way for me to get out of this mess?' he asked because, again, she was easy to talk to.

'Umm, well, no. You were born to it.'

'Same as you were?'

She nodded, a smile tugging at the corners of her lips. 'I fear I am part and parcel of your mess.'

'You make it sound as if we are helpless against what other people have decided for us.'

'Perhaps we are destined for one another.' At that her smile burst wide on her pretty lips and he knew she was jesting about it.

Her sense of humour over the situation put him at ease.

He straightened up, squared his shoulders and gathered his courage for what awaited him at the mansion glittering in the sunshine below.

Chapter Five

'Percy was in a fine huff.' Mother drew a shawl about her shoulders. 'Such a vain peacock. Now that the true heir has come I can say so.'

Eirene, Mother and Father sat on the back terrace taking a few moments at the end the day to speak privately of today's events and to enjoy the sounds and scents of summer twilight.

Mother chilled easily in the evening, even at this time of year, so she was bundled into a coat with a blanket over her legs. Her health was improving, but slowly, Eirene thought. If they returned to London, she feared it would grow worse again very quickly.

Now that everything had changed she did not know what to expect for their future.

The new Viscount did not seem eager to embrace their betrothal. She could hardly blame him. One day he had been happily sailing the seven seas, punching opponents in the boxing ring and the next…

Well, it was safe to say he was not happy about any of it.

Especially about discovering he was all but a betrothed man.

Just because their fathers had wished for them to wed did not mean he would go along with it. He did not even know his late father and was not obliged to fulfil his desires.

'I'm relieved the estate will not fall into Percy's hands. His nature is not suited for taking care of it as he ought to.'

'As far as that goes, we do not know that Joseph—Fletcher, I mean…he did make it clear he wished to be called Fletcher…but we do not know that he is suited either,' Mother pointed out. 'The boy was raised on a ship. I do not know that it qualifies him to run an estate.'

'As I understand it, he was in charge of the ship. He and his uncle captained it together,' she said in his defence.

'But he was also a boxer. I recognised him right off. I gained a tidy sum when he won his match against the bigger fellow.' Father patted his coat pocket as if it still contained his winnings. 'At least in the end, Percy came around and greeted our new Viscount graciously,' he said.

'He seemed to.' Mother shook her head, frowning. 'I am not so sure it was genuine. You always did give him more credit than he deserved, my dear.'

'Only because I knew I would need to deal with him as the Viscount and my son-in-law.'

'I was there when Percy first met Fletcher,' Eirene pointed out. 'He might look as though he accepts the turn of events, but I am not so sure of it.'

'He did lose a great deal,' her father pointed out. 'The title and you, my girl. And all in a day.'

'The fortune that was to come with me more like it.'

'Our feelings about your marriage remain the same as they did with Percy.' Mother reached out, touched Eirene's chin and nodded. 'You need not go through with it. We can all return to London and carry on quite nicely.'

Except that they could not. Eirene would never endanger her mother's health by returning to London's wicked foul air.

While they might find another place in the countryside to live, it would not be home. Warrenstoke might not legally be theirs, but it was home in their hearts.

'I had a dream,' she said in a rush.

She was nervous telling them even though she knew they would believe her. 'I dreamed of Fletcher. In it I knew him as my husband.'

Mother and Father looked at each other, speaking in that silent language that long-married people had.

Mother nodded, then Father spoke. 'How did you feel about it? In the dream?'

'In the dream I was happy, but that does not mean I will feel the same way if I do wed the Viscount.'

'If? But you dreamed it. Surely you will.' Father nodded, seeming certain.

'Just because in the past my dreams were that way, does not mean this one will be. Fletcher Larkin does have some say in matter.'

Deep down she thought they were right. In fact, more than ever. For a time she feared her dreams conflicted with each other. As it turned out, they did not.

A dream was something to be counted upon.

At the same time... 'I do not have the feeling that Fletcher intends to wed me. I have known of your arrangement with Viscount Warrenstoke since I was born. Poor Fletcher has only just discovered it. I imagine all this is a great shock to him.'

'Oh, but surely he is delighted?' Mother said. 'Any man would be.'

Eirene would feel better if she had half of her mother's confidence.

What she hoped for and what she knew were not the same thing. The new Viscount might be bound to the title, but he was not bound to her. Not really.

'I think he will return to his ship when he gets the chance.'

And what would become of her then if she married him and if, as her dream suggested, she was in love with him?

Fletcher had stated clearly that he would not be poetic over love. Only over whales and his beloved ocean…and perhaps buxom Penny.

While it might be her fate to marry him, she must be careful not to fall in love with him.

Falling in love with Percy was not something she had ever feared. It would never have happened. In fact, the more time he spent away from home, the happier she would have been.

When it came to Percy, the most she had ever hoped for their marriage was that she would tolerate him.

'Gerard, my dear, is there nothing you can do to make Percy leave Warrenstoke?' her mother asked as if reading her mind.

'He is family, so I do not see how it can be done without causing offence.'

Apparently she was going to have to continue to tolerate him.

'I think once our girl is wed to the Viscount, Percy will give up all hope of what he hoped to gain and go home to Liverpool.'

Which meant that, if Fletcher Larkin did not choose to marry her, Percy would not leave?

At least…perhaps…as long as the true heir was in residence, Percy would not cause trouble.

She hoped.

Fletcher had hoped to have a private word with Eirene tonight before everyone retired. He hadn't got the chance, not with having to make the acquaintance of so many people.

Aboard ship he had made a point of knowing everyone, from deck hands to first officer. The estate should not be any different.

As he understood it, Warrenstoke was his by birth, whether he wanted it or not. This was not something he could decline or walk away from.

He did not know how long he would remain here, but as Viscount he was responsible for the place for the rest of his life.

Having hired a captain for the *Morning Star*, to care for it while he and Uncle Hal were landlocked, he figured he could do the same thing here when he and his uncle returned to the sea.

There was only one problem with this ideal solution.

He was expected to take a wife. That wife, as it turned out, he owed a great debt to.

It was the greatest of coincidences that they had even crossed paths again. A coincidence he would not have minded if not for the fact that a marriage was expected between them.

Not expected by him, though. He could not wed her, then leave her in the care of someone else, even if that person was her father. Not only that—where there was a wife there might be children.

Having grown up separated from his father, he would not have that for his children. The odds of them having someone like Uncle Hal to raise them were unlikely.

Eirene Smythe seemed a lovely, bold lady, but that did not mean he would offer his life to her.

His reason for coming here was to benefit his uncle. To purchase the ship they had always dreamed of having.

What he needed to do was speak with Miss Smythe and find out what she thought of their possible betrothal. They had not got around to discussing it earlier today because of the unhappy arrival of Percy. He would bet a winning purse that she did not want this marriage any more than he did.

Damn it, but he could not speak to a woman he could not find. In this huge house he could wander about all night trying to find her. He supposed he could ask, but it was late and most of the staff had already retired.

Since he was not ready to go to his appointed chamber, with the lofty name of the master's quarters, he would go for a walk outside where the stars would look the same as they did at sea.

Wandering down hallways, through this room and that, he felt as though he was sneaking about in someone else's home. He had to remind himself that this grand place belonged to him. He had every right to go where he wanted to go, at any time he chose to.

Just now he chose to walk in the garden. He was not used to gardens, but he thought he would enjoy this one.

So far it was inviting, beautifully dark and still. Garden paths did not rock in the comforting way a ship would, but they were nice none the less.

It was good to have a private place to go.

A sound caught his attention. He stopped to listen because the crunch of his footsteps on the path drowned it out. It was a voice. It was singing.

He grinned, then bit his bottom lip to keep from laughing aloud. He was not ready to let the singer know he was listening.

'Oh, Penny, oh, Penny, oh, where did she go? She left this old port to find a new home. She wandered for weeks then she wandered some more, but poor Buxom Penny just—just…well what did she do?'

Looking up, he saw Eirene standing on the balcony of what must be her chamber. She looked pretty, her silhouette soft in the light that spilled out of her open chamber doors.

As beautiful as a masthead was what she was.

'If you come down, I'll tell you,' he called, but softly so he would not wake anyone.

'I cannot come down now.'

'Then I shall come up.'

The trellis looked sturdy. Three storeys was not higher than the mast on his ship.

So up he shimmied. His supposed intended looked outrageously shocked.

He must be breaking a few rules of etiquette. No doubt he would break many more before he and Uncle Hal made it home to the sea.

But if the lady would not come down, he must go up.

'Stay right where you are,' she said when he would have looped his leg over the balcony rail.

She dashed into her chamber. When she came out again she wore a robe with a blue ribbon at the collar tied under her chin. He could not recall seeing a woman look half as charming.

'We need to speak.' He hoped she would invite him over the rail, but she did not.

'In the morning. You should not be hanging from my balcony. It isn't safe.'

'Safer than hanging on to the ship's mast. The balcony isn't swaying.' Although he wished it was. Only a short time on shore and he already missed the motion.

'If you fall to your death, Percy will be in charge of Warrenstoke…and in charge of me.'

'I won't fall, I promise. But being in charge of you, as in marriage, is what I wish to speak with you about.'

'Yes, I think a conversation is in order since we are… but then it is I really and not we. I have been betrothed to Viscount Warrenstoke since I was born. And you are now he, so, yes, it is we after all.'

She seemed awfully willing to accept this state of affairs, but he could not possibly be held to an agreement like this. 'We must have some choice in the matter. I doubt you wish to wed me any more than I wish to wed you.'

She blinked, bit her bottom lip. Surely he had not injured her feelings by speaking the truth?

Having only recently met, they were not in love, barely even friends, so how could he have offended her?

'Surely you do not wish to marry someone you do not love?' How could she?

'I am the daughter of a viscount. Love plays no part in whom I wed. Except that I do love Warrenstoke… the estate, I mean, not you.'

Life had become too confusing. He had fallen head-long into a world he knew nothing about.

'And so you would marry me, regardless. What if I am a wastrel?'

'If you were a wastrel, you would not bring it up. But, yes, of course I would marry you. First I was to marry Henry, then Percy and now you.'

'You, Eirene Smythe, are not a piece of property to be passed around. I am surprised you accept your fate without question.'

'Not without question. But, yes, I do accept it.'

He thought he heard wood creak. If the trellis gave way, he could leap on to the balcony. What he was not going to do was leave here without finishing this conversation.

'What if I am not willing to go through with this ancient plan? I do not intend to remain at Warrenstoke longer than I need to. You must understand that.'

'Firstly, the plan is no more ancient than I am.'

'That was a figure of speech. Is there a secondly?'

Her hair was loose. She flicked a hank of what looked like smooth cream and strawberries over her shoulder.

'If you did go through with your obligation to marry me, I would not fall in love with you. And for the very reason you just gave. I will not give my heart to a man who is not here so you need not worry about that.'

'Then why marry me?'

'If you think you can run Warrenstoke from which-ever port you land in, you are quite wrong. The estate needs someone to take care of it every day. Too many people's livelihoods depend upon its success.'

'I will hire someone…a captain of sorts.'

'That will not do. Warrenstoke needs someone who

belongs to it. Someone who loves it and not the wage he will receive.'

'It seems like you are suggesting I hire you.'

'No. What I am saying is that you marry me and my father will run Warrenstoke. The same as he has been doing since Henry left us.'

Left us? Perhaps she had chosen that phrase on purpose because the word 'died' was harsh and his grief was so new.

He supposed he was grieving. Only not in the way the people who knew his brother were. His grieving had to do with what was lost of his past and a brother he did not quite recall.

It was all damned confusing, though, to grieve for a life one did not have when one preferred the life they had.

'May I tell you something, Fletcher?'

He nodded. Not that what she had to say was going to change his mind.

'I come with a great deal of money. Whoever marries me will get it. Until earlier today, Percy assumed it would be him. If you do not marry me, he will keep assuming it. He will see me, and all that I have, as his.'

Slow and steady anger boiled up the back of his neck at the thought of his cousin going after Eirene. He owed the lady too much to put her in such a position.

But marrying to solve the problem was extreme.

'I never planned on marrying anyone, Eirene. My life is all wrong for having a wife.'

'I always planned on marrying the heir to Warrenstoke. Everything about my past has led me here.'

'Any man would be lucky to have you...not Percy. I

don't mean him. But you are lovely and should not be willing to just give yourself away. You are not property.'

Now he had done it. Moisture dampened her eyes.

'You should go now. If any one sees you, you will have no choice but to marry me. In case you ever did.'

'What do you mean by that? I do have a choice.'

'Never mind.'

Spinning about, she went into her chamber, closing the doors with a quiet click.

Never mind? He did have a choice and it was not to marry. If it came to choosing a wife or choosing a life at sea, there was no question what he would pick.

For his uncle's sake, if for no other reason, he would go back to his ship.

The world might consider Viscount Warrenstoke to be his father, but Uncle Hal was the one to have lived the role.

Besides that, his future had been determined by another person's choice once before.

From now on his future would be decided by what he chose.

On the way to the breakfast room, Eirene walked down the wide corridor where family portraits hung.

There were benches scattered along the way where one could sit if one wished to.

Fletcher sat on one. He was staring so hard at one portrait that he did not notice her until she sat down beside him.

'Good morning,' he said. Blinking his eyes quickly, he nodded, then swept his hand towards a portrait.

'Is this my mother?'

'Yes. I've often thought how beautiful she was.'

'It is not something I remember, but I see it now. She looks as fresh as if she was just out of the schoolroom. I wonder why my father kept her portrait hanging here with the rest after what she did.'

'My father tells me he cared very much for her… and you. But she never adjusted to her life here. It was never her choice to move an ocean away from home and she was homesick every day. I imagine you are in something of the same position, aren't you? Taken away from the life you love.'

'It does not compare. I'm not an eighteen-year-old girl. And I was born here. Not that I remember much at all.' He shrugged. 'Which of these fine old fellows is my father?'

'That one, between your mother and his first wife.'

'Henry's mother?' He looked at her portrait for a moment and then shifted his gaze to the portrait of Henry.

'He doesn't look much like his mother. I think we both take after our father.'

'I see the similarity, but also the differences.'

'My brother and I led different lives. But of all these men…' he scanned the portraits one by one '…Henry is the one I remember, but only in a vague way.'

'It's no wonder. You were so young. But maybe once you are here for a while memories will come back to you.'

After a moment they rose and walked to the breakfast room.

Mother and Father were already eating.

While Fletcher went to the side table to fill a plate, she kissed her father's cheek and then her mother's.

Looking out the window past her mother's shoulder, she spotted Percy sparring with a tree trunk.

She dreaded him coming into breakfast. He was bound to bring the cloudy weather with him. No one could cast gloom as well as Percy did when he was in a mood. No doubt he would be in one.

To her surprise, when moments later he did come in, he was smiling.

That was the last thing she expected to see. Yesterday, he had been incensed over the turn of events. Seething under the skin was what she thought. But then all at once he seemed to get over it.

While he had appeared congenial in company last night, she believed his acceptance of losing Warrenstoke to be insincere. Surely he wore a deceitful mask over his emotions.

Here he was, though, making pleasant conversation to everyone. He was especially pleasant to Fletcher.

A shivery little chill tiptoed up her spine. This was not the real Percy Larkin. She felt anxious in his presence in a different way than she had before.

Percy would not give up what he believed to be his with a smile. He had revealed the violence within him when he'd squeezed her shoulder, giving her a warning... a painful one.

If anyone else was wary of him, they did not show it. For now she would keep what he'd done to herself. There was no point in stirring the hornet's nest. Perhaps he would go away on his own.

As odd as it was that Percy was acting civilly, it was even odder that Fletcher spoke to his cousin as if they really were long-lost relatives reunited at last.

Everything was as cheery as could be.

Nothing could be more confusing.

The Larkin who wanted Warrenstoke and now could

not have it was much too amiable with the Larkin who had it and did not want it.

Caution was clearly the order of the day.

'Well done, Lord Warrenstoke.' Lord Habershom snapped the accounts ledger closed. 'You are learning quickly.'

Learning that he would rather be keeping the ship's journal was what. While there was a great deal of clerical work involved in running a merchant ship, there was more involved in running an estate.

Behind the desk where Lord Habershom sat was a large window.

Everyone who walked past it distracted Fletcher from what he needed to be paying attention to.

Spending this much time indoors nearly made him itch. When the day was bright and sunny, and he could see it was, he needed to be out in it.

'In time you might wish to hire an accountant to see to all this.' Eirene's father tapped the leger with his finger. 'But you will need to know it all before you do. There are those who would swindle us. Not all accountants are above board.'

'I would not mind hiring you.' The man knew everything about Warrenstoke. Even though he himself was a viscount, he did not seem to be above bookwork.

'Hire me?' He shook his head. 'I would not be able to take a wage. Besides, there will be no need to once you marry my daughter. We will be family, after all, and I will carry on here for the pleasure of it. It makes your father happy to see me sitting in his chair, that is what I believe.'

'Eirene and I have not agreed to wed.'

Lord Habershom stood, indicating they were finished with the books.

'We shall see, shan't we?' Lord Habershom shot him the strangest grin.

There was nothing to see except that he was going to remain here for as short a time as he could, then take up the life he himself decided to have, which was at sea, not on land.

The Viscount clapped him on the shoulder. 'And now I have an appointment with your uncle to ride about the estate.'

'Ride? As on horses?'

'It is the best way to see it all, or most of it.'

'Uncle Hal does not ride.' No...he sailed.

'He is eager to learn, though. Your uncle seems to be a very decent man. I look forward to getting to know him better.'

'The most decent man I know. But I'd wager you will never make a horseman of him.'

'How much?' Lord Habershom had a good smile. Like Uncle Hal, he was a man to be trusted.

'A friendly sum.'

They agreed on an amount, then walked out of the office.

Going outside, Fletcher took a deep breath of air, the same as he did whenever he came from below decks into the sunshine.

This was not so different than that, except he was walking on solid ground and not a shifting deck, and he was looking at green grass, not green waves.

He took a stroll beside the stream, trying hard to remember something of his life here.

The only good, solid memory he had of this place

was recent. The memory of Eirene, standing in the water, skirt and boots tucked into each of her elbows and water lapping at her calves, was so fresh he did not have to close his eyes to see it.

Leaving the stream, he walked up a green hill with trees at the top. Something about it felt right. Perhaps he had climbed it before many years ago.

Nearing the top, he found he was not alone. Eirene waved at him from the crest.

'Hey there, pretty lady,' he said, then sat down beside her.

'Good afternoon to you, too.'

'There is an amazing view from here,' he remarked. There was the majestic one spread out before him and the lovely one seated beside him.

Eirene Smythe was simply a pleasure to look at. Just now her hair was more strawberries than cream. Her eyes drew his attention, their expression being a mixture of boldness and softness. And the slight hint of a dimple in her chin made him happy.

Ah, but it was her smile that nicked him in the heart. So wide and genuine, he figured he could look at it for ever.

He really could, couldn't he? If he were not set on going back to the sea, back to his real life.

Which he fully intended to do. There was his uncle to be considered as much as himself. They were both seamen, not landlubbers.

'This is the best place to sit on the whole property.' She lifted her face to the sunshine, smiled and closed her eyes for a moment.

She did not seem to be worried about getting freckles

as many women were. He liked freckled faces. Kissed by sunshine was what he always thought about them.

'Your brother used to come here. I tagged along and when I got tired he carried me the rest of the way up. I must have been about four years old, and he was…let me think…fifteen, perhaps?'

Fletcher went soft inside all of a sudden… It seemed like…yes, there it was, a memory. He remembered being carried up the hill…or was it dragged by the arm? Either way, he remembered Henry laughing…he was laughing, too.

'You have a faraway look in your eye, Fletcher. Are you recalling something?'

He had to nod because if he tried to speak the words would get tangled in his throat.

'Good, then. Perhaps more memories will come.'

She sat silently beside him as if visions of the past would suddenly cram his mind.

Nothing did, but it did not matter greatly. In the moment he was happy to be sitting in the sunshine beside a pretty woman.

Out in the distance he spotted two men on horseback.

'Can't be!' He squinted his eyes—still the image did not change. He saw what he saw.

'What can't be?'

'Your father and my uncle.' He pointed to them trotting up a slope. 'Riding horses.'

She shot him a puzzled look. 'I am certain it is them.'

'My uncle has never ridden a horse in his life. He's a sailor.'

'He seems to be taking right to it.'

'I suppose. I only hope they don't…' Stunned, the words dried in his mouth.

'Go too fast?' she added helpfully.

It was what they were doing though, trotting towards the crest of a hill as if his uncle knew how to. As if he did not look like a buoy bobbing on waves.

A second later the horses ran faster, their long legs pumping and their tails flying out behind them.

'Don't worry. My father would not let him do it if he was not ready to. I'm sure he is safe.'

'No, he is hanging on and—'

And then he could not speak, could hardly think, only remember. An image of a streaking tail, of hooves hitting the ground, galloping across…the dining room table?

Lurching to his feet, Fletcher went around the back of the great old tree they were sitting in front of. There ought to be a root sticking up out of the ground.

Yes, that one!

He scraped dirt from under the root. His finger poked something firmer than dirt. Not as hard as a stone. With care he dug it free.

'What is it?' Eirene must have followed him. The ruffle on the hem of her skirt brushed his sleeve.

She bent over to get a closer look at what he held in his open palm.

'Pearly.' Even though he was looking at small wood horse in his hand, he could not believe it. 'My father carved it for me. I don't know why I buried it, but I remember doing it.'

She squeezed his shoulder, her small hand warm but solid and encouraging.

He felt something tickle his knee where he knelt. It was probably an insect, but he imagined it to be a tender root growing into the soil of Warrenstoke.

What he ought to do was yank the root out because this wasn't his place. His new title, and who his father was might indicate it to be true, but his place was the sea…so was Uncle Hal's.

'I wonder what I can do to help you remember.' Eirene tapped her chin, drawing his attention to an enchanting dimple.

It might be helpful to remember his past, to make peace with what his mother had done.

Had she not taken him away, he might have been happy growing up at Warrenstoke with his brother and his father. How was he to know?

His mother had made a choice and he had lived with the outcome of it.

That outcome being that he had a wonderful life growing up aboard the *Morning Star* with his uncle.

'I would like that,' he said.

Remembering would be fine, but he would be the one to choose where his future went from here.

'Come with me.' Eirene stood up. 'I have an idea.'

'Where are we going?'

'I cannot say. The idea is to have memories spring upon you unexpected.'

Eirene Smythe was unexpected. This time he was spending with her would one day be a memory. He was damned certain to make sure he would not forget this time with her.

Twenty minutes later she led him through tall stable doors. The building was made of stone, solid as could be. He imagined it would not have changed much since he was a boy.

In the dim interior, he glanced at the horses, listening to their welcoming whickers.

'Well?' Eirene asked. 'What do you recall?'

'Nothing.'

She looked so disappointed he wished he had, if only for her sake.

Sitting down on an overturned barrel, she gave a great sigh that lifted, then dropped her bosom.

He shifted his gaze to a horse watching over its stall door. If he meant to return to the sea, which he did, he did not need to be dwelling on how pretty Eirene was. Or how nice kissing her would be. That would be a good memory to take back to the *Morning Star*.

Didn't matter, since he was not going to kiss her. It would not be right, not with her hoping for a betrothal between them.

'I only thought that since you remembered the carved horse, a real one might spark a memory.'

'No, not a single one.'

'I have one.' She shrugged one shoulder, looking wistful. 'Henry used to put me on the saddle in front of him. We would gallop to the village and he would buy me a stick of barley sugar or a pie…or, well never mind. I should not go on about my memories when you do not have them. He is your brother.'

'Was my brother.'

'Is.'

A stableman came in, leading a saddled horse. He led it to a stall and then went about removing the saddle and brushing the animal down.

Fletcher opened his mouth to argue the difference between the 'is' and 'was' when it came to the dearly departed, but she spoke first.

'My point is, if you can remember him, he will become real to you. Then you will have your brother with you always.'

'I do not remember that he took me riding.'

'Very well, let's visit the kitchen. Surely you pestered Cook for treats together. Boys are always hungry, as I understand. And even if you do not recall anything, we shall pester Cook for a treat.'

She rose and walked ahead of him out of the stable. Pausing at the door, she glanced back, waving her hand for him to hurry.

As far as he was concerned, he already had a treat. Being in Eirene Smythe's company was a great treat.

And as far as memories went, he thought he would enjoy the new ones he was making with her as much as the ones he might or might not recall.

New memories, old memories…he would carry them all back to *Morning Star*.

Chapter Six

Fletcher kept the carved figure in his pocket the same as he had as a young boy. Even after so long the weight felt familiar, comfortable.

Damned if he knew why it should. But when a man whose job it was to get him dressed set his pants on the bed, Fletcher had tucked the little horse in the pocket.

Maybe having it there would spark another memory.

He was early coming into the breakfast room. Not earlier than his cousin, though. Percy sat behind a plate heaped with enough food for two men.

Ships' rations would never allow for such indulgence.

Percy swallowed whatever he was chewing, then said, 'Good morning, Fletcher. May I say again how glad I am that you have come home at last?'

He could say it a dozen times and Fletcher would not believe him.

'I appreciate your warm welcome.' Damned if either of them meant what they said. What they were doing was a dance of sorts like boxers did when they circled one another, sizing the other up before fists started flying. 'Given that you expected to inherit Warrenstoke, it is gracious of you welcome me so warmly.'

Percy bit a corner of toast, chewed, then swallowed hard. Fletcher could well imagine the words he swallowed with the toast.

'Titles come and go at the whim of fate. We all expected Henry to be Viscount, of course. I am only glad you were located. Imagine having no family at all? If not for you, I would have no relatives. Not living ones, anyway.'

'It is a relief to know you do not resent me for claiming my place. But I wonder…how do you feel about Eirene?'

'Lovely woman, of course, but wilful.'

'You are not disappointed that she will not be marrying you? You were nearly betrothed, were you not?'

Ah, right there, Fletcher sensed that he had landed a punch. Percy's jaw began to tic, a sure sign he was chewing on anger, not breakfast.

Anything else they might have to say to one another would have to wait. Eirene, along with her mother and father, entered the breakfast room. Uncle Hal followed steps behind them.

Conversation became easier once the Habershoms joined in. They spoke of the new foal in the stable and the recently bloomed flowers in the garden.

Uncle Hal went on about how he looked forward to going riding again. If he longed for the *Morning Star*, he did not mention it. Surely he missed it as much as Fletcher did.

'Eirene.' Lady Habershom shot her daughter a wide smile. Mother and daughter looked much alike when it came to their smiles. 'We need to host a house party so that people from all around will have a chance to welcome our new Viscount, and to celebrate that he has been brought home safe to us.'

Eirene cast him a glance which said as clearly as words that she understood he would hate having a party. She offered a small shrug. It was good to have someone on his side.

Any second now she would tell her mother what a bad idea it was.

'That is a wonderful idea, Mother.'

What was that? Damned awful was what.

A party. Worse, a house party. Even he knew those could go on for days.

'It is a perfect idea, Lady Habershom,' Percy declared. After that, his jaw was no longer ticking.

'"It was the best of times, it was the worst of times…"' Eirene was happy that Mother had decided to leave Poe on the shelf today in favour of Dickens. '"It was the age of wisdom, it was the age of foolishness, it was the epoch of belief, it was the epoch of incredulity…it was the season of Light, it was the season of Darkness, it…"'

Mother sighed. 'Why, those words might be written for our own times, don't you think?' her mother asked.

A motion through the window caught her attention.

Fletcher? Why was he waving to get her attention?

Mother must have seen her gaze wander. She glanced over her shoulder, out the window.

'Oh!' Her mother yawned. 'I am ready for a mid-morning rest.'

'It will not be mid-morning for another hour and a half. We have only just finished breakfast and did not even get though one sentence of *A Tale of Two Cities*.'

'Well, it is a very long sentence and now I am weary. Ring for my maid, will you, dear?'

As soon as the maid had come to take her mother to the morning room, Eirene hurried out of the house.

Fletcher stood in the same spot she had spotted him through the window.

'Can't you talk your mother out of this?' he said without preamble.

'I fear not. It is only right that you be welcomed into society.'

'What if I do not wish to be welcomed? I will not be here long enough to make it worthwhile.'

'What you wish has nothing to do with it.' Having grown up a daughter of society, she knew this to be true. Poor Fletcher had grown up as free as a bird and must now feel as if his wings were being ruthlessly clipped. 'Society has rules of behaviour which must be observed…or at least appear to be observed.'

A hank of hair fell across his face which he scowled through.

Quite boldly, she reached out and tucked it behind his ear. 'There, that is better.'

'Nothing seems better to me.'

'Are you aware that you are snarling at me?'

'I might be snarling, but not at you.'

'Since I am the one you are looking in the eye, you are definitely snarling at me.'

His shoulders sagged as he shook his head. 'I beg your pardon. It is the damned party I meant to snarl at.'

'It need not be so awful. With the right attitude it will be great fun.'

'Will I be required to dance and make polite conversation to strangers at this event?'

'I am afraid you will.'

'Then how can you say it will not be awful?'

Poor Fletcher. He truly looked alarmed.

'Because I will teach you all you need to know in order to survive it. Not only that, you will have a grand time.'

'Grand,' he repeated, but with a snort.

'Shall we begin now? My reading time with Mother was cut short so I have a few moments.'

'Tomorrow. Right now I am to ride about with your father and meet the tenants.'

'Ride about? On a horse?'

'You are laughing inside, aren't you?'

He spun about and began to walk away, but then stopped, looking over his shoulder.

'Thank you for offering to help me, Eirene. I will try my best not to be a beast of a student.'

She watched him walk towards the stable. As a student he might be a challenge. One, she had to admit, she was looking forward to.

Turning, she walked leisurely back towards the house, stopping to smell a violet, pausing to admire the colours of a butterfly. It was a beautiful morning and there was no reason to hurry.

There was not, until she spotted Percy leaning against a tree trunk, arms crossed over his chest and staring at her.

Malignant was the only word she could think of to describe the expression on his face.

Were Mr Poe still alive, he could write a story about

Percy Larkin as he appeared in the moment. She must be wary of encountering him alone.

In the past she had considered him merely vain and annoying. Now she knew the darkness in him went deeper. In that moment at the stream when he discovered who Fletcher was, he had dug his fingers into her shoulder with the intent to cause her pain.

With his eyes shooting invisible arrows at her, she was not certain it was safe to walk back to the house alone. No doubt he was imagining punching her with the fist he was clenching.

Reasonably, she knew he could not act on it. He would be banned from Warrenstoke if he did.

Still, rather than take the path to the house, she took the one Fletcher was on.

Slowly, though. She did not want Percy to know he had unnerved her. Putting on a casual air, she bent to pluck a yellow rose, then continued after Fletcher.

Once she caught up, she handed him the rose.

'I am suddenly in the mood to go riding.'

Bouncing over the countryside on horseback was one way to shove the house party to the back of his mind. Keeping a seat on the horse kept his attention occupied. The animal swayed back and forth like a ship did, but that was where the likeness ended.

A ship did not have a mind of its own. It went where the helmsman steered it. A horse might take it in mind to dash away and this poor sailor would be left hanging on for dear life.

This was a sorry show. Settling himself in the saddle, he firmed his back and resolve. If his uncle could do this, he damned well could, too.

'You are doing splendidly,' Eirene said brightly. 'It is as if you were born for it.'

'If I was, it was too long ago to do me any good now.'

His companion looked comfortable in the saddle, as relaxed as if she were a gull riding air currents, as pretty as the rosebud she had tucked into the button-hole of his shirt.

It was supposed to be he and Lord Habershom going to meet tenants, but no sooner had he and Eirene walked into the stable than the Viscount recalled a meeting he had forgotten about.

He handed over the visit with the tenants to his daughter who, Fletcher had been informed, knew them even better than Lord Habershom did.

Given a choice, he would have taken both of them with him.

Meeting tenants, folks who looked up to him for their livelihoods, was daunting. He might be called Viscount Warrenstoke but it was the last thing he felt.

The first introduction had been awkward. Fletcher was used to being in charge aboard ship. The needs of a deck hand were vastly different than the needs of a land tenant.

Having muddled his way through the first introduc-tion, he rode on to the next feeling slightly more con-fident.

Eirene assured him that everyone would be thrilled to meet him and it seemed to be true.

Visit by visit he began to get a feel for their needs. The people he met were kind, welcoming. Truth be told, he supposed he had more in common with them than those he was supposed to be peers with.

As they rode from home to home, a growing sense of his responsibility to these cottagers niggled at him. It was not going to be the easy thing he had imagined to leave them and go back to the sea. He would need someone reliable to fill this role once he was gone.

The most qualified person was one he could not hire. Nor could he ask him to remain and volunteer out of affection for the estate.

As his father-in-law, Lord Habershom would gladly do it. That was the impression Fletcher had got, anyway. But damn it all! He could not have a father-in-law without marrying the man's daughter. He could not in all good conscience wed a lady and then abandon her for the sea.

As they came over the rise of a hill, the next cottage came into view. Its rundown condition made him forget the saddle blisters he felt coming on. The cottage was in shambles. It was missing roof tiles. Shutters with peeling paint hung cock-eyed at every window.

'Does no one live here?' he asked.

While the other cottages they had visited were painted white, had neat yards and tidy gardens, this one did not. The door looked like a plank of splintered wood. Weeds sprouted instead of flowers. One window was covered by slats, indicating the glass was broken.

'You wouldn't think so,' Eirene answered.

The reason it was in this condition became apparent the closer they got to the cottage. At only one in the afternoon a bearded, unkempt man sat on the porch in a chair. The chair had one leg shorter than the other three which put the fellow at an odd angle. He leaned sideways, cradling a brown jug in his arms as if it were a cherished child.

There was a child, he saw, about ten years old. If there was one thing she was not, it was cherished.

Eirene let out a frustrated huff. 'Henry gave him money for repairs, but you can see where he spent it.'

On keeping the jug filled.

The little girl did not seem to notice them riding into the yard. Poor thing was trying to coax a cow into the pen in the yard. It was a stubborn giant of a beast which resisted being put away.

It must know that a slip of a girl could not force it. Clearly the girl's father was not going to do anything but sit on his porch and watch her struggle.

Closer now, he could hear her pleading with the cow to move. No matter how she yanked and hauled at the lead rope, the animal stood stubbornly outside the gate.

The man shouted at the girl to get the beast inside, then fetch him something to eat.

'Floyd Mathers has not been sober a day since his wife passed away. That was five years ago.'

'I'll have a word with him.' Grief was a cruel thing, but there was no excuse for him neglecting his child.

All of a sudden the girl sat down in the dirt, covered her eyes and began to weep, the lead rope around the cow's neck dangling from her fingers.

Fletcher knew a thing or two about cows, having transported them upon occasion.

He dismounted the horse, wishing he did not look like a bumbler. Not that it mattered since his feat of awkwardness had already been witnessed by his other tenants. And this one, as glassy eyed as he was, was not likely to notice. Not the girl either, weeping into her small hands as she was.

'You are getting better at this, Lord Warrenstoke,' Eirene called after him.

It was then that she appeared to notice them. She stood up, dabbing her cheeks with the backs of her hands.

'Good afternoon, Willa,' Eirene said.

The child glanced back and forth between him and Eirene. After a hesitation, she dipped him a curtsy. Poor mite could not seem to manage a smile.

That one, hesitant curtsy got to him in a way that nothing else had. This child, ignored by her father, had no one to care for her.

No one but him. He was Warrenstoke and so she did, by rights, have him.

'It seems you are having trouble with your animal, little lady.'

She swiped her sleeve across her eyes. 'Florrie is the most stubborn beast, sir. She will not go until she wants to. Last night she stood in this spot until after dark. Papa was angry about not having dinner ready, but—'

Dinner? That was the man's concern?

'Here, let me have a go at the beastie.'

She handed him the rope. In the past he'd had some success with sweet-talking animals who feared boarding ship.

First thing, he spoke gentle nonsensical words into the cow's fuzzy flicking ear. Then he patted her neck.

'Come along now, Bessie,' he crooned.

The cow stepped placidly into the pen behind him.

'Maybe she doesn't like being called Florrie,' he suggested. 'Bessie is a good strong name for a cow.'

'I will call her Bessie, my lord.'

Close up he noticed how thin the girl was. It was a

pitiful father who thought more of nursing his jug than he did providing for his child. Just as shameful, he expected his child to take care of him.

The man was about to discover that a drunken tenant would not be tolerated any more than a drunken sailor was.

'Do you have any brothers? Any sisters to help?' Pray that she was not the oldest and required to care for siblings as well as her father.

'No, it is only me and Papa.'

'I will have a word with your father. But here...' He dug deep into his pocket where a few coins clinked against the carved horse. He pressed them into her hand. 'Take this to the village and get some sweets and whatever else you wish.'

The village was not far away, but he would have enough time to say what he needed to without her overhearing.

'Thank you, sir.' She dipped him another curtsy then skipped towards the village, a smile on her face as a child ought to have.

Pressing his point was easy. He snatched the jug from the man's arms, then emptied it on to the dirt. This got Mathers's attention, hopefully enough to heed the reprimand Fletcher lashed him with.

It got the attention of a pair of men walking past the cottage. They stopped, staring. One of them nodded in approval, the other shook his head in disapproval. It's how Fletcher interpreted it.

Not that it mattered what they thought. Only that the little girl was better taken care of.

He mounted the horse. This time seemed easier than the past dozen times he had done it.

From where he sat he had a view of acres of grass waving in the breeze. Nestled in a copse of trees he spotted the roof of the estate house. The contrast between this cottage and the mansion struck him hard.

The reason the cottage was in the condition it was sat slumped on the porch in his chair.

It was Mather's fault. None the less it seemed wrong that Warrenstoke had such abundance while one of its own went hungry.

One of his own.

'Willa is such a sweet child,' Eirene said while they rode away. 'Until her mother died, she was as pampered a child as could be.'

'You know everyone here rather well, it seems.'

'You will, too, once you have been here as long as I have.'

Which he would not be. Although it was his intention to return to his ship, the thought of leaving did not have the urgency it had in the beginning. Sailing away from his responsibilities would not be the simple thing he had first thought.

Somehow meeting Willa, seeing her need, moved him in a way he did not fully understand.

'I will speak with the kitchen when we return and make sure food is sent over to Willa. Sending money will be worse than wasted, I fear.'

'I see something in you, Fletcher.' Eirene arched a brow at him, smiling.

'What?'

'It's only that, seeing your natural way with the tenants, I believe your bloodline is showing. You are an excellent Warrenstoke.'

He could not deny that in a small way it did seem

natural. Not because of bloodlines, but because of experience. Having been in charge of the crew of *Morning Star* was what made this feel somewhat natural.

One thing was different, though. Aboard ship he had never had a lovely and intriguing lady standing beside him at the helm.

Introducing Fletcher to the tenants yesterday had been an important step in teaching him his role as Viscount. This afternoon would be another step, although vastly different than the one yesterday.

'Step into my world, Fletcher Larkin,' Eirene told her reluctant pupil when they entered the large empty ballroom.

Given the narrowed gaze with which he answered, one would think she had invited him into a snake pit and not on to a dance floor.

It was understandable that the ballroom was intimidating to a man not used to such extravagance, being as large and glittery as it was. More than a dozen chandeliers hung from the ceiling. Even though they were not lit, afternoon sunshine streaked through glass doors running the length of the south wall, casting rainbow prisms across the floor and walls.

This was one of Eirene's favourite places to be this time of day, besides on the hill or walking in the stream. She could not teach Fletcher to dance in the stream, could she?

Then again, why couldn't she?

It would be better for him to learn here where he would actually be dancing. There was a great deal of sense to it.

But there was sense the other way, too. Feeling a

fish out of water, so to speak, would Fletcher struggle to learn and not enjoy dancing when the time came to do it?

And it would come to it in three weeks' time. No one could plan an event more quickly than Mother could, even when not at the tip-top of health.

'I know you are not happy about this party, Fletcher, but Warrenstoke needs a reason to celebrate. There has been too much sorrow lately. Now that you have been safely delivered home, it is only right we do so.'

'People will only be let down once my uncle and I return to our ship. Seems wrong to get their hopes up and then let them down.'

'Are you certain going back is what your uncle wishes? As far as I can tell he is enjoying living here. It is what he told my father, at any rate.'

'He is as anxious to get back to the ship as I am.'

'Perhaps he is. But come with me. You do not look yourself with rainbows glittering on your nose.'

'Wherever we are going will be better than this.'

He followed her out of the house, walking beside her across the meadow to the stream.

Once under the shade of trees, near the gurgling murmur of water, she noticed the corners of his mouth relax, his shoulders sag as his tension released.

Funny how water made all the difference in his sense of well-being. If only she could arrange to have a fountain magically placed in the ballroom, Fletcher might have a good time at his party.

Naturally, he would need to learn to dance first.

'Take off your shoes,' she said, sitting on the same log they had used before.

While he yanked off his shoes and stockings, she turned her back and did the same.

She tied up her skirt at the hip, which was not an easy task, then stepped into the water and reached her hand out, wriggling her fingers for him to join her.

'What are we doing?' He waded in, grinning. 'Guess it doesn't matter as long as we aren't dancing.'

She took his hand, placed it on her waist.

All of a sudden her insides turned fluttery. His fingers were firm…the heat of his hand seeped through her dress. How odd. Nicely odd, though. She had never had that reaction to a dance partner before.

'What are we doing, Eirene?' His smile was warm, ripe with mischief, all in one teasing glance.

Gathering herself, she refocused on the reason she was standing barefoot in a stream with his hand on her person. She was serious about teaching him to behave in a ballroom.

'We, my friend, are going to dance.'

'There's no music. Got to have that.'

She placed her hand on his shoulder. 'Of course there is music. Just close your eyes and listen.'

He shrugged, then, after a moment with his eyes closed, he smiled softly in a way she had not seen before.

'I hear it now.'

'Good, now just sway a bit to the sound. Imagine this is the deck of your ship and let your body react to it.'

His eyes popped open and he gave her the oddest look. It was a frown, yet not an unfriendly one.

She got the oddest shiver. When had a shiver ever been warm…made her feel soft and yearning rather than cold and frightened?

Then, eyes closed once more, he began to sway.

'Excellent. Now move your feet side to side as if you are gliding.'

'Hmmm,' he murmured. 'Like manoeuvring on a slick deck?'

'I suppose so. I have never done that to be able to make the comparison.'

He stopped suddenly, opened his eyes and pinned her with a pure blue stare.

'Never been on a ship's deck?'

'I have, once or twice. What I have not done is glide about on a slick one.'

'Tomorrow, then. We will go to the seaside.'

'Alone? The two of us?' She shook her head. 'Until we are engaged we will need a chaperon.'

'That makes no sense. We are alone here without a chaperon.'

True, but the warmth pulsing under her skin pointed out why one might be needed. Not that she was going to forget her morals and fall into his arms…well, she was in his arms, but she was teaching him to dance so it made all the difference.

'We are at home so a chaperon is not required. But we cannot parade about in public without one.'

'The life of a gentleman doesn't seem genuine,' he said. 'From what I can see, it's all about appearances.'

'Isn't it that way on board your ship? Don't you need to appear to be in control of everything even when the condition of the ocean says you are not? Appearances are important.'

'And so I must appear to know how to dance?'

This might not have been the wisest place to teach

him after all. The odds of him ever dancing midstream were remote. She only meant to put him at ease.

However, she was far from at ease with his hand pressing the curve of her waist, distracting her from studious instruction.

'I will ask Father to come with us to the seaside,' she said.

He stopped swaying.

'And your mother. Seems to me it would do her good to get out.'

'Oh, I don't know. I worry that it will be too much for her.'

'It won't.' He let go of her, stepped on to the bank. 'Nothing like good salt air to promote one's health.'

'Your lesson isn't finished yet, Viscount.'

Up on the bank, he looked down at her...held her gaze for a long time without speaking.

At least not speaking with words. He was telling her something, though.

No man had ever given her such a simmering gaze and so she might be mistaken in its meaning. But if she was not mistaken, well then, the moment was intensely intimate. It felt akin to a kiss. Not of the lips, no...but of the heart.

She touched her fingers to her heart, hoping she was not wrong...but, no, that was not right. Of course she hoped it was wrong. No woman wanted to fall in love with a man who would sail away and leave her heartbroken.

Oh, dear and drat! That was exactly what she had been in her dream. In love with him.

'That is Captain,' he replied. Somehow he managed to grin and look serious all at once. 'Come, Eirene, the sun is setting and, as you said, appearances are important.'

'And dreams are not?'

He reached a hand down to help her up. 'I have no idea what you are talking about.'

'Oh, but of course I mean my dream of turning you into a proficient dancer which will make you a happy dancer.'

'I shall practise diligently in order to make your dreams come true.'

Chapter Seven

As it turned out there were five of them going to the seaside: he, Eirene, Lord and Lady Habershom, along with Uncle Hal.

During the hour-long carriage ride, Fletcher was surprised to see how quickly his uncle and the Viscount had bonded with one another.

Eirene had said as much and now he saw it with his own eyes. To look at them, one would think they had been friends for ever. He recalled his uncle having acquaintances, but living as they did, going from port to port, he had never made any particular friendships.

A viscount and a crusty sailor? They were an unlikely set of companions.

It was good to know that not all proper gentlemen were stuffy and ruled by rules.

If Fletcher had to become one of them, he would be like Eirene's father.

Or perhaps his own? He would like to think his father was like the gentleman sitting across from him, but how was he to know?

Casting his mind back as far as he could, he tried to recall the man, but could not.

'I would like to see a ship like yours, Hal,' Lord Habershom said. 'If one is in port.'

'We will search one out. I need to stand on deck again, get the sea back in my bones. I am becoming a content landlubber in short order,' Uncle Hal declared with a great smile.

'You are?' Fletcher could not believe he heard what he had.

'The air is drier inland. More comfortable for this old body.'

'It's not that much drier and we are not all that far inland,' he pointed out.

He could scarcely believe this was his uncle speaking…the man who had been a sailor all his life and raised Fletcher to be one, too.

Uncle Hal, a landlubber?

The reason for coming here was to obtain the funds to get them a new ship.

Most of it was, not all.

Discovering his past had been a part of the reason, too. He was still who he had always known himself to be, Fletcher Holloway, sailor and fighter, but now he knew he was also Joseph Fletcher Larkin, Viscount Warrenstoke. Now, with a few memories returning, he wanted to know all of who he was.

Going back to where he belonged without remembering where he had come from would be a mistake. Without his memories, well, dash it all, he would be constantly wondering.

'Your father enjoyed sailing.' Lord Habershom nodded, smiling. 'You probably don't know you had that in common with him.'

That was something! It was not only from Uncle Hal that he had learned a love of the sea, then. Now that he thought about it, maybe he did feel it in his blood. He'd always taken to the sea in a way which went deeper than simple learning.

'Oh, the great times we had taking out his sailboat… you remember it, don't you, my dear?' Lord Habershom asked with a grin at his wife.

'Like it was yesterday. Of course we never took Eirene. I feared taking her out on the water. Oh, but you were raised on the water, Fletcher, and look how well that turned out. But now fate has delivered you to us and we could not be happier about it.'

It had been hired detectives who delivered him to Warrenstoke, not fate. He would have said so, but they had reached their destination.

The coachman opened the door. Uncle Hal stepped out first, gave a hand to Lady Habershom and helped her down with great care. The lady was frail, but Fletcher thought she handled the journey in glad spirits.

A happy attitude and sea air could only lead to better health.

Fletcher made sure he was the one to help Eirene down. Having held her when they stream danced yesterday, he wanted to hold her again.

Hang it all if he hadn't spent the night remembering how nice it had been. Sure didn't want to miss a chance to touch her again, although, given there were three chaperons, touching her would not have the intimacy it had at the stream.

'Well, now…' Lady Habershom reached out and patted her daughter's cheek '…the gentlemen and I will have a bite to eat in that lovely pub over there. You take our young man and make your dream come true.'

Lady Habershom looked stronger by the moment. He was glad he had asked for her to come along.

'Your family has the oddest way of saying things,' he pointed out while they walked towards the dock. 'What did your mother mean about making your dream come true?'

'Oh, that...' She glanced away, seeming to give her attention to a flock of seagulls flapping around a barrel of fish. 'My dream of teaching you to dance, what else? I think aboard ship would be the best place since it is what you are comfortable with, but we shall make do with this swathe of sand.'

'Let me speak to the Captain of the *Moon Glider*. I know him. He might allow us to come aboard.'

As luck would have it, the crew was on land for most of the day. The Captain welcomed them to borrow his deck. Got a good laugh when he discovered the reason, too.

The ship smelled like fish. Hopefully Eirene did not mind too much. The sea was easy today so the ship rocked in a gentle, comforting way.

Eirene stood beside him, pointing to his feet, then illustrating the steps he was to take. This seemed a more serious lesson than the one yesterday. He paid close attention to her instructions.

Starting off, he stepped on his own toes. Then he stepped on hers which was a feat since she stood beside him.

After a while, when the natural vibration of the deck and the regular creak of the rigging found its place in his bones, he began to feel looser. She had told him to count steps, then he forgot to and the dance took over... feet, legs and even his arms.

'Now let's try it face to face.' She directed him to touch her.

Could a person grin with his whole body? Apparently so.

He placed one splayed hand on the small of her back, felt the rise and fall of her breathing. Each time she took a step, ribs and muscle moved delicately under his fingertips.

Gradually something changed. Waves slapping the hull and gulls calling as they circled overhead created a sort of music which flowed though him. In his mind it bound the two of them in some way, body and spirit.

Dancing, he decided, was a form of courtship.

And something else. Sweet, sensual seduction, was what…which was to be performed in front of a ballroom full of onlookers!

The emotions stirred up by dancing were far too intimate for anyone to be watching. He did not even want Eirene to see them and she was involved in this as much as he was.

At least he thought so. How was he to know if each whirl made her heart spin the way his did?

He looked deeply into her wide blue eyes, trying to figure it out. All at once she blinked, stepping away from him.

'Have I made your dreams come true already?' he asked, disguising the state of his heart with a playful tone. He did not wish to have her look too deeply and see how touched he had been by the moment.

Touched and shaken. Dancing this way was not meant for common seamen. It could lead to romance which could lead to marriage.

Marriage might be well and good for gentlemen, not for sailors.

Looking away from her, past the docks to a row of houses facing the sea, he saw one having a structure on the roof where a sailor's wife would go to gaze out at the ocean. Where she would pace and watch for her husband's return.

It was called a widow's walk.

As a viscount, he would be in a position to offer marriage. But never as a sailor.

He was a sailor.

'You haven't yet.' She gave him an odd smile and shrugged one shoulder. 'But you are dancing very nicely now. It is time for you to learn something new.'

'What does that mean? Not yet?' He took her elbow, led her to the rail. It had been some time since he'd seen the roll and swell of the ocean. As always, its immensity amazed him. 'You and your parents say the oddest things at times.'

'Do we? What odd things?' She held his gaze as if she were trying to decide how much to say about the odd things.

'Things that seem to make sense to all of you...but I feel left out of some secret.'

'Oh...that.' Now she looked away.

He lifted her chin with his finger, turning it so that she could not evade the matter.

'There you go again! What does "Oh...that" mean?' She blinked, bit her bottom lip. 'And that time you said, "In case you ever did"? That was a strange comment to make.'

'I suppose it was.'

'And when your father out of the blue said, "We shall see, shan't we?", it sounded mysterious to me. And now your mother talking about making your dream come true? Why is it that I feel this all has to do with me?'

'Because it has everything to do with you.' She

shrugged as if what she said cleared everything up when all it did was make it more confusing.

Gulls screeched overhead. A stiff moist breeze caught the brim of her hat, yanking it away from her face. It dangled down her back, held only by the yellow ribbon at her neck.

The ribbon tickled his fingers. The temptation to kiss her tickled his mouth.

All he had to do was dip his mouth to hers. Damn it, though, even one little kiss would make it a hundred times more difficult to leave this lady when the time came. There was no use pretending it would be easy, even without crossing the line between friendship and romance.

'Do you intend to tell me why?' he asked, jerking his attention back to the moment at hand.

She was taking a long time deciding. He wondered if he would have to pry whatever it was out of her. Not that he expected it to be anything earth shaking, but he was curious about what the Habershoms' half-spoken comments had to do with him.

'It has to do with our marriage.'

'The marriage which is not going to happen? That marriage?'

'I'm sure you are right.' She turned her chin, freeing it from his fingers. Too bad. He liked the smooth feel of her skin and the indentation of the dimple under his thumb.

She clutched the ribbon, took a long breath in and out.

'Just because my dreams have always proven true in the past does not mean this one will.'

'Dreams!' This was about a dream? 'What sort of dream?'

'The sort in which I saw you as my husband.'

'We did meet in a surprising way. No wonder it gave you a dream.'

He'd had a couple of his own about her.

'It couldn't be that.' She tied the ribbon under her chin in a bow. 'No, I dreamed of you before I met you. You were standing on the deck of a ship, looking down at me, and I knew you were going to be my husband.'

'How did you know?'

'I felt it in my heart. In my dream you were my husband. I was in love with you.'

'That, pretty lady, is pure nonsense…bilge water.'

'Perhaps, but it is also the truth. Why do you think I sent Percy's man in the wrong direction? Would I do that for just any stranger with a bloody lip?'

Why had she done it? He had never been able to figure a reason. It was a puzzle which he had never been able to piece together.

'I recognised you, that's why. What a heartless thing it would be to turn over one's future husband to be beaten and robbed.'

'Robbed, maybe.' Probably not beaten.

'I'm sure you are right. However, my parents believe the dream. I have had a few dreams of that sort before. None more important than the one having to do with you, though. I will admit, we were all relieved when we discovered it would not be Percy getting Warrenstoke.'

'Percy getting Warrenstoke? Eirene!' He held curled his fingers about her upper arms. He was not certain if it was to ground her or himself. This conversation made his mind whirl. 'What about him getting you? You would have wed him had I not come back, wouldn't you?'

'It would have been my place to wed him.'

'The same as it is your place to wed me? Him or

me? It makes no difference to you? As long as you dreamed it?'

She raised her arms, slipping free of his hands, then took a step away.

'But I never dreamed of Percy. Only that I would marry the heir to Warrenstoke. All my life I believed it would be Henry. It was the agreement our fathers made, after all, even without my prophetic dream. But then we lost Henry. And there was Percy to take his place.'

The grief shadowing her eyes told him how much she had cared for his brother. Oddly enough, he envied her sadness. He wished he remembered enough about Henry to grieve like she did.

'Surely your parents would not expect you to marry Cousin Percy. I refuse to believe that.'

'You are right, they would not. That is not why I would have married him.'

'Ah, but you would sacrifice yourself for what our fathers wished? You are worth more than being a sacrifice, Eirene.'

'I suppose it all depends upon what one is sacrificing oneself for.' With that she spun away from him, walked stiff backed towards the gangplank.

'What is it? What would you sacrifice yourself for?' he asked, striding up behind her.

She stopped, pointing her finger at the row of shops and restaurants on the far side of the dock.

Her parents and Uncle Hal sat on a bench in the sunshine.

'For her.' She lowered her hand, casting a glance at him over her shoulder. Moisture stood in her eyes. 'My mother nearly died in London. Her physician said she would if she did not leave the city. We need to be here for my mother's sake and for Warrenstoke's, too.'

He walked beside her down the gangplank to the dock, thinking this was the oddest conversation he had ever engaged in.

'After your father died, Henry needed help learning his new role as Viscount,' she said, shooting him a sidelong glance under the brim of the hat. 'It has been my father keeping the estate from failing ever since.'

'I am aware of how valuable he is to Warrenstoke, but you…you ought to have a choice in your marriage, not blindly wed whichever heir is at hand.'

'Wed the heir or lose my mother. If you think I have a choice, please do tell me what it is.'

'You can continue to live here even without marrying the current heir.'

'You?'

On the spot all he could manage was to shrug. He bore two titles, Captain and Viscount. He could not offer marriage without knowing which title he would wear.

But why had he even wondered? He damned well did know who he was. Captain Holloway was what he was called by his sailors.

They were within yards of the bench. He caught Eirene's arm.

'I like you, Eirene. But I cannot marry you. Being wed to a seaman is no life for a woman.'

'Do not think you are obligated to. You are not bound by a dream that I had.'

'And our fathers' arrangement for us to wed? Do you think I am bound by that?'

He hoped she did not. He would not let his future be determined by someone else again. His mother had done it, so had Uncle Hal in keeping mum about who he was. He would not, now, allow it to be determined by a father he did not remember. Less still by another person's outlandish dream.

'I think you should do what you wish to do.'

He damn well would. Yet he would not forget what she said about the dream. Especially the part where she was in love with him. He had to wonder…would she really come to love him if he married her?

Even if a part of him thought he would like that, unlike Eirene, he was not going to live his life based on a fantasy or an agreement which their fathers had made.

'You and your family do not need to leave Warrenstoke. My father and my brother would not wish for you to. I think I am right about that.'

'Unless we marry there is no reason for my family to live here. My parents and I will find another place in the countryside.'

'I am inviting you to stay. I do not wish for you to go.'

'Why? It makes no sense. If you do not wish to marry me, we must go.'

He could not explain why. It seemed that she was supposed to be here, probably more than he was.

'As long as you live at Warrenstoke, I can keep Percy from bothering you.'

'I cannot imagine how you will if you are away, merrily sailing the ocean blue.'

'I will send him away.'

'For what reason? He is your kin. You cannot simply send him away.' She placed her fingers on his arm, cocked her head and shook it at the same time. What an endearing gesture. 'Besides, sending him away will not help my situation. You know that a great deal of money goes with me when I wed. He will want it even more because of losing Warrenstoke. I am afraid he will only follow me no matter where I go.'

If he married her, then she and her money would be beyond Percy's grasp. But he and Uncle Hal had their own dream. They were not living his father's dream, not Eirene's, either.

And yet, she would not be here had their marriage not been anticipated. Eirene's father would not have kept the estate from failing were it not for the fact that his daughter was expected to become Viscountess Warrenstoke.

He owed them both a great deal. The question was, how much? His career as a seaman? Uncle Hal's happiness?

Was he willing to give away the life he wanted because of a dream which Eirene and her family believed in?

Of course not. It would be absurd to believe that a dream could influence one's future. And as for the rest…he should not be bound by an agreement his father had made.

Henry might have been willing. Fletcher was not.

'Well!' Eirene kicked the hem of her skirt because it dragged when she walked and it was slowing her down. If she were in charge of the world, women would not be bound by them, but allowed to wear trousers the same as a man did. 'But you are not in charge of anything, are you?'

She mumbled her thoughts while walking past the portrait gallery towards the library. What she needed was to escape into a book, to go somewhere long ago and far away. Perhaps she could spend a few moments as a Viking shield maiden. Or an opera singer who enchanted everyone with her beautiful voice.

The weather had taken a gloomy turn with fog rolling in from the coast, making the day damp and dull, unfit for walking outdoors.

'Not all days are sunshine and bird song.'

After what happened yesterday at the dock in Margate, she decided this was one of them.

Fletcher had not reacted well to discovering her dream and his part in it. He was alarmed, no doubt. Everyone wanted to think they had some control over their lives.

And yet...

'I do not know why it should bother you so much if you don't believe it,' she said as if speaking to him face to face.

She was the one who ought to be bothered. The man the dream had given her was not at all the one she would have picked of her own free will.

A fighter...a rough-and-tumble seaman who would return to the sea as soon as he possibly could?

A man who could not even dance?

Oh, but that was not all the way true. He had danced on the ship. For a few lovely moments they had drifted together, one with the music, such as it was, and with each other.

And then he had pressed her about unguarded comments. There was nothing to do but tell him the truth.

'I wish I hadn't. But you were involved at the heart of it and so what could I do?' she told the him who was not there.

She glanced about to make sure no one was nearby and listening. The long hall was empty except for the dearly departed of Warrenstoke.

She carried on, muttering whatever she wished to. It did help to gather her thoughts, hearing them spoken aloud.

She paused in front of Henry's portrait. 'You never knew of my dream. And yet you were willing to marry me because it was our parents' wish. You, my friend, understood duty and honor. Not everyone does.' How could brothers so resemble each other from the outside, but inside be as different as sugar was from lemon? Before her was the image of Henry's sweet smile to prove it was true.

'Your brother's smile is not sweet.'

She would not say exactly what Fletcher Larkin was aloud, but she thought it none the less.

Rough, uncourtly, a brazen tease with no proper manners...strong, brawny and well built, fascinating really and altogether appealing.

'What he is, is confusing.' She turned away from the portrait to continue down the hallway. Several steps along the way, she stopped, glancing back at Henry.

'And I like him rather well,' she whispered.

Even though she would not have chosen him in the beginning, there was every chance she would do it now.

But choice was the very thing she did not have. He would make up his own mind about marrying her and apparently he did not wish to.

'And, my friend, even if your brother does wish it one day, in a choice between me and a life at sea, he will choose the sea.'

She came to the library, opened the door and stepped inside.

'I am doomed,' she declared rather dramatically.

A rustling noise came from the area of the couch. A head popped up over the back.

'That is dramatic. Perhaps I can save you from it.'

'Oh, hello, Percy. I did not realise you were here.' She would not have come if she had.

It made her stomach twist in a dizzy, half-nauseous turn. Only a short time ago she had been willing to marry this man. She could not imagine how she would have managed it, not now knowing who he really was. Having got a glimpse of his dark heart, she could not stomach the idea.

'No better place for a nap, I've found.'

'I will leave you to it, then.'

He leapt from the couch, placed himself in front of her and the door, smiled with straight white teeth.

'I am at your service, Eirene. What can I do to erase your doom?'

Go away without causing any trouble, would have been the honest answer.

'It isn't as dire as doom. In my boredom I was being dramatic. I simply need a book to distract me from the gloomy day.'

'Your fiancé is not up to keeping you entertained?' He scratched his chin, appearing to be in deep thought. All at once he brightened and gave her a Cheshire cat grin. 'Oh, but I have not heard a betrothal announcement, have I?'

'Your ears cannot be everywhere at once.' She hoped.

'You would be surprised at what I hear and what I see.'

'Then have you seen a book on the shelves to keep one entertained on a dreary day?'

The look he gave her raised the fine hairs on the back of her neck. The entertainment he was clearly thinking of was not to be found within the pages of a book. At least not a respectable book.

'I'm more of a napper than a reader,' he drawled.

He reached behind her, caught the doorknob and slowly drew the door open.

With a nod he stepped around her, then went out of the library.

Why, the cad! She could not put her finger on exactly what he had said to reveal himself as one. On the surface his words had been polite.

But he was one, none the less. It was what he did not say, but surely wanted to, that made him a cad.

She felt rather as if she had encountered an angry wasp in the garden which had buzzed about her head and then flown off.

An image popped into her mind, odd but accurate. She saw a bee and a wasp engaged in battle. The bee was Fletcher and the wasp was Percy.

In nature wasps could be dangerous to bees. If the bee colony was weak, the wasps would attack.

Thank heaven that Fletcher Larkin was not weak. As long as he was here, Percy could not harm Warrenstoke.

How long would that be? Clearly, Fletcher heard the call of the sea louder than he heard the call of the land.

Chapter Eight

Sometimes when the sea was calm and the stars bright, Fletcher liked to hang his hammock on the deck of the *Morning Star*. Something about it felt like being rocked to sleep in his mother's arms, not that he could recall such a thing, no one could.

Imagining it had always been soothing, though.

There was no reason he could not sleep here on his balcony. He dragged some of the bedclothes out. It proved to be an easy matter to fashion a hammock of them.

It was not a starry night. Fog had pressed down on the estate all day long. He was not one to mind fog though, since it occurred often at sea. With a content sigh, he relaxed into the curve of the sheet hammock, folded his hands behind his head.

This might be as close as he got to sleeping aboard ship for the time being, but it would do.

Gazing up at the swirling mist, he thought about Eirene's dream. People dreamed all kinds of things, mostly bizarre but not threatening by the light of day.

If only he had not asked Lord Habershom about

them after dinner tonight, he would not be wasting his thoughts on dreams.

He had tried not to laugh when Eirene's father told him a story of a three-legged dog and how it trotted into their lives after Eirene had dreamed him.

An odd coincidence was what that was. Not at all proof that he was destined to wed where he did not choose.

The fact remained he did not choose to wed at all.

And that was the end of the matter.

Once and for all.

No more said.

Aw, dash it. He sat up so quickly that he nearly tipped out of the hammock. He caught the balcony rail where one end of the sheet was tied, steadying his balance.

He'd never fallen out of a hammock before—damned if an unexpected vision of Eirene's smile would make him do it now.

Damned if he would allow troubling thoughts get him off balance, either.

There were plenty of those to knock him about if he allowed them to. They buzzed about his mind like flies on a fishnet.

One persistent thought was that if he ever did marry he hoped it would be to a woman like Eirene Smythe. If there was another like her. He had never met a lady such as her before and was not likely to in the future.

If he did decide to wed, now would be the opportunity to do so.

He could not imagine Eirene and her family leaving here. They were as much a part of the estate as the streams and the hills were. Much more a part of it than he was.

What, he wondered while staring at the fog, would become of Warrenstoke when they left? When he and Uncle Hal also left?

The only one who knew the place well enough to keep it going was Lord Habershom. More the shame he could not hire the Viscount. The only way to keep him on was to wed his daughter.

Eirene was lovely, he thought a great deal of her. Too much to leave her always watching for him to return from the sea.

An owl hooted from somewhere in the milky night. At sea, there were no owls and yet the sound seemed familiar. It was strange and intimate all at once.

A memory was trying to push forward. He closed his eyes, trying not to drive it away by looking too hard.

'Do you hear that, my boy?' A voice came from far away, but grew clearer, word by word. 'Even in the fog it is hunting. What a marvel of nature…' The voice in his head faded, but the feeling he had of sitting on his father's lap, leaning into the strong arms folded about him, remained.

What, he had to wonder, would his life have been like if his mother had not taken him away?

He could not change the past, did not regret it, either.

Only, he did wonder.

A few more memories came to him, tacked on top of one of the owl. They were fleeting, but welcome.

It was a relief to have a few things about Warrenstoke take their place in his memory. A feeling of home was making a crack in his heart.

Before he could think too deeply about it, something else occurred to him.

Why had he not thought of it before?

His mother had a family in New York. Had she ever made it home to them? If so, why had she ended up with Uncle Hal? He could only guess that they knew nothing about what had become of her, or him. Who were those people? Did they grieve the loss of their daughter and grandson?

For the first time he questioned his uncle's decision to withhold the truth of his past. Didn't mean he was any less devoted to the man who raised him, though. Everyone made mistakes in life.

Now that they were here at his ancestral home, did Uncle Hal regret it?

Did Fletcher regret it?

He could ask himself that question a hundred times and still not know the answer.

What he did not regret was learning about his brother and his father...or meeting Eirene.

No matter what happened from here on, no matter where life took him, he would not regret having shared this small slice of life with her.

'You could have the whole pie, Brother.'

What? Where the blazes had that come from?

Wherever it was, it startled him so badly that this time he did fall out of the hammock.

It took a full minute of sitting on the floor of his balcony blinking, looking about to convince himself that it had come from his own brain.

Nothing more than an odd, scattered thought.

There was no pie.

Not for a man like him.

Three days passed in which Eirene saw very little of Fletcher. He spent most of his time with her father in the office or riding about the estate, learning about the land and its tenants.

The house party was now only a couple of weeks away and she still had things to teach him about societal manners.

Not that she wanted him to change too much. He was interesting just as he was. Charming and bold all at once.

Still, with guests expected, a bit of polish could not hurt. Out of loyalty to the former Viscount and Henry, she felt duty bound for Fletcher to be presented at his best.

If she could find him, she would teach him the proper way to greet a lady.

As it turned out, she did not have to search too long.

Voices came from the half-open door of the study.

She paused to listen for a moment before she made her presence known. She would not want to intrude at an inopportune time.

'I won't wear this!' she heard Fletcher say. 'Feels like I'm a crab that outgrew its shell.'

Oh…yes, she remembered now that the valet had ordered new clothes befitting a man of Fletcher's station. Apparently they had arrived.

'You look a proper gentleman, my boy,' she heard his uncle point out.

'I'm not one.' This was as near a growl as could be.

'Let me look at you a moment longer before you rip off that cravat.'

'Better hurry or I'll suffocate. Cursed noose is what it is.'

Eirene covered her mouth, smothering a laugh. She wanted to hear a bit more of this before she made herself known.

'Son…' Hal's voice grew softer, the teasing gone from it '…you were born for this.'

'If that was true, you'd have told me about it a long time ago. It's only because I was found by the detectives that you admitted it. If they hadn't come, we'd be at dock in New York right now, not being smothered by our clothes… You are wearing the same thing I am, Uncle. Why aren't you twitching?'

'I feel elegant. Reckon I had hidden hankering for the finer life.'

'Damned if I believe that for a second. It almost seems like you want to be held hostage by a fancy suit.'

With the way Hal and Father were getting along so famously, it would not surprise her if Hal was developing a fondness for life at Warrenstoke.

'You know I love life aboard ship. But the truth is, it's a hard way to live. You might be surprised to hear it, but I like being on land.'

'You always made fun of landlubbers.'

'I was wrong. About that and about keeping you from your home and family.'

The conversation had come to a point where it was improper for her continue listening.

She did not wish to interrupt the clearly important things they needed to say to one another.

Tiptoeing backward, she pressed her skirts close to her legs so they would not rustle.

She bumped into someone.

'Father?' she whispered.

'Indeed, it is me.' Clearly, he felt no need to lower his voice. 'I have come to see what the Viscount's valet has purchased for him.'

Fletcher stepped into the hallway. He tugged at his shirt collar.

'Instruments of torture is what.'

Oh, but he looked dashing for someone being tortured. This very moment might not be the time to point it out.

Poor Fletcher had no idea of how the ladies at the party were going to fawn all over him. As far as they knew this handsome Viscount was ripe for marriage.

Perhaps she should not teach him to be a gentleman after all. Looking at him now, more attractive than any man she had ever seen, she experienced a flash of possessiveness.

What an odd sensation. She could not say she had ever felt one like it.

'It is the price we must pay, my boy.'

Fletcher's brows lowered. His eyes stabbed blue daggers at Father. 'Pay for what?'

'For being born to responsibility.'

'I was not— But even if I was that is not how I was raised. If it weren't for my brother—'

With an oath, Fletcher stomped past them.

If not for Henry dying, he would not be here at all was what he surely meant…there would have been no reason for him to be dragged from the way of life he loved.

Hal entered the hallway, shaking his head. 'This is my fault. I never should have kept him from his family.'

Her father hurried up to him, patted him on the shoulder. 'Nonsense, my friend. He is the man he is because of what you taught him over the years. All he needs is a little more time to accept it.'

There was a great deal Fletcher would have to accept, was what she thought.

Judging by the way he looked brushing past her, he had no intention of taking his place at Warrenstoke.

Which meant he had no intention of marrying her.

'If you will excuse me,' she said.

Moments ago, she had come looking for Fletcher to give him instruction on proper decorum at a society event. Now she thought he needed something far different.

She only hoped she could find him and give him whatever it was he needed.

Fletcher fled the house, clawing at the black satin noose around his neck. All he did was fix the knot tighter.

He was a sailor and knots were second nature to him—not this one, though. This one hated him, meant to do him in.

At least it was not raining today so he could escape to the garden, pace along winding paths lined with trees.

He liked it here, liked the stream and the hilltop. There were places on his estate which were beginning to speak to him of home.

If only he did not feel this softening towards the estate was a betrayal of the *Morning Star*.

Uncle Hal did not seem to have conflicted emotions about any of this. As unlikely as it seemed, Fletcher suspected his uncle would be just as happy to remain on land.

It had never occurred to him that such a thing could happen. Uncle Hal, a landlubber?

A movement on the terrace caught his eye.

Ah, Eirene hurrying out of the house, looking this way and that. Probably searching for him. He had left them all in a huff.

He yanked his collar, tugged on the tie. He waved to

Eirene so that she did not wander uselessly about looking for him.

Spotting him, she smiled, lifted the hem of her skirt and hurried towards him.

Eirene was not the only person outdoors. Percy stood at the corner of the terrace, deep in the shadow of a tall bush. His sharp gaze followed Eirene while she ran past him unawares.

He wished Percy would give him a reason to send him away. He reminded Fletcher of a cat lashing its tail while patiently waiting to pounce.

Since Fletcher did not wish to alarm Eirene, he did not point out that Percy had been watching.

He walked towards her, met her several yards from the terrace steps.

'Walk with me.' He took her arm and led her deeper into the garden away from where his cousin could see them.

'You look like you need some help.' She pointed to his neck.

'Damned thing means to kill me.'

She laughed at that. Indicated that he should stand still.

Her fingers fiddled at his collar and in a moment he was free. The wicked black tie dangled from her fingers.

What he wanted to do was kiss her...in gratitude.

'But I do have to say it, you look dashing.'

Dashing, was it? He wasn't sure how that made him feel.

Better than gentlemanly. Dashing indicated adventure.

Very well, dashing—he would accept that.

Didn't mean he was going to kiss her, though. There was too fine a line between gratitude and passion.

Walking with her might not be a kiss, but time in her company was always welcome. And it would take them out from under Percy's dark gaze.

'Let's go to the hill. I think you need some freedom after being nearly killed by your new clothes.'

They walked in silence for a time. A good silence. One in which friends could just be.

He tried to think of when Eirene had crossed that barrier from acquaintance to friend. It had happened gradually so he could not quite put a moment on it.

'I remembered a moment with my father.'

'That is wonderful news!' She clapped her hands, took a happy skip. 'Is it private or would you like to share it?'

'It wasn't much. I was sitting on his lap and we heard an owl...but I was happy.'

'What we need to do is discover more happy memories.'

Coming to the top of the hill where he had discovered the carved horse, he wondered if it was possible.

'Any ideas on how to do that?'

'Well...' Three delicate lines crossed her forehead when she scrunched her face in thought. She sat down. He sat beside her. 'I might have one. What if I tell you a few of the things Henry and I did together and maybe something will jolt a memory lose?'

'Even if it does not, I would like to hear what you did together.'

'When it rained we spent time in the library. Henry read me books. If he was ever bored by it, he never let on. But really, what did an adolescent boy have in common with a little girl?'

'You were to wed. You had that in common.'

'Neither of us gave that a thought back then.' She laughed as if she were looking back at the two of them when they were young.

He had to admit to envying her that.

'Once we were outside we did more of what he wanted to.'

'Climbing trees? Catching insects?'

She shook her head. 'I did not care for insects. But rolling downhill… That was great fun.'

'Let's do it.' Even if it did not spark a memory, it would make one. After the morning he'd spent he could use a bit of outlandish fun. What could be more outlandish than a pair of adults rolling downhill like a pair of carefree children?

'We will stain our clothes.'

He took off his jacket, tossed it behind him.

'You are lucky to be able to get rid your clothes so easily. It would be tea time before I ever got down to my petticoats.'

None the less, she rose to the challenge by tucking her clothes this way and that. In the end she had the lacy under-things rucked outward and the outer fabric in.

'You've done this before,' he stated.

She nodded, grinning. 'You should roll up your pants legs like Henry used to do. We would have caught the dickens from the laundry lady if we came back with grass stains.'

'I do not know how you could…' He remembered a woman standing over him shaking her finger. He was rather sure it had had to do with dirty clothing. 'How you could avoid getting them.'

'We could not, but it was worth a scolding.'

With that Eirene lay down on the grass, her arms stiff at her sides.

'Are you ready?' she asked, looking up at him.

He could not speak at once because gazing down at her, watching her breathing hard with excitement, made him think this was the worst idea he'd ever had.

'For the rolling downhill race?' she added when he did not answer over the lump in his chest.

'It's a race, then?'

'Of course. Where would be the fun if it were not?'

If things were different between them, if he was not going back to his ship, he would show her what other 'fun' they might have.

But he was. So race it would be.

Lying down on the grass with the top of his head inches from hers, he tensed his muscles to engage in competition.

'Go!' she cried, then started to roll.

She was quicker at first. He saw her rolling a full six feet ahead. He put more effort into flipping over.

'Slowcoach!' she called though a burst of laughter, but it was another voice he heard along with hers.

Henry used to say the same thing. A memory re-called and a memory made.

If anyone was close by enough to see them, they would think them caught up in lunacy. They would not be wrong. He could not recall a more delightfully insane moment in his life. He closed his eyes, focused on gaining speed without becoming dizzy.

All of a sudden he hit something, rolled on top of

it and stopped abruptly. The something was curvy… womanly. He opened his eyes to see Eirene looking at him, pleased and grinning.

'I won,' she murmured while reaching for the hair dangling over his eyes. Her gaze grew soft, tender when she brushed it back.

The moment was far too intimate for comfort.

'I surrender to your superior skill, Miss Smythe.'

Her lips were too close, yet he made no move to rise. The urge to kiss her was too damn strong.

He felt her chest rise against his when she asked, 'Did it work? Do you remember anything?'

Ah, two things. He rolled away, sat up.

'I did, in fact.'

She sat up, too, looking eager to know what it was.

'Slowcoach. It is what my brother used to say to me when we rolled down this very hill.'

With a great grin she hugged him around the neck, then let go quickly.

'Oh, I beg your pardon. I got carried away with the excitement…of you remembering, I mean.'

'And the thrill of victory, no doubt.'

'That, too, of course.'

He stood up, chewing over the other thing he remembered.

Warrenstoke was not really his home. The *Morning Star* was and he was returning to it as soon as he could manage.

He reached a hand down to her. 'We should get back. It must be time for tea by now.'

As light as the mood had been a few moments ago, it dimmed the instant they climbed the terrace steps and encountered Percy. It was nearly as if having seen him and Eirene go off together, he'd waited, watching for their return.

'Good afternoon, Fletcher… Eirene.' There was no mistaking the accusation, the sneer in his cousin's voice when he said her name.

Damn it. He only now noticed the piece of dry grass in Eirene's hair. Percy's gaze was focused on it. Fletcher could hardly brush it away without bringing more attention to it.

'Eirene tripped coming downhill.'

'You really ought to be more careful, my dear. Anything could happen.'

Eirene flinched when the churl called her 'my dear'. It hit him hard, recognising she was afraid of Percy.

'No need to worry, Cousin. I will be here to make sure it does not.'

He hurried her inside, feeling the worst of men.

Yes, he would be here. But not for ever.

The next morning, Fletcher caught up with Eirene in the portrait corridor on the way to breakfast.

'Can you spare me an hour today?'

'Can you spare me three? I still have a lot to teach you before the party?'

'After breakfast, then.'

The hour they had spent over the meal seemed to stretch for ever. There was something he needed to teach her that was urgent.

Once outside in the garden she asked, 'Should we go to the hill or the stream?'

'You pick,' he answered unbuttoning the cuffs of his sleeves and rolling them up to his elbows.

'The waterfall, then.'

'There's a water—wait...it's at the head of the stream...it empties into a pool?'

'You remember?' She clapped her hands.

'I fell into it once. My brother dragged me out.'

'No! So did I. Henry dragged me out, too.'

'Seems like we kept Henry busy.'

It took little less than half an hour to reach the fall and the pool.

'I remember this...the way it looks and how it sounds.'

'I wonder if you left a toy here, as well?'

He shrugged. He did not recall leaving anything, but perhaps?

Stooping, he drew his fingers through water so clear he could see stones even at the deepest part of the pond. Then he looked up into the most expressive eyes he had ever seen. He was not certain what they were expressing, but something was going on behind them.

'I owe you, Eirene.' He stood up, shaking the water from his fingers.

'Because of the tie? You would have freed yourself from it and, really, it would not have killed you.'

'It would, but that isn't it. I owe you a lesson, for all the lessons you have given me.'

'Will you teach me to steer a ship or find my way by studying the stars? I'm sure you know those things.'

He would rather teach her that. This lesson was more urgent.

'Right now am going to teach you how to defend yourself.'

'Do you intend to attack me?' She fluttered her fingers at her throat, in mock fear.

'Not me…just any fellow who comes along and acts like a brute.'

'Percy is who you mean, isn't it?'

He nodded. 'I won't always be nearby, so you must know how to deal with him if you need to.'

'I do not think he would act violently towards me,' was what she said, but her eyes said something else.

'He won't think that you will act that way either. It gives you the advantage in the beginning. It might be all you will need, though.'

'Very well.' She danced about on the balls of her feet, hands clenched as she hit the air. Then she twirled. When her skirts settled she said, 'I am ready to learn to punch now.'

'You will not be punching. You will be learning to duck and feint, to avoid grasping hands.'

'That sounds important to know.' It looked as though she was trying to hide a smile, so he wondered how serious she was about learning the lesson.

'It isn't so difficult if you understand what to look for. There will be warning signs just before I reach for your shoulder.' He made the move with exaggeration, then grabbed her. 'It would happen faster, but did you see the subtle shift in my stance?'

Nodding, she copied his move, grabbing his shoulder. 'Ha! I've got you now, villain! Don't move a hair if you wish to survive.'

Next he presented the assault from different angles, showed her in which direction to duck from each one.

She was a quick learner, which was good. However, he would feel better if she were not so light-hearted about it.

Now it was time to teach her what to do if she did not escape a grasping hand.

This was not going to be easy. As lessons went, this was not one he was comfortable teaching a lady.

Didn't mean she did not need to know it, though.

'The thing is…' This would be a great deal easier to explain if Eirene were a boy. A boy would understand how effective the manoeuvre was with no more than a word of explanation. 'In the event you do not avoid your opponent, you will need to fight back. You will not be using your fists to do it.'

'Teeth?' She clacked hers and growled.

He shook his head, grimacing to the bone. 'Knee.'

'Oh?' She blinked at him, clearly puzzled. 'My fist is closer to the reprobate's nose.'

'Aye well, it isn't his nose you are going to hit.' He wondered if it had been this hard for her, teaching him to dance. 'The thing is, if you need to do this you will already be trapped. You would run away otherwise. That leaves your knee as your only weapon.'

'If I am not to hit his nose with my knee, what am I to hit?'

'Another place, far more sensitive than a nose.'

'Why are you sweating?'

Sweating? It was a wonder he wasn't trembling and pressing his knees together.

'You must think me a great dunce not to know, but I have never had the need to defend myself before.'

'And you still might not, but you need to be prepared.'

'Very well, what is it I do with my knee? Besides run, which at this point, you say, I am not in a position to do.'

He cleared his throat. 'How much do you know about a man's anatomy?'

'They have a head, two arms and two legs, same as I do.'

'It is the parts that are not the same that I am speaking of. What do you know about them?'

If her blush grew any redder, he figured her cheeks would catch fire. At least she did appear to understand what he was referring to.

'I do not have first-hand experience, naturally, but I do have an idea what you are speaking of.'

Her gaze dipped. She blinked, looked back up. She knew enough, then.

He swept his hand in front of the spot she had cast a brief look at.

'Exactly that. It is your target.'

'I could not possibly.'

'Of course you can. You are going to do it to me, once I show you how.'

'I would rather not.'

'I'd rather not prance about a ballroom either. Doesn't mean I won't do it.'

'Are we bargaining? Because if we are—'

He grabbed her, held her to his chest so that she could not move.

'What other weapon can you use against me?'

She wriggled, tried to lift her arms, but he held her tighter.

'Not your fists. Teeth? Maybe if your assailant is careless enough to expose a spot to be bitten. A woman needs to fight smarter than a man.'

He let go of her so suddenly he had to catch her wrist to keep her from toppling backward into the water.

'Do you see why now? A knee to the ball—groin, I mean, might disable man long enough for you to find a rock or whatever is at hand to smash against his head. You should be looking when you first sense a threat, before he grabs you. If you haven't spotted it beforehand, just give him a knee, then run…and scream.'

'All right. Grab, smash, run and scream—I will remember that.'

Here was the part of the lesson he dreaded. The better she learned it the harder it would be on him.

'Let's practise the move,' he said. 'Like this.'

He rolled up his pant leg, bent his knee. 'If you can get your skirt up the blow will be more painful. Then just jerk up your knee fast and sudden. Surprise is important. If he suspects and turns to the side, it won't work as well, maybe not at all. A direct hit is what you want.'

He demonstrated by kicking his knee at the air.

'Now you do it.'

She kicked her knee. Petticoats erupted.

'Were you unable to lift your skirt?'

'If the time comes, I will do it.'

She was probably shy about exposing her undergarments…but damnit!

He grabbed her again. 'Free yourself!'

She looked at him, her expression disbelieving. 'You wish for me to hurt you?'

There was nothing he wished for less than the pain about to momentarily cripple him. 'Yes. Can you reach your—?'

All of a sudden he was on the ground, gasping and cursing.

Then Eirene was beside him, kneeling with a rock gripped in her fist.

'You did say surprise was important.' She dropped the rock. 'It is why I didn't answer about the skirt, but I did manage to lift it. Oh, but I'm so sorry. Can you breathe?'

No, only gasp. She stroked his hair as if that might somehow help.

'I would run and scream, but I cannot leave you like this.'

'You…did…well.' Better than he expected. 'Proud… of…you.'

Gradually, his breath came back. He braced his hands on his knees, slowly straightened, managed to smile at his student.

'I'm so, so sorry.' Patting his hair must be her way of wiping away his pain since she could not pat him where it hurt.

He had to admit, it was a pleasant distraction from the injury.

Catching her hand, he squeezed it to show his approval.

'You did everything I told you to, Eirene. Damned if there is a single reason for you to be sorry. You were brilliant.'

She wriggled her hand out of his fingers. 'I did not feel brilliant.'

He managed to laugh, but shallowly. 'Anyone on the wrong end of your knee will not feel brilliant, either.'

'I have to say, Fletcher, you are a dedicated teacher.' She gave him half a smile. Sweetly poised between pride and regret, it shot straight to his heart.

'Praise heaven you are a quick learner and I will not have to teach that lesson again.'

Although he still ached with the jab she'd delivered, he did not move away from where their knees brushed together.

This was the oddest time to realise how much he enjoyed touching her.

Not the oddest locale, though. The waterfall and the grassy swathe around the pool gave him a peaceful sensation way down deep. Something special must have happened here once. It teased his memory, dancing just out of reach.

Ah, but Eirene was not out of reach. Unlike a foggy, distant memory she was flesh, blood and present.

And only an outstretched arm away.

He had taught her to dodge an advance. The question was, would she dodge this one?

Eirene faced Fletcher, knee touching knee, looking him over to be sure she had not hurt him some awful way he would never recover from.

How could she have done that to him? Just because he insisted did not mean she had to do it.

He did not seem to think an apology was necessary, but she most certainly did.

The last thing she wished was to cause him pain.

Regret notwithstanding, she was also proud that she had managed to disable a foe. Not that he was a foe. But had he been, she would have taken him down and struck him with a rock.

It was odd, though—even though she hadn't hit him, his eyes were beginning to get a strange look, soft and fuzzy.

'You have the most peculiar look in your eyes, Fletcher. Can that sort of injury...' she did not mean to drop her stare at the sore spot, but since it was the area of concern…well, she did '…go to your brain? Maybe we should sit for a while and then call for a doc—'

'Eirene…' He touched her lips with one finger, then shook his head. 'My brain is fine, the rest soon will be.'

'Good, then. We will sit here and enjoy the sound of the water and…' His gaze was getting odder by the second. Odd in a nice way, a flutter-belly way 'Frogs…'

'You have the loveliest…' he touched her chin, drew her towards him, his mouth coming close…closer '…soul of anyone I have ever met.'

What? Soul, not lips? Did he mean to intimately compliment her or to kiss her?

A lovely soul was all well and good, but it was a kiss she wanted.

Yes! A kiss from the man who was destined to be hers whether he accepted it or not.

Oh, but then he did kiss her. How very, very, lovely… She sighed, but the sound was muffled against his lips. She put her hands on his shoulders, drawing closer.

His strong arms curled around her back, drawing her against his chest. There was no mistaking how hard his heart was thumping. Surely now he recognised what they were meant to be to one another.

It was a long simmering time before he moved his mouth from her lips to her ear.

Was he about to declare his affection, or perhaps his love? Or that he decided to stay at Warrenstoke and claim his title…claim her?

How would she answer? They were growing close, but it might be too soon—

'No kiss will ever come close to this one, Eirene.' Hot breath skimmed the shell of her ear.

Her hands were still on his shoulders, so she pushed him back. What had he meant by that?

Not that it was for her to care what and yet…

'Between us?' She scrambled backwards on her knees, putting distance between them. The look in his eyes was not the one she hoped to see. 'Or between you and the hundreds of women you will kiss after you sail away and leave me?'

Chapter Nine

That night Fletcher sat on an iron bench in the garden until every lamp in the house went out.

Eirene's was the last window to go dark. That had been nearly an hour ago.

Was she dreaming? About him…about what he would do or not do?

For all he knew his future was being written while she slept.

The question she had asked him at the falls after he kissed her had been plaguing him all day.

What the blazes had he meant, saying what he had?

He intended to express that kissing her had been wonderful, a moment he would always treasure.

Then all of a sudden it had been about the future.

Not his future, not her future. But their future together.

She had put the question to him and after nearly a minute of him staring at her, silently stunned, she rose, then ran away.

They had not shared two words in private since.

He would have answered her right off if he had known what to say.

Not that he meant to apologise for kissing her. He well knew an apology was not what she was asking for.

What she wanted to know, and what he still had no answer for, was what his intentions were in giving the kiss.

He wanted to, that was one reason. It was what had prompted him in the first place. Seeing her lips so pretty and inviting, the mood of the moment and the perfection of the setting…what man would not want to kiss her?

Then, the instant he did it, he recognised this kiss was different. The thought that struck him was, she tasted like home. Home in a way that Warrenstoke and even the *Morning Star* were not.

Couldn't deny being unsettled at the notion.

It was as if her crazy dream had somehow leaked out of her, then into him through the kiss. Which was absurd, he knew. Yet when she asked him that question he truly did not know the answer.

Would it be the best one they ever had? Or would this kiss rise above any he had in the future…from his hundreds of kisses.

Sitting alone in the dark, he had to smile at that. Did Eirene think he did nothing but put into port and seek women to embrace?

She thought rather highly of his masculine skills if she did. His smile shifted to a full grin.

If a man in his situation did wish to marry, the lady sleeping upstairs would be his choice.

That was key…his choice, not predestined by some confounding dream or chosen for him by someone else.

As far as choices went, he had made his before he ever set foot on Warrenstoke land. That choice had been a new ship and a life at sea.

The life of a seaman was what he had always known, what he had always loved.

And yet that was not the truth. He'd had a life here before his mother took him away. Had he loved that life?

If he had been happy here…and he was beginning to remember things to make him believe he had been… would returning to the sea be as perfect as he remembered?

Life changed. What one wanted of it changed along the way.

So, what did he want?

Not only that, what did Eirene want of her life? In her heart, what was it she really wanted?

She knew what was expected of her by their parents' decree and seemed willing to go along with it. As preposterous as it was, her dream also dictated to her what her future would be and she seemed willing to go along with that, too.

Aside from dutifully fulfilling an obligation, what was it that she wanted for herself…of her marriage?

She had told him that in the dream she was in love with him.

Which did not mean she was happy about it.

What if they did wed and she loved him, then he left her to go to sea. She might very well end up unhappy to be loving him.

His grin slowly sagged, the good feeling he had a moment ago dripping away like melting wax.

How in the flaming blazes had a simple kiss turned so wrenching?

He knew what Eirene would say. Probably her mother and father, too.

They were meant for one another, their futures bound

by a dream, or whatever hocus-pocus it was that controlled people's futures.

It was going to take more than one remarkable, quite poignant kiss to convince him that was true.

Two kisses, perhaps? Four or seven? Nothing would be proved by kissing her seven times because if he did that, it would be because he was in love with her.

A love resulting in the logical progression of their relationship. Not destiny, but choice.

The greatest mystery in this situation was that he was giving the idea of being in love any thought at all.

Forcefully, he shoved the matter out of his mind. No woman of his was going to spend her nights pacing the widow's walk on her roof.

Passing by her chamber window, Eirene looked down to see Fletcher sitting in the garden gazing intently at her window. She turned off the lamp. Standing beside the curtain in the dark, she was free to watch him watching her.

Her lips went warm and tingly all over again. She licked them, but his distinct masculine flavour had faded.

It was a silly thing to do, stand here and stare, but she was alone. No one would ever know of it. Nor would they know how calf-eyed she was in the moment over him.

Calf-eyed and nipped by Cupid's arrow. She leaned against the window frame, sighing.

No one truly believed in Cupid and his pointed little arrow.

Some people, she thought, narrowing her eyes at the man sitting on the iron bench, did not believe in dreams, either.

Not yet, he didn't. He was probably confused as to why he had kissed her the way he had. It was understandable. She had been confused, too, at first. Oh, yes, delightfully fuzzy for a while, grinning and flushed all over. It had taken a few hours to gather herself.

Concentrating on common things such as discussions about the party menu with Mother and Cook, having tea, and reading, it took all those things to make her feel like herself again. Eirene Elspeth Smythe, grounded in reality and trusting in dreams.

She blew a kiss down to Fletcher in the dark. She did not expect him to see it.

It was only one more thing he could not see.

What he probably saw was his bright shiny new ship cutting across the Atlantic.

Nothing could be more at odds with her dream.

His ship? His land? What would he choose?

For as much as she would like to think nothing could stand against the power of her dream, she did wonder.

He was a strong-minded man.

She spun away from the window. Flopped backwards across her bed.

The memory of his kiss made her go flip-floppy.

It left her questioning things she had long held true.

Why, oh, why did she have to be wondering if love assigned in a dream was love at all? It was not as if Fletcher had walked her dream with her. He had not shared the loving feeling it gave her.

Dreams were complicated wee things. In the moment she was confounded by them.

Did the special dreams make things happen or simply show her in advance what was to be?

She did not know. What she did know was that tomorrow she would begin teaching Fletcher proper etiquette when meeting a lady.

Not that she wanted him to meet a woman who would become infatuated with him. No indeed, all she wanted was for him to make a proper impression.

Truly, though, it was but part of the reason for the lesson.

The bigger part was that she wanted to spend time with him. Even if she had never dreamed of him she would want to be with him.

Fletcher Larkin was unlike any man she had ever met. He was a bold man with a tender kiss. He was a rascal with a possessive kiss. He was a viscount and a captain, who gave himself away in a kiss.

He might not realise he gave himself away, but since she had been on the other end of it, she rather thought he had.

Standing in the library listening Eirene explain proper greetings to the rhythm of rain tapping at the windows, Fletcher decided he would rather be somewhere else.

If there was one thing he did not wish to do, it was to learn how to greet a debutante, or a widow, or any of the other ladies Eirene assured him would be competing for his attention.

To complicate matters, if there was one thing he did wish to do, it was to spend time in Eirene's company.

It had been three days since he had kissed her. During that time he had only encountered her in passing.

Lord Habershom had kept him busy going over the estate's accounts, visiting the stables and exploring the property.

He and the Viscount had spent a great deal of time

riding over hill and dale. Fletcher wondered if this was the Viscount's way of subtly encouraging him to fall in love with the estate.

Clearly Lord Habershom and his family were in love with it. But they had something he did not.

Strong memories…roots. If Fletcher had a recollection of his father the way that they did, well, damn it, he might love it here, too.

It was becoming clear that Uncle Hal enjoyed life at the estate. Maybe he liked not having the stress of keeping his crew safe, of making sure the cargo would earn enough to cover the expenses. It was hard to imagine that Uncle Hal enjoyed riding horses as much as he enjoyed skimming waves.

Fletcher's intention in coming to Warrenstoke had been to ensure his uncle's happy future. He could not have imagined it would be on land and not aboard ship.

It was inconceivable that Fletcher would leave his uncle here. This was not how he had pictured how life would go.

He wouldn't worry about it so much if he thought the Habershoms would be here to watch out for him.

He bit off a curse, swallowed it whole. The only reason for them to remain here and care for his uncle would be because he had married Eirene.

Damn it if he would have the heart to ride off and leave both a wife and an uncle behind.

What he needed to do was remember more of his life here with his father and his brother. To get a sense of home.

If he could do that, it might make a difference in his desire to return to the sea. Perhaps he would decide to stay if he could feel his roots growing into Warren-stoke soil.

If he did stay, he would court the lady now standing beside him and illustrating the proper posture required when formally greeting a lady.

Proper wasn't how he first met Eirene. He'd come close to tripping on her and then asked her to keep his hiding place a secret. He'd looked anything but a gentleman that day.

Even though he appeared a sweating, half-wild miscreant, she had not given him away.

He knew now why she hadn't. He also knew her to be a great-hearted lady who might have kept his secret even if she had not believed she knew him.

Eirene jabbed him in the ribs to bring his attention back to the task at hand. And no mistake, this was a task.

She bent at the waist. Imitating a man's deeper voice, she said, 'It is a pleasure to meet you, Lady Most-Worthy.'

He shook his head, felt how shaggy and ungentlemanly his hair must look. However, he did not intend to cut it in order to look a proper sort.

'Lady Most-Worthy will not approve of me, no matter how much I behave like…' he pointed at her, grinning '…like you.'

'Not me, the gentleman I am portraying.'

'Who is he? What is his name?'

She anchored her fists at her waist, curled her fingers and frowned until her brows nearly met. 'Lord Stubborn-as-a-Rock.'

'I foresee trouble for those two.'

It occurred to him that there must have been trouble between his parents, too, otherwise his mother would not have left here, abandoned her husband and taken her child.

Funny that Uncle Hal had mentioned his mother often, but never his father. What was it he'd been told the few times he'd asked? Oddly enough he could not remember. He had simply put his uncle in his father's place, then gone on with his life. His happy life.

Now that he knew he had had a father who had loved him and grieved his loss, everything seemed upended.

Until he filled in the gaps of his memory, he did not fully know who he was. Viscount or seaman?

'You are thoughtful today, Fletcher. Perhaps we should carry on with this lesson another time when you can give it your full attention.'

'I'm sorry, my mind is preoccupied.' He sat down on the couch. There were flowers in the hearth today. With a nod he indicated the spot beside him, inviting her to sit. Eirene sat in the chair across. 'I was wondering if more memories of my life here will come back.'

'Perhaps you should not force them to. They might come easier if you don't. May I suggest you make new ones instead? The present day will eventually become a memory, after all.'

Sitting here with Eirene would become one. This was far from the only memory of her he would take with him when he returned to his ship.

One recent memory pressed upon him now, cherished and stressful at the same time. Even now he could smell the scent of her skin when he'd kissed her, feel the rise of her bosom when she sighed against him.

'Eirene, that question you asked me?' Her cheeks turned pink so he knew she understood what he meant.

'I didn't answer it because I did not know what the answer was.'

'I thought not.' She folded her hands together on her lap, tipped her head and held his gaze.

'I still do not know what to say. Only this one thing. No matter what happens, I will not be kissing hundreds of women, just to be clear on it.'

'That might have been an exaggeration. I only hope you will remember our kiss after all the tens you might have in the future.'

'Tens?'

It might be a lonely life if that was all he had to look forward to.

'Yes, unless you decide to marry me. Then I will kiss you more than ten times.'

Her smile reassured him she was speaking in jest.

Jest or not, the prospect did make him feel like smiling. With her, he suspected he would never be lonely, whereas going back to sea without his uncle would be lonely.

Would he then long for this place and these people the way he now longed for the sea? The last thing he wanted was to live his life longing for a different one.

'You are looking melancholy again,' Eirene pointed out.

'Not melancholy…only going over deep thoughts.'

'You would be, of course. You have a hard choice to make.'

'It would seem so. The thing of it is, at the beginning of all this I did not consider there would be a choice. Uncle Hal and I were going back to the sea. Now I wonder… you must have noticed how he has taken to life on land? I think he would rather stay here.'

She nodded, stood, then came to sit beside him. 'He told my father he wishes to.'

Suspecting it was one thing. Hearing it spoken aloud cracked his heart down the middle. He and his uncle had held a common dream for so long, Fletcher could not understand how he could have given up on it.

Eirene caught his hand, held it without speaking.

She did not need to speak. Her fingers, warm and gently stroking his, said far more than words. It was her heart doing the talking, his heart doing the hearing. What it heard was that she understood how conflicted he was…how confused. Even sensed how, in a way, he felt betrayed.

What she told him without words was that he was not alone.

Her fingers were small, soft, yet at the same time strong.

He had never spoken in silent communication with anyone before.

In touching him, she had opened her heart for him to take comfort in.

There was only one way to let her know that he heard, that he understood.

He squeezed her hand.

And then he kissed her, lightly grazing her lips.

With that one quick whisper of a gesture he revealed more than he wished to.

Not to her since she already believed they were destined to love one another, but to himself.

Ever since he'd first come across her at the wheelhouse, he'd liked her, was grateful to her.

That had not changed, but something had.

Without a word being uttered something shifted between them.

He knew she felt it even though neither of them had uttered a word.

He stood up, nodded, then walked towards the door. He was going to need time alone to understand what had just changed, what it meant to his future.

Everything? Nothing?

'Don't worry, Fletcher. This will all come out right in the end.'

He wished he had a dream to guide him. Her certainty that all would be well must be reassuring.

'You really do believe that, don't you?'

'I do.'

'You put a great deal of faith in a dream.'

She shook her head, a smile playing at the corners of her mouth.

'No, Fletcher, it is you I have faith in. I have given a great deal of thought to my dreams lately. What I wonder is if they influence what will happen, or are they some sort of a reporting? Say, like seeing a headline in the *Daily Chronicle* before it goes to post. The paper is only saying what already happened.'

'Let's say for example, then, that I decide to grab my uncle and go back to our ship. Then the *Daily Chronicle* reports Viscount Warrenstoke has left England. But what if I changed my mind and did not go? Even though it was printed, it would be wrong. Would it be the same thing with your dream?'

'Maybe. It is complicated, I know.' She stood up, fluffed her skirt and smiled at him. 'Of course you are in control of what you do or not do. My dream was meant for me, not for you.'

'It's hocus-pocus.' He was not half ready to admit that could be true.

'Bilge water to be sure. No one would blame you for thinking so. Even I wonder if it is mumbo jumbo at times.'

What a surprise to find he was smiling at this absurd conversation.

But if it was not mumbo-jumbo, he figured…was nearly certain, in fact…that he would not mind it if she loved him.

Chapter Ten

Fletcher's mother was buried in New York, her resting place a shady corner in a kirk yard.

This afternoon he was to visit his father's grave, Henry's, too.

Eirene rode beside him, quiet, thoughtful. Every now and again she smiled, seeming far away in her thoughts.

No doubt she was visiting the many memories she had of his father and his brother.

The Warrenstoke cemetery was located on the furthest corner of the estate, he'd been told.

It was a gloomy day, fit for visiting graves.

Good company took the edge off the nature of the ride across the countryside.

'This might be the one place on the estate I have not seen.'

'We did not wish to rush this visit,' Eirene said. 'You were not ready to grieve when you first came.'

'But you think I am now?' He did not want to grieve. Grief hurt.

'No one ever is, are they?'

'It's different for me. My memories of my family are

too vague for grief. For cutting grief, I mean. I will pay my respects and be sorry they died.'

'I believe they will know you came.' She turned that soft, faraway smile on him. 'And they will be glad of it.'

It was a nice thought. He hoped it was true.

By now he was familiar enough with the estate to recognise most of the hills, meadows and streams they rode across.

He was even becoming more comfortable with having a horse under him rather than a deck.

They approached a hill he did not recognise.

They rode around the base of it, then crossed a brook. On the far side of the water was a copse of shady trees. Under the trees a white fence circled some tombstones, most faded with age.

Two of them in the back of the cemetery were still bright. It might be where his brother and his father were buried.

'Here we are,' Eirene announced even though it was clear they were.

Fletcher dismounted, then helped Eirene off her horse.

He held her waist for a second or two longer than he needed to because this visit was more stressful than he had let on and touching her gave him comfort...courage even to face—

What was it? Hello? Goodbye? A wicked, hurtful combination of the two.

She held his hand while they walked towards the gate.

'Isn't it peaceful here?' Eirene's voice was soft, comforting when they walked under the rose arbour at the entrance.

Maybe it was peaceful if all one paid attention to

was the sound of chirruping birds, the rush of water from the stream and the rustle of the leaves overhead.

If one went by how one felt, peaceful was not it.

'It is for me,' she said, probably sensing he did not feel the same way about the place. 'I came to terms with their deaths years ago. Now when I remember them, it is with a smile.'

'Whereas I cannot remember them.' Those vague shadows he saw on occasion did not count as remembering.

There were so many graves in the cemetery. Following Eirene towards the back fence, he noticed the dates. Generations of his family were laid to rest here.

Until recently his only family had been Uncle Hal. It was the oddest sensation, knowing every name engraved on these stones made up who he was.

He read a name, Hyrum Larkin. This Viscount had died eighty years ago to the day. Did Fletcher have anything from him? His smile, his eye colour? Or his love of this land?

Wait…where had that come from? Fletcher liked the land, but he loved the sea.

When they came to the graves of James and Henry Larkin, he and Eirene stood silently, gazing down.

He slid a glance at her. As he expected, she was smiling. He envied the memories which would allow her to look back that way. When Fletcher looked back all he saw was nothing.

'I will wait for you by the brook.'

He was about to say he would go with her, but then did not.

Although he did not know any of the people buried here, he was a part of them. He could not say he heard their voices calling him to sit for a while, it was curiosity about them more likely.

"'Seventh Viscount Warrenstoke, Henry Larkin.'" He read the name he was looking at aloud while he sat down on the grass. "'Loved by All'."

That must make Fletcher Eighth Viscount Warrenstoke. He picked a white flower growing at the base of the headstone, thinking he would probably never have a marker in this quiet cemetery. In all likelihood he would be properly buried at sea.

He took a breath, slowly in...slowly out. He closed his eyes and rolled the stem of the flower between his fingers.

He heard someone crying. A child.

Wouldn't do any good to look around and see where the child was. The child was him, the crying coming from his memory.

This one was not foggy, but vivid...hurtful.

'I want my papa!' he had wailed, sensing something was wrong on the night his mother took him from his bed.

He remembered kicking and trying to scream, but his mother had had her hand clamped over his mouth. As young as he had been, he understood his mother was taking him away.

Away from Father, away from Henry. Away from home.

She had scolded him, warned him to be quiet. But he wanted his papa to come and get him out of the carriage his mother had put him in.

After what seemed to be a long time of being jostled about on the seat, his mother gathered him against her, hugged him and wiped his tears.

'Don't cry, Fletchy, we're going home now.'

Home to Father and Henry. Exhausted, he fell asleep.

When he awoke, he was not home but being carried on to a ship.

He looked at his father's grave marker, seeing the man again on that last night, but earlier in the evening. He had been sitting on his father's lap, feeling strong arms wrap him up.

'You, my boy, are going to grow up to be a man among men. I will be proud of you every day.'

'He's going to be a rascal, Father,' Henry said, looking up from his spot beside the hearth, holding a book and grinning.

Fletcher remembered now, he and his brother had the same smile.

'I'll be your heir, but he will be your favourite.'

At that Father said he had no favourite, but loved his sons, each for their own qualities. He was not sure what Papa had meant by that. Only that it made Henry laugh, get up and tickle Fletcher's ribs.

'Even if I have a dozen more brothers, I'll like you best, Fletchy.'

Then he remembered his mother getting up from her chair. Snatching him out of Father's lap, she had led him towards the stairway.

The last thing he saw of his father or his brother was a glance back over his shoulder while they waved him goodnight.

Footsteps on the grass jerked him back from the past. He realised he had tears dripping off the end of his nose.

Eirene... He did not need to open his eyes to know she sat down close by beside him. A sense of silent understanding came to him. Without a touch it felt as if she placed her arm around his shoulder.

'I cried when she took me away. I did not want to go.'

'My father was there that night,' she whispered. 'I have heard the story. He heard you crying, but did not think anything about it. Children cried. He thought perhaps you must have had a nightmare. In the morning they discovered you and your mother were gone. Your father never got over it. The way my father tells the story, it helped when I was born. I imagine having a baby around will do that. So, our fathers made the marriage agreement in the hopes that uniting their families would begin the healing of losing you.'

Fletcher swiped his face on his sleeve. Curiously, he was not embarrassed that he had wept in front Eirene.

'I wonder if my bother minded having his future decided for him.'

'Being born first decided his future.'

And Fletcher was expected to carry on with it. To be everything that his brother would have been.

If only he were more like Henry. Perhaps then he would be willing to give up the future he dreamed of for the one he did not.

From what he understood of his brother, though, Henry did want the inheritance. Was accepting of his duty.

He stood. Eirene came up after him, then they walked out of the cemetery.

Passing under the arbour, he caught the scent of roses. Interesting that he had not noticed them coming in.

When he helped Eirene into the saddle he was struck again by how touching her, even if briefly, was soothing.

Not only soothing…there was more to it than that.
He did not allow himself to dwell on what it might be.

They crossed the stream, rounded the hill and then
rode across land he was growing quickly familiar with.

Going back, he saw the meadows, the trees and the
green hills. The roof peaks of the cottages.

The strangest thing was, he had a sense of belonging to all this in a way he had not had on the way to
the cemetery.

Now he remembered there had been a time he loved
his home here, had been devastated when his mother
took him away.

And something else he remembered after his mother
took him away. They were at sea, he wasn't sure for how
long, but he could no longer see land. But his brother
had taught him to swim, so he thought he could make
his way home.

When he thought no one was looking he jumped off
the ship, intending to swim back to his father.

Looking back, it was a wonder the jump hadn't killed
him. Since he was not nearly as good a swimmer as
his little boy ego thought he was, he floundered in the
swells. Luckily, someone had been watching.

Uncle Hal jumped overboard, caught him, then shimmied up the side of the ship on a net the sailors let down
for them.

First thing after getting home…back to the mansion, he meant, he was going to find Uncle Hal and
thank him.

'Life is an odd fish,' he muttered.

'It is,' Eirene answered. 'But what do you mean specifically?'

He had not known he said that loud enough to be

heard. It was a private thought, more than anything. But since she had heard he would tell her.

'Only that if Henry had not died, your father would have had no reason to have hired men to find me. I might have gone all my life not knowing who I was. No one would have known.'

'We knew who you were. You were never forgotten.'

Why the blazes did that make him want to snivel again?

On the ride home from the cemetery Fletcher had asked her the oddest question.

Did she know how to swim?

She admitted she did not. Fletcher insisted that was a skill she must have. No one was truly safe without knowing how.

What he insisted was that she needed to know how to swim more than he needed to know how to dance.

And so it was agreed that they would make a trip to the waterfall and pond where he would teach her to swim.

Although she had agreed, she considered this a waste of valuable time. It ought to be spent teaching Fletcher how to survive in society. The party was coming up rather quickly and she wanted him to have the skills he needed to relax, to feel comfortable enough to enjoy his party.

As wise as her point was, it did not hold up against an afternoon of 'fun', fun being in the opinion of her companion.

Even the argument she presented that in the event she did fall into deep water, knowing how to swim would not save her because the weight of her clothing would be enough to drown her, was dismissed as nonsense.

To which she replied, having never worn a lady's gown, he would not understand how it could happen.

And yet here she was at the pond, wearing an out of fashion bathing gown which had once belonged to her mother. She must look an odd sight with a knee- length wool dress and Turkish-style bloomers to match.

Not as odd as Fletcher did in what looked like striped undergarments.

If she never learned to swim, that would be just fine.

Fletcher would not budge on his position that knowing to swim was essential. If she ever went sailing aboard his ship, he insisted, she would need to know how.

She could not imagine what circumstance would put her aboard his ship. Either he would sail away and leave her here, or he would stay and marry her and she would remain here.

Either way she did not see herself aboard his ship. In the odd event she was, she would be very careful not to fall overboard.

Fletcher waded into the waterfall's clear pool, ripples of water licking at his knees. He grinned and waved for her to join him.

She dipped in a toe. 'It's too cold.'

'Only at first,' Fletcher said. 'Already, I am as warm as can be.'

That could not possibly be true, but she stepped in up to her ankles.

When she hesitated to come deeper, Fletcher waded back, took her by the hand and brought her into deeper water. 'Isn't this delightful?'

Warm was delightful, cold was not. Wet wool was misery.

'Tell me again, why must I learn to swim?'

'So you will not drown.' Fletcher took her other hand leading, led her in up to her waist.

'If I stay on land I will not.'

Fletcher dipped beneath the surface of the water, then came up sputtering and grinning.

'You might have occasion to be aboard ship,' he said. 'Your mother can swim. Your father told me she learned in this very pond.'

No doubt in the very swimming gown clinging to Eirene's skin and making her itch. Truly, she did not wish to remain shivering in the water for a moment longer.

'What was it your father said when we left the house?'

'Do not breathe when you are under water.'

'He also said he felt comfortable leaving you in my capable hands.'

She could hardly forget him saying that.

Capable hands? What an interesting thing to say. She cast a sidelong glance at Fletcher's large, rough, capable hands.

His brows arched and his grin flashed.

Capable hands, indeed. He did not need to touch her to teach her to swim. An explanation would do—

Quite suddenly, her feet were swept out from under her and she sank beneath the water.

Oh, but then Fletcher's arm came under her knees, his other arm around her back, and he lifted her.

'What you will learn first is to float.'

Blinking water out of her eyes, gazing up at his smile while she lay cradled in his arms, she was already floating.

'Relax your back. Pretend you are drifting to sleep.'

With one hand, he supported her between her shoulder blades. With his other hand, he supported the small of her back. 'That's good, just let yourself go. You won't even notice when I move my hands away.'

Oh, she would notice. Even through itchy wool she felt the heat pulsing from his fingertips. Oddly enough, the water did seem warmer all of a sudden.

She glanced up, waggling her fingers in the water, as if they were fins. 'Like this?'

'Close your eyes so you do not sink. And don't talk.'

He smiled at her, his lips twitching at the corners, his gaze tender...or something like it. Unless he was just happy to be in the water and the look had nothing to do with her.

'Eyes closed,' he repeated. This time he frowned so she obediently squeezed them shut.

Water dripped, plip, plop, plip, when he lifted one hand out of the water.

He stroked her eyebrows.

'You are too tense. You must relax all over or you will go under.'

'It is unnatural to float on top of water.'

He must have dipped his face closer to hers because she felt his breath, smelled his wet skin.

There was no way this would work. How was a woman to relax when she was about to be kissed?

But then, surely she was not. This had only to do with teaching her to float.

'Let your limbs go soft, pretend you are air...a bubble skimming over water. You will like it. I promise.'

She concentrated on breathing, on drifting, on becoming a mindless bubble.

As soon as he removed his hands from her back she

would sink. The weight of her soaked bathing gown would drag her down, mental attitude notwithstanding.

'It's nice, isn't it?'

His voice was beside her now, not above.

It was nice. His voice was getting further away than his arm could stretch which meant…she was bobbing about on her own!

This was blissful.

She cracked open one eye. Saw him on his back floating several inches away. Now and again their feet would bump, his shoulder would graze hers.

One could fall asleep like this. What a delightful way to spend an afternoon.

All things considered, learning to swim was much more pleasant than she expected.

'Somehow I missed my invitation for the outing.'

Percy's voice was like icy water being dumped on her lovely moment. It made her flounder and sink.

Fletcher caught her arm, steadied her until she got her feet under her.

'No matter, I'm here now to join the fun.' He stomped to the edge of the water, probably thinking the expression on his face was a smile. That was the last thing it came across as.

'Of all the bad luck,' Fletcher declared. 'We just finished Eirene's lesson. Lady Habershom will be expecting us for tea.'

'But I would like to see what you learned, my dear.' She truly hated when he called her that. 'Won't you show me?'

'I learned that this water is cold and wet wool is itchy.'

'I would never have guessed, seeing the pair of you

bobbing about quite prettily. Won't you show me how to do it?'

Percy was not wearing a proper swimming garment, but started to unbutton his shirt as if he intended to undress and join them in his small clothes.

'Cousin, do not tell me a grown man such as yourself does not know how to float?'

Percy's lips thinned, tense looking even though they were curled in a smile.

'But I do, naturally. I'm accomplished at it normally. But it has been a while since I had time to indulge in the pastime. Show me, Eirene. You looked so…' His lip curled in a way that gave her a shiver on top of the one she already had from being in the water. 'So skilled.'

'Your mother will be waiting to take tea with you,' Fletcher said. 'Go along and I'll refresh my cousin on how to float.'

She doubted if Percy could float even with the best instruction. Anyone could see how tense he was.

'I would not wish to make any of us late for tea,' Percy snapped. He swallowed his irritated tone at once. She wondered if anyone else had noticed it. 'Tea is a good way to spend time together in the afternoon. All of us family, or nearly so.'

This time Percy's smile was quick and wide and completely insincere.

An hour later during tea, Percy was so congenial she wondered if she had read more into his previous mood than was there.

And yet, she knew him too well to believe he was not up to something. He would never let go of Warrenstoke with a sip of tea and a smile.

* * *

The wind was up. Fletcher went outside, walking around the corner of the house to secure a shutter which slammed into the wall outside the library.

By the last dim light of day he watched grass on the hills being blown this way and that, sometimes nearly flat.

It brought to mind rough seas.

His ship rode easily over erratic waves.

He feared his tenants' cottages would not fare as well against the violent weather.

Floyd Mathers's roof was barely attached as it was. First thing in the morning he would ride over, bring a crew to fix it. Floyd deserved to live in the conditions he created. Small Willa did not. As long as he was at Warrenstoke he would see that she was protected.

What about after? Who would be here to make certain the estate and those living here were protected? It was not as if he could sprout wings and fly between his ship and his estate.

What he could do was marry Eirene. If he did that, her father would run the estate in his absence and all would be well for Warrenstoke.

'Damned, cursed...' he mumbled while securing the shutter.

It wasn't right for Eirene to pay the price of him following his dream. He would never ask his wife to give up her happiness for him to have his.

How long would it take for her bright, lovely spirit to turn sad, burdened and constantly watching for her husband to return?

He cursed all the way back to the front door since no one would hear him with the wind snatching his words.

By the time he came inside he had managed to cast a net around the worry and store it in the back of his mind.

He went to the library for a peaceful sit before dinner.

Or perhaps not. His cousin was in the library, lounging on the couch.

'Percy.' He nodded, then walked to the chair which was furthest away.

There was a fire in the hearth this evening, the flowers having been moved to a table near the window.

'Good evening, Cousin.' Percy nodded back at him.

There was not much doubt in Fletcher's mind that Percy had come to the waterfall earlier today because he did not wish to be left out of anything having to do with Eirene.

Which meant he was watching her. He'd thought so, but this afternoon was the final proof. It had not been random coincidence that Percy knew where they were.

The man was jealous of Fletcher's growing friendship with Eirene. Not because he desired her for who she was, but for the funds that would come to whomever she married.

His cousin's interest in Eirene gnawed at his nerves, made them feel raw, irritated.

It seemed to Fletcher that Percy was a cat sitting in a corner swishing its tail, waiting for the dog to leave the room so he could pounce upon the mouse.

Not that Eirene was a mouse, or that he had grudge against cats. There were several useful ones aboard the *Morning Star.*

'You and Eirene looked rather…cosy, shall we say, floating about in the pond the way you were. I trust you will not act in any untoward way where she is concerned.'

Fletcher's blood began to rise, heated in the way it was before a boxing match. Percy's comment invited a skirmish and no doubt about it.

Verbal but real, none the less.

Percy took the first jab. 'A man like you? You understand, I cannot be too careful when it comes to her.'

A deflection was called for, a side step. 'Do you really know how to swim, Percy?'

Now for a cross to the jaw.

'I got the feeling it was only a boast.'

Percy's jaw clenched. He'd hit the mark. 'I shall challenge you to a swimming race one of these days, Fletcher.'

'Shall we wager on the winner?' Upper cut delivered.

Percy blocked the blow with a laugh. 'I've learned that lesson. You cleaned out my gambling funds once already.'

'It was a fight fairly won.'

In boxing terms they were dancing about one another now, avoiding what was at the heart of their battle.

'I should not have sent my man after you. I apologise for that.'

Judging by the narrowed glare in his cousin's eye, this was not surrender. Percy was not a subtle soul. He gave his thoughts away by a glance or expression, by the quick, angry grinding in his jaw. What he said was not what he meant.

'I accept your apology, Cousin. No harm was done.' Fletcher did not say what he meant, either.

Feint for feint.

'But what are your intentions towards Eirene? She is expecting a proposal.' Gut punch.

Percy landed the blow where Fletcher was most vulnerable.

'My intentions are my own to know.' With that honest answer, Fletcher took off his gloves, laid them aside for the moment. 'But rest assured, Percy, I will never harm Eirene.'

'I believe I hear dinner being announced. Shall we get to it?'

Percy went out of the library first.

Fletcher followed behind, bruised and confused.

He knew he belonged at sea…and yet he could not, at the same time, disavow Warrenstoke.

Chapter Eleven

Eirene went to the ballroom, determined to direct her mind to practical, busy matters.

The problem being, all she could think of was floating. Even after four days she could not get the sensation out of her mind.

If the moment presented when she was certain to be alone, which was unlikely to happen with the details of the house party pressing, she would go back to the waterfall. She would strip down to her shift...wait, this was a fantasy so she would strip down to nothing and then float about, bobbing and blissfully unaware of anything but cool water below and a dapple of warm sunshine from above.

No worries, no lurking Percy, Mother was healthy, and no handsome heir who could not make up his mind between Warrenstoke and the Atlantic Ocean.

Supported by a bed of water, she might allow herself to drift to sleep. Being so relaxed, the last thing she would do was sink. Her blood would pump through her veins as sweetly languid as syrup. Her thoughts would be clouds, no more than wisps in the blue.

How lovely. How utterly delightful and unobtainable.

Being alone at Warrenstoke these days was nearly impossible. There was always someone popping up here and there.

So many details needed to come together to give Fletcher a proper introduction to local society. Many of them would remember his disappearance and be happy to celebrate his return. Others would attend because they were curious.

So much to do!

But—

She glanced about. In this very moment she was alone. While she could not float on water, she could do it on a dance floor.

She picked up her skirts, held them wide. She closed her eyes and began to spin, to step and glide to the music…which she had to sing herself.

She chose a tune, a waltz. Then added the words.

'Oh, Penny, oh, Penny…' There had to be more words than she had heard Fletcher singing. Where did that buxom lady roam? Poor Penny needed to find a home. 'She came to the green hills, of Warrenstoke place, a lovelier spot she would never…grace?'

She twirled faster.

'Oh, Penny, oh, Penny,' she sang, now breathless. 'She found her new home…never more did she roam!'

Someone clapped, then laughed.

Fletcher! That just went to prove she could not count on being alone.

'It was kind of you to give Poor Penny a home.'

She was breathing too hard with exertion to do anything but nod.

'I expect she will be happy here. I think she might

have become tired of seaports and sailors,' he said with only half a grin, which somehow came across as even more fascinating than a full one.

'In that case, she shall have the best room,' she managed to say over her laboured breathing.

The half of his expression which was not a grin seemed troubled.

'Is something bothering you, Fletcher?'

He shrugged one-shouldered. 'Perhaps, but it can wait. Since I am here and you are here, shall we practise on a proper ballroom floor?'

Clearly he did not wish to discuss what was on his mind, but if he wished to improve his dancing, good then.

He placed one hand at the small of her back, caught her other hand, held it in the position she had taught him to.

'Oh, brilliant!' She was more than a little proud of him.

'I have yet to take a step.'

True, but her comment had to do with the delightful way his fingers pressed her back. He did not need to know it, though.

The truth was that he still had a great deal to learn, but he caught on to the basics quickly.

And then he led her around the floor. Masterfully, skilfully…as if he were well versed in the ballroom.

'What happened?' Just when she caught her breath she lost it again. This time not from exertion.

'I've been practising in my chamber before bed.'

'How could you possibly learn by yourself in your chamber?' Most people required hours upon hours of professional instruction. 'It is as if you were born for this.'

His answer was to flash her a grin. 'Innate talent.'

Mid-whirl, he stopped dancing.

'Honestly, though, I do not know what I am meant for.' He drew a strand of straggling hair back over her ear. His fingers lingered at her temple feeling warm, intimate. 'I used to, but now—'

His fingers drifted from her temple to her lips. 'What I wonder is if I was meant for this…all of this, the estate…for you?'

'You are the only one who can know for certain.'

'Oh? I thought you were the one with the answer.'

'I was the one with a dream. You are the one who must decide his future.'

'There's the trouble right there. It isn't my future I'm deciding, is it? It's your future and my uncle's. If I choose the *Morning Star*, what happens to everyone who lives here?'

'I'm sorry you are in this spot, Fletcher.'

'Are you?' He bent his lips to hers and gave her a kiss. Tender and quick rather than long and ardent. 'Because I am not sure I am.'

In the moment a maid entered the ballroom, carrying a bucket and a mop.

She dipped a curtsy, then covered a smile with the back of her hand.

'We will get out of your way,' Fletcher told the maid.

He stepped away from Eirene, grimacing. 'I wonder if tales spread as quickly here as they do aboard ship.'

'The estate is bigger, but there are more mouths to spread stories and eager ears to listen to them.'

They walked out of the ballroom, elbows nearly

touching. Once in the hallway Fletcher paused in front of a potted palm.

'I don't mind what people say. I doubt if they will be mean spirited about what the maid saw. I mind how my cousin might take it.'

'Does it matter what he thinks? Not really, I don't believe so. There is nothing he can do to you. You are the Viscount.'

'I only wish there was some way of making him leave Warrenstoke.'

'I do not see how you can unless he does something to warrant it. So far he is behaving as well as anyone.'

'To appearances. But there are sharks under the surface of the ocean that can't be seen until a big dorsal fin slides past the ship.'

'What do you do when one does?'

'We catch it and eat it.'

'We cannot do that with Percy, but at least he is not behaving too badly.'

There had been that one time when he pinched her shoulder. He had caused her more fear than pain. But it had been a warning.

'Neither is a shark, until he is. You remember what I taught you?'

'I'm not likely to forget. You were a dedicated instructor.' He'd definitely gone the second mile which she ought not to be smiling at.

'Aye, well. I hope you never need to use it. If you do, though, give it all you have. Don't let my pain go to waste.'

'You were so gallant, Fletcher.'

'Wasn't what it felt like to me.' He shrugged, turned and walked down the hallway, leaving her with the image of his deeply dimpled smile.

* * *

Fletcher found his uncle in the most unlikely of places.

The stable.

He had put off this conversation for as long as he could. Earlier, he wanted to talk to Eirene about his uncle, but decided dancing with her would be better.

Now it was time to talk. There was no damn way he could make a decision about his future without knowing how his uncle felt.

Sail away or remain here? He needed to understand his uncle's feelings about it before he made a decision.

He feared he already knew. Uncle Hal might rather live on land. Fletcher needed to hear the words from his uncle's mouth, though.

Remaining at Warrenstoke was the last thing either of them meant to do in the beginning. Then, there had been one clear course of action. Come here, receive the means to purchase their new ship.

It had taken only a day to know things were more complicated than he first thought.

In the beginning, before he had found the carved horse under a tree root, before he had ridden about meeting tenants who were his whether he chose them or not, before he met a lady who dreamed she loved him, whether he chose it or not, everything seemed simple.

His and Uncle's Hal's dream of a new ship had been a good one, but now…somehow the idea didn't sparkle as bright as it used to.

Uncle Hal spotted him, waved him over to a stall.

'Fletcher, my boy, what are you doing out here among the hay bales and the horses?'

'Looking for you. Never knew you liked horses so much.'

'Ha! Surprised me, too. But just look at Blue Boy here. He's magnificent, don't you think? Long clean lines...pretty as a new ship.'

'He's a beauty, Uncle.' It was easy to understand why he would think so. But to compare the animal to a new ship? 'Can we sit for a while and talk?'

Uncle Hal patted Blue Boy's sleek neck. The horse whickered, nudging his arm.

They sat down next to each other on overturned barrels. It seemed the most natural thing in the world to do even though they were in a stable.

How many times in the past had they sat just this way, but on the deck of the *Morning Star*?

'Feels like old times, doesn't it?' His uncle slapped the side of the barrel he sat on, grinning.

'It hasn't been all that long. Can't say I'd call them old times. But you like it, though? Being here?'

'A man can't do the same thing all his life. He changes. Things that used to come easy to me no longer do...so, yes, Son. I like it here very much.'

Fletcher took a minute to let that settle. Accept the change, as best he could. Life was changing. It was hard to see Uncle Hal as an older man. He had always been strong, in charge of his world.

'I'll tell you something.' Uncle Hal waggled his brows as if he was about to divulge a great secret. 'I never had a friend until I came here and met Viscount Habershom.'

'That can't be true. The crew thinks the world of you. The Captains we meet when we make port speak highly of you. You go with them to pubs! And there's me, you have me.'

'No one means more to me than you do.' Uncle Hal

clapped his shoulder. 'But the crew are employees, they come and go. And the Captains? They come and go, too. I have a passing comradery with them and they with me. It is different with Lord Habershom. Brothers more like. Same as it was with him and your father. Interesting it would turn out that way, isn't it?'

It was interesting. He could not deny it. Both his fathers and Eirene's father, close as brothers?

Nothing of this was what Fletcher expected to hear, not what he wanted to.

'Some people just get on in a different way. I think you know what I mean. It's like the way you feel different about Eirene than the way you do about the crew.'

'I do not see the comparison,' he said even though he did. Saw it as clear as hay dust floating in the stable.

'Do not try and hoodwink me, Son. You haven't got away with that since you were seven years old. Fool yourself if you must, but not me.'

He was not here to fool anyone. Only to learn what was what when it came to his uncle.

'Will you remain here when I go back to the *Morning Star*?'

His uncle glanced at Blue Boy, who cast them a curious eye over the stall gate.

'Well, now, I was hoping you would not go back.'

'Our ship is my place. It's where I grew up.'

'This is your place, too. I should have brought you home first thing.'

He would have missed so much if his uncle had done that.

'No, you were right not to. No boy ever grew up better. I loved our life at sea.'

'Are you so certain you will not love your life here? It's where you were born…it is who you are.'

Uncle Hal regarded him silently for a moment as if trying to decide whether to say something or not.

'I nearly married once…did you know that? But, no, you would not. I never mentioned it.'

'That's a big thing not to mention.'

He shrugged, gave Fletcher a faraway smile.

'She was a beautiful woman. I loved her, but I loved the sea, too. I believed I could not have both.'

'Uncle, you made the sensible choice. You had a good life.'

'A wonderful life, but the truth is, I made a wrong choice. If I'd picked Mary, I'd be a husband, have five children. Four girls and one boy. It's what she had in the end, four girls and a boy. She also had a man who put her first.'

'Is that why you raised me? To take the place of the son you did not have?'

'No. It was more that your mother was the daughter I did not have. She did not trust her father to keep you safe and she did not want you to return to Warrenstoke. So when she begged me to keep you, I did. Do not think I regret doing it, Son. Not for myself. But I was wrong to keep you from your family.'

'I don't regret it either, Uncle.' Not regret…but he did wonder. What would his life be, if it had gone another way?

'Not yet, maybe. But one day you might, and if I'm not with you then, I'm telling you now how sorry I am for hiding you from your father and your brother.'

What kind of not together did he mean?

'Sounds dire.' His uncle was ageing, but not doddering. He was a vision of good health. He'd learned to ride a horse as if he was the one to have been born to it.

'I don't mean to die if that's what you are thinking. I'm only just starting to have fun.' His uncle let out a great laugh. 'I only meant that if you choose a life at sea, I will not go with you.' He arched his bushy grey brows. 'Maybe I will help raise your children.'

Well, curse and damn it! 'I do not have children for you to raise.'

'But you could if you make a better choice than I did.'

'I didn't hunt you down to discuss children who do not exist. Only to find out how you felt about staying here.'

'Aye, well, now you know. While you are at sea getting knocked about in your cabin by a storm, I'll be right here, happy in a comfortable chair with my toes toasting by the hearth.'

It would be lonely without his uncle. The *Morning Star* would not be the same without him.

'I'm glad you have taken so well to the land. I'll be thinking of you and your warm toes when I'm getting soaked on deck.'

'And I'll be telling your sons and daughters how the moon looks reflecting off the ocean's surface on a clear night. And the way the water ripples just before a whale rises.'

'Don't think I do not know what you are doing.'

'Reminding you of the fun I will have with your children and you will miss?'

'Given that I have no children, it will not work.'

'Worth a go, wasn't it? Good thing our Eirene has better bait than I do.'

Bait? He would not call it bait!

But she did have something. And it drew him, made him question everything he thought he wanted.

Children? It was his uncle who brought them up.

It was Eirene who kept them toddling about in his mind.

'I believe our young Viscount is ready for his debut.' Eirene's mother watched Fletcher through the breakfast room window while he walked in the garden with his uncle.

They were laughing together. She was relieved to see things were easy between them now that Fletcher knew his uncle was going to remain at Warrenstoke.

Father had confided to her and Mother what Hal had told him about staying. It would be a harder separation for Fletcher than for Hal, she feared.

Already, Hal had made friends with everyone from the stable boy to the butler. In the event the Habershoms did not remain here, Hal would be still happy at Warrenstoke.

While he would miss his nephew, she did not think he would be lonely.

Eirene was nearly sure the same could not be said of Fletcher. He would dearly miss the man who had raised him and loved him as his own.

But would he miss her? In order to miss someone a person needed to care about them.

Since he did not wish to marry her, he must not.

But that seemed wrong. He did not act as if he didn't care for her. The hours they spent together were special, warm and happy.

More and more he seemed torn about where his place

in life was. From what she could see, with each memory that came back to him, the more divided he was.

'Where are you wandering, my girl?'

Into a fog of uncertainty was where.

She was confused about many things when it came to Fletcher Larkin, but at least not his readiness for the coming party.

'He is as ready as he can be, Mother. He hates formal wear and might appear to be angry at his tie, but he dances like a dream.'

'Your dream, Eirene?'

'You know he was.'

'But that is not what I mean, at all. When I see you look at him, he is who you would choose even if you did not dream him.'

'I am not his choice.'

Mother waved her hand in front of her face, laughing.

'Do not worry about that. Love will find a way.'

'But is it love? If it is forced by fate, maybe it isn't true.'

Oh, but when they kissed it was wonderful, not in the least forced.

'What do you see when you look inside your heart? Obligation or joy?'

'Worry, Mama. Even with the dream I don't know anything for certain.'

'From all we have experienced your dreams are a reflection of what happens. Which means he will choose to stay.'

'I used to believe that. I only wish I was as certain of it now as I used to be.' She glanced out the window. Fletcher and his uncle were on the path leading to the stable. Her mother was smiling at her when she shifted her gaze back. 'If he does not choose Warrenstoke or me, will I recall the dream differently? Or at all? Maybe that dream will just go away as if it had never been.'

She crossed the room to her mother, leaned across the back of her chair and hugged her neck.

'I think, right this minute, I am more confused than Fletcher is.'

Her mother reached back and stroked her hair, clicking her tongue.

'Forget the dream, Eirene. As I said, love will find a way. I promise.'

'He would need to love me for it to find a way.'

'That is precisely why you should not worry. I see what I see.'

Which was more than what Eirene saw. But then, if she closed her mind and only felt with her heart? Perhaps... it might be that Mother was right.

Chapter Twelve

Sitting in mist heavy with drizzle was comfortable. It reminded Fletcher of the ocean where mists and fog were commonplace.

This morning it slid in off the ocean, reaching far enough inland that he could nearly smell fish. If he closed his eyes he could imagine ships bobbing in the harbour as vividly as if he were standing on the shore looking at them.

Didn't want to close his eyes, though.

Not when he was sitting in a sheltered arbour with Eirene and he could look at her instead.

This time last year, if anyone had told him he would rather look at a woman than the ocean, he'd have laughed his ribs sore.

Last year seemed a lifetime away.

'So,' Eirene said. 'The guests will be arriving in two days. Are you ready?'

He shook his head, then nodded.

No? Yes? Eirene had taught him all she could. He wanted to get this right for her sake, at least.

'I won't know until it happens.'

'I already know.' She nudged him in the ribs with her elbow. 'You will intrigue your guests. It is not every day that a sea captain becomes a viscount. Also, the older people will remember when you disappeared. This will be the homecoming they never believed would happen. It will be a great celebration.'

And if he disappeared again, this time by his own choice, what would they feel then? As he was coming to learn, viscounts belonged to their land as much as their land belonged to them.

'The ladies will be intrigued?' he asked, striving for a lighter subject to occupy his mind.

'Utterly. You are a gentleman and yet not all the way civilised. They will not have met anyone like you before.'

'Is it required of a lordly fellow like myself to be all the way civilised?'

'I hope not. And if it is, you will rebel. You are perfect as you are. Wait and see, everyone will think so.'

One thing everyone thought, and he knew because he suddenly recalled it, was that his father and mother were graceful dancers. Just now he saw them in memory whirling and swirling about at a ball they had hosted.

He and his brother had had a great adventure that night. Henry had led him by the hand while they crept from potted plant to potted plant in a stealthy invasion of the ballroom. Finding a bushy shrub, they crouched behind it.

Lying on their bellies, chins propped in their hands, they tried very hard not to laugh. Shiny boots and ruffled hems swirled past their line of sight. They had to cover one another's mouths to keep their giggles from bursting out whenever toes got stepped on. What he remembered, too, was that his mother was smiling at his father. She looked happy. Not like a woman who was soon to run away.

He might never know why she had done it since he could not remember and his father was not alive to tell him. But perhaps Lord Habershom would know, given how close he was to Father.

'Eirene, I wonder…has your father ever mentioned if he knows why my mother ran away?'

'Not that I recall. It happened before I was born and I do not remember anyone talking about it. But you must want to know.'

He nodded. 'I just remembered something new… old, I mean. I remember my mother and father dancing. Both of them were smiling. It could not have been long after that she took me away.'

'It is puzzling. But right now it's getting too damp to remain outside. Let's go find my father and ask him if he knows why.'

She stood up. He did, too, catching her hand when he did.

Mist touched his face feeling damp and cool. Familiar.

It dotted Eirene's nose and the corners of her smile. What he could not help but wonder was, what would mist feel like on lips? What did it taste like?

Not fish…green was what it was. He was not certain who kissed who first, but green was the flavour.

Had his whereabouts never been discovered, had he never come home, he would never have known.

He liked knowing. If he went back to sea, everything would be familiar. If he remained at Warrenstoke, so much would be new.

Eirene was right about it being damp, though. If he continued to kiss her, she would catch a chill. If he meant to survive the party, he needed her to be with him, not in bed sneezing.

They had just made the terrace steps when a man approached, running across the garden. At the same time another man came out of the house.

'My lord!' A tenant, Mr Arnold as he recalled, hurried forward.

At the same time, Percy rounded the corner of the terrace closest to the garden. A nasty suspicion drew his attention from the tenant for an instant.

Had Percy been watching him and Eirene? It would not be the first time.

'Sir, we need your help in the village.'

'What is the trouble, Mr Arnold?'

'It's Floyd Mathers, sir. He's off his head with drink, throwing rocks at folk's front doors.'

'This is where being Viscount is a nuisance.' Percy grinned when he said it. 'Always seeing to other people's problems. Glad it's you and not me.'

'Lucky thing, isn't it? Me and not you?' A shadow skittered across Percy's expression. Eirene probably saw it, but Arnold was unlikely to recognise the underlying tension.

Poor Arnold had his own troubles in the moment.

'Please hurry, sir, before someone gets hurt.' Mr Arnold glanced towards the hill that separated the village from the mansion.

'Let's go do something about him, shall we?'

He clapped Arnold on the shoulder, then trotted beside him towards the village.

He glanced back over his shoulder because he did not

like leaving Eirene alone with Percy. They were within steps of the house. He believed she was safe enough.

His duty in the moment was to his tenants. He could hardly leave them in danger.

He was doing what Henry would do in this situation. Didn't know how he knew it, but somehow he just did.

'Can't say I would want to be Mathers, would you?' Percy said opening the terrace doors. 'Our new Viscount has a vicious pair of fists. I lost money because of them. But you will remember, won't you?'

'I shudder to think how much you lost. But what you do with your money is not my concern.'

'Isn't it? Has the Viscount asked you to marry him? For all the time you two spend cosied up together, I would have expected him to. But do not fear, my dear. When his attentions all come to nothing, I will not hold a small indiscretion against you. Certainly you are not the first woman he has led astray.'

'Percy Larkin! I will have you know I have not been led anywhere, astray or otherwise. And since I have no intention of marrying you, you need not overlook anything.' If only he would do something outright awful to get himself banned from Warrenstoke. 'If you will excuse me Percy, I need to speak with my father.'

'Until next time then, my dear.'

'Until then.' *Unless I see you first*, she added but in her mind.

She found her father in the library, sitting beside Mother next to the window. There was a chair close to the fireplace, so she sat down there.

'Father, I have something to ask you. Do you know why Fletcher's mother ran away?'

A glance shot back and forth between her parents. Mother nodded.

'I know, so does your mother.'

'And yet the one who ought to know does not,' Mother pointed out.

'Fletcher, of course.' Her father set aside his book and started to rise. 'I shall speak with him now.'

'He is in the village. Floyd Mathers is causing trouble. Fletcher went to take care of it.'

Sitting back down, Father gave a smile which took in her, Mother, and all the books in the library. 'He will be every bit the Viscount that his father was.'

'Indeed he will,' Mother said. 'Just as long as it is what he chooses.'

Father's grin slipped. 'He will choose it, won't he, Eirene?'

'She does not know and we will not press her about it. What will be will be.'

It was late when a knock rapped on Fletcher's door.

He opened to see Eirene dressed in the gown he had last seen her in, but without the customary bustle lifting the back of her skirt...and she was barefoot.

It nearly seemed as if she had undressed and then quickly dressed again, but not all the way.

'Is something wrong?' There must be or why would she be here at this hour, her toes peeking out from under her skirt.

'No, not wrong...only I have discovered some things. Things you have a right to know.'

'Sit with me by the window.' He indicated a pair of chairs in the bay. She hurried to one and then flopped down on it.

'I spoke to my father about your parents. He wanted to speak with you himself, but Mother was a little under the weather and so they retired together. Father asked me to speak with you.'

He sat down in the other chair and a good thing. All of a sudden his legs grew wobbly, as if he were standing on deck during a storm.

The clock in his chamber ticked away half a minute while she looked anywhere but at him.

'I hope she is not ill,' he said, breaking the silence.

'No, only weary from everything going on. She will be well enough by morning.'

'What is it your father wished for you to tell me?' It was hard to ask with his heart halfway up his throat. 'I assume it has to do with my mother. Eirene, do you know why she did what she did?'

'Yes…my father says your mother was homesick for New York, but even more for her mother.'

Homesick meant lonely—had her husband and her son not been enough to fill her sad space?

'I know.' Eirene squeezed his fingers which were gripping the arms of his chair. 'It sounds simple, not much of a reason to take you and flee. But you must understand she was barely out of the schoolroom when she was sent here to wed your father. As I understand it, her own father was so eager to be related to a title that the weeping and the protests of the women in his home meant nothing to him. Your grandmother's pleas to wait a few years went unheeded, as if they meant nothing.'

'The same as later, my father's tears must have meant nothing to my mother.'

Eirene stood up from her chair. She sat down on his

lap then with a gentle touch, pressed his head to her shoulder.

He wrapped his arms around her, seeking comfort.

'Well, from what my father had to say the situations were not the same. From what your mother used to say, her father was a cold man and cared nothing for anyone, only his ambition to secure business contacts in England. What your mother wanted was to heal her broken heart. So it is not the same thing, Fletcher.'

'Was my father such a cold fellow that he could not heal her broken heart?'

'Your father was a warm, loving man. It is only that your mother could never really see what he offered. I was told that she cried all through the wedding ceremony. My parents were both there. My mother tried to comfort your mother, but it was no use. The one person your mother wanted at her wedding was not there, her own mother.'

'Her parents did not attend?'

'Your grandmother was too sick with grief to travel. Your grandfather, though, we do not know why he did not.'

'I wonder—why was my father willing to marry a sobbing bride?'

'Mama says that once he saw her he fell head over heels. She was an exceptionally lovely young woman. Before that, though, when the betrothal was arranged, he had already agreed to it because the marriage worked financially for both families.'

He rubbed his ear against her shoulder. The fabric was soft and smelled like her which gave him courage to hear the rest.

'Sounds heartless to me.'

'It did to your mother and grandmother, too. But in society's eyes it was an excellent match which made a great deal of sense.

'I told my father about how you and Henry hid behind the pots at the ball that night. Can you believe he remembers? He says you were full of the dickens. You and Henry were having such great fun he didn't have the heart to remove you. Later on the butler did.'

'I'm glad I remember that time with Henry.'

'Our fathers had a good chuckle over it. And my father agrees that your mother looked very happy that night. Apparently she loved nothing more than dancing. It must be where you get your skill from.'

'Skill, is it? I only manage not to trip on my feet,' was what he said, but he did like thinking he got something from his mother besides being abducted. 'If she was happy, why did she run? I do not understand it.'

'Ah, well, there was a reason. Your father regretted what happened for the rest of his life, you should know that. But you see, your mother asked to go visit her mother. Your father would have allowed it, but her own father refused. Said she needed to adjust to her new life and would not be welcomed home.

'When your mother appealed to your father, he told her she must respect her father's wishes. Mama says your mother had a wilful streak. She would not be denied what she wanted and so she took you and off she went. Once she got to America you can guess what happened.'

'My grandfather turned her away.' Easy guess.

'He did and that was not the worst. He did not allow her to see her mother. That part they learned from the investigators your father hired. After that is when they lost track of her.'

'Because my uncle hid her aboard his ship.' No wonder she attached her affections to Uncle Hal so readily. 'She must have felt betrayed by my father as much as she did her own.'

'How could she have felt any other way? I can imagine she considered her husband and her father to be cut from the same cloth. Both of them keeping her from her mother and breaking her heart.'

'I suppose she must have been bitter at having no choice in what happened to her.'

His mother must have felt something of a fish in a barrel. No control over her life and no way out.

She did what she felt she had to do. He did not condemn her for it.

He, her son, also wanted to have a choice for his life. He could not see that he was so different from her in it.

'Thank you for telling me, Eirene.'

He held her closer, not wanting to let go. She was lovely, soft and comforting…and more.

Now was not the time to indulge what might be more. He wondered if there would ever be one.

'Well, it's ten-thirty.' He lifted her off his lap.

'Yes, it is late. My maid will be waiting.' She bent to kiss his cheek. At the doorway, she paused, looking back. 'I would like to say one more thing, Fletcher.'

'And I would like to hear it.' He stood, came towards her.

'It's only that there are things which happened in the past and they were not right. Your mother should have been allowed to see her mother. You should have been allowed to be raised by your father and with your brother. I only hope those things which you were help-less to prevent do not burden you now. Life is lived in the moment. We should cherish it. That's all. Good-night.'

Fletcher stepped in to the hallway, watching her walk away. It was true that life had dealt him a hard blow in his youth.

But now? He had never had a better friend than Eirene Smythe.

And what she said about being raised by his father? While he thought he would have liked that, he had two men who now filled the role.

What he felt when it came to fathers was blessed.

Would he stay here with these men?

Or would he return to the life he had before? A life he wanted, but feared would not be the same.

Unlike his mother, he did have a choice.

Fletcher sat up in his bed with a jolt. Sunlight streaked past his curtain and on to his bed which meant he was late in rising.

He might have slept even later had it not been for the sudden sense he had of being watched. This was not a new sensation for him, but he had not had it since com-ing to Warrenstoke.

He glanced about. He was alone, yet he knew the sensation was not false.

Tossing the bed clothes off, he got out of bed and strode to the window to look out.

Down below in the garden there was only one per-son poking about.

Eirene. She was not looking at his window, but rather cutting flowers and putting them into a basket. Getting ready for tomorrow and the arrival of guests, he thought.

He could not determine what caused the foreboding tickle along his nerves, but it grew more troubling by the second.

His chamber door opened.

'Good morning, my lord,' his valet said cheerily.

The ill feeling persisted, but it could not be caused by his valet. The fellow was a fountain of good cheer at all times.

'Good morning, Henson.' He looked back at the garden. 'I hope my late rising did not keep you from—'

A movement caught his eye. Not Eirene, she was bent over a flower bed reaching for a yellow bloom.

It was a bush swaying that caught his eye. It did not quite hide Percy's crouched form.

Henson held out his robe. Fletcher snatched it, then ran past the slippers on the floor.

He had never felt danger threatening anyone but himself before. Perhaps Eirene was right and they were connected in some woo-woo, hocus-pocus way. There was no time to ponder such a mystical notion now.

He burst on to the terrace, saw Percy speaking to Eirene. She was discreetly inching up her skirt.

Percy leaned in close enough for Eirene to feel his slithery words as well as hear them. She half expected to see a forked tongue slip from between his lips.

For the last minute and a half, he had chattered on about how she needed to be careful of Fletcher. How his cousin was a violent man and one to be wary of.

What she knew was that Percy was the man to be

wary of. Especially lately. He'd become more cunning in the way he hid behind congenial words.

Not outright threatening, they were all the more menacing because of it.

What he was saying outright was that when Fletcher showed his true colours, Percy would step in and marry her.

'You are standing too close to me. Go over there.' She pointed to a rose bush six feet away. 'I will hear you plainly.'

'But you smell so much sweeter than a rose, my dear.' He took a step closer.

A position, he did not seem to realise, that put him exactly where he needed to be.

'Have you sniffed that rose?' She gathered up her skirt, scanned the ground for a rock. 'If you went over to where I suggested and smelled the rose, you would not say such an untrue thing.'

'You do understand my meaning was not—'

'Good morning.'

Fletcher's face popped out from behind Percy's shoulder. If she had ever been more relieved to see him, she did not know when it was.

Percy might look the bigger man, but it was Fletcher who loomed larger in the ways that counted.

'I was just looking for you, Eirene,' he said.

Clearly he had not been for very long, given that he was not yet dressed. He was barefoot, his robe gaped open to expose his chest, every bare, muscled inch of it. Quite clearly his valet had not seen to his hair. It hung every which way across his face.

Through a mass of blond strands she saw a fight

pulsing in his eyes. He must have seen her speaking to Percy from his window and come tearing downstairs.

It was just as well her defensive move had not been necessary. It would be better to save the manoeuvre for a time when there was no way out but that one. Percy would not fall for it twice.

She released the hem of her skirt. Fletcher gave a whisper of a nod, probably to acknowledge that he understood what had been about to happen.

'I was late waking up.' He shrugged as if that explained his state of undress. 'I hope you are not offended by my appearance.'

'Umm, no.' Surprised, yes. Relieved, completely. Not offended, far from that.

'You forget yourself,' Percy grumbled at her. 'You are a lady. Of course you are offended! What will your father think when I tell him of the Viscount's behaviour?'

He wanted to hurt her again. The itch to do it flared in his eyes. It took all she had not to recoil and hide behind Fletcher's back.

She smiled when she wanted to cower because if she did not, he might believe he had succeeded in making her feel his victim.

'I meant to escort you to breakfast, Eirene.' Fletcher extended his elbow to her. 'I hope I still may?'

'Of course.' She looped her hand through the crook of his elbow. His arm was strong, supportive and she found the courage to say, 'Percy, come along and join us, won't you? We can tell Father how inappropriate the Viscount is, together.'

Percy's face grew pale. He clenched his fists.

Perhaps she should not have taunted him with that

last. It was rather like waving a red cape in front of a bull. This bull was probably down to his last ounce of self-control.

'I'm sorry, Percy,' she said while clinging tighter to Fletcher's arm. She must do what she could to diffuse his anger or it would be a miserable day for everyone. 'Surely you are hungry. Come and eat.'

'I did not mean to offend you, my dear.' He did not mean the apology any more than she did. The fact that he called her 'my dear' was the proof.

Percy knew there was a line he could not cross. He walked just this side of it. If he did cross it, he risked giving Fletcher reason to expel him.

For now Percy was in control, but how long would he be? That was what worried her.

Percy walked ahead of them without looking back.

'He was hiding in a bush, watching you. I saw him from my window.' Fletcher covered her hand, squeezed it. 'What did he want?'

'He told me to be careful of you. That you were a violent man and I should be wary.'

'I can be when I need to. But you have no reason to be wary of me.'

Well, she did need to be. Only, not for the reason he was speaking of. The man was too distracting, walking beside her half-dressed the way he was.

If she loved him, gave him her heart and he chose the sea…well, how would she get over it? She was not certain she would.

'I wonder if you should put on some clothes before we enter the dining room.'

'I'm the Viscount and I can do as I please.' He flashed a teasing smile.

She thought he meant to distract her from the encounter with Percy.

'That is not quite right, Lord Warrenstoke. You cannot do all you wish to. People watch everything you do, listen to everything you say.'

'Same thing is true on the *Morning Star*. Captain is always scrutinised.'

When they approached the breakfast room door, he prevented her from going inside. He cocked his head, listening. Then, seeming satisfied, he nodded.

'I hear your father's voice. You may go inside.'

She started to, but then he prevented her again.

'Be very careful not to be alone with Percy.'

'I am trying to.'

He kissed her cheek and let go of her elbow. 'Try harder.'

Chapter Thirteen

Try harder?

There was something she was trying harder to do. That was go to sleep. After the encounter with Percy this morning, it was difficult to relax.

Every time she closed her eyes she saw Percy's fat lips too close to her face, heard his slithering voice saying wicked things about Fletcher.

He was up to something, although she had no idea what it could be. But every time she tried to relax, she grew tense again.

What she needed to do was pace. Even if it was only up and down the corridor outside her chamber.

That should be safe enough. Percy's chamber was on another level of the house and all the way in the east wing.

Opening the door, she listened. When she did not hear anything, she stepped out, barefoot and as silent as the stars.

The stars she wanted to see. Surely they would calm her.

This was her home...well, not exactly, but it felt like it was, and it might be one day.

She had every right to go where she wished to go.

Fear of Percy Larkin began to give way to another feeling.

She was offended, incensed!

Who was he to call her 'his dear'? Not only did he not mean it, but she was not his in any way.

And who was he to keep her from looking at stars?

What time was it anyway? Not so late that there were not still a few servants going about the business of closing the house for the evening. Perhaps some of them even getting ready for tomorrow and the arrival of the guests.

Chances are she was not really alone. In a home this size someone was always busy doing something.

It would be perfectly safe to go to the conservatory.

While creeping along the corridor she did hear rustlings, occasional footsteps.

It only went to prove that people were about and she was quite safe.

More than likely, Percy was snoring away in the far wing of the house.

In only moments she would be gazing up through the conservatory ceiling and seeing…stars? Yes, them, but also Fletcher as he looked this morning.

She tucked the thought away, intending to bring it out and savour it once she reached her sanctuary.

Coming to the conservatory door, she opened it, came inside and closed it again, as silently as a fairy flitting across blossoms.

Yes, a flitting fairy. Adopting that attitude ought to restore her sense of well-being.

She caught the hem of her robe, twirled, smiled and imagined Fletcher's bare chest, his messy blond hair, and oh, those eyes which captured her heart and made her sigh.

She stopped twirling, looked up at the stars and thought more about his eyes. Behind the messy strands they had a fierce, manly gaze. When he looked at her it was as exciting as a touch.

But she had seen them look tender before, too, which made her feel soft...lush? Yes, lush it was.

When he looked at her with mischief winking in his eyes, in his dimples, it left her delightfully undone.

Had buxom Penny met Fletcher in her seacoast village, she would never have wandered from home.

'I do believe I am in love with you, Viscount Warrenstoke.'

She had known she would be from her dream, but now, in the face of loving him as a flesh-and-blood person, dream love grew foggy.

Loving Fletcher Larkin in the here and now was so much richer. No wonder she wanted to dance and swirl. She'd heard of walking on air and decided it was true. She was half certain she did not feel the conservatory stones under her toes.

Clap...clap...clap. The sound echoed across the conservatory.

'What are you doing here?'

'Ah,' Percy drawled. 'I was restless, wondering how I might finally get you alone.'

Oh, dear, they could not be more alone.

'I thank you for saving me the trouble.'

'I do not know what you might have to say to me which could not be said in company.'

She had an idea what, she just needed to keep him distracted while she looked for a stone.

'Oh, my dear, in company I am not free to speak baldly.'

No stone, drat. If it came to it, and she was rather certain it would, she would need to run.

'If we are speaking baldly, I forbid you to call me your dear.'

'You…my dear…are in no position to deny me anything.'

Not yet, but if he took a few steps closer she hoped to be.

'I would like to know what you need to say that was so important it kept you from sleeping.'

'We will talk and then get to the reason you are lifting your nightgown.'

Oh, drat. There was no discreet way of getting it up.

'The reason I am lifting my gown is to scratch my knee.'

'Still,' he licked his lips. 'I have something to ask of you…not ask, demand.'

This would work in her favour, probably. He would misunderstand why she let him get so close.

'Asking is ever so much more civil. The results are better.'

'What I am demanding is my rightful place at Warrenstoke.'

'You have it already. It is as cousin of the Viscount.'

'I was meant to be Viscount. It is who I will be. Had that bloody fighter not been found, I would be by now.'

'Since he was found, I do not know what you want me to do about it.'

'You must contrive a scandal of some sort which will result in him being put away.'

'I will not do that.'

He rushed her, grabbing her shoulders. 'This estate is mine...you and your fortune belong to me.'

She was as frightened as she had ever been in her life. If Fletcher's instruction did not work on Percy the way it had on him...well, she was not confident of her next breath.

Lift, slam!

Percy fell to the floor, bellowing.

She ran.

Straight into Fletcher's arms. He set her behind him, backed her out the door.

'Go to your chamber, Eirene. I will deal with him.'

'In a sense, you already did.' Why did her voice have to be shaking? Probably because she had used all her courage getting Percy on the floor.

'That was all you. But did he hurt you?'

He'd scared the wits out of her, but she was not the one writhing on the floor.

'No. More awful words, that's all. I promise I did look for a stone, but there was not one. So I ran, just like you told me to...but I am so grateful you came. I'm still shaking.' She held out her hand, not ashamed for him to see. 'Will you walk me back to my room?'

He cast a glance back at Percy. 'I'll deal with him later. Come now, we will go to the library. I do not wish for you to be alone until we decide what's to be done about him.'

'You sound so in command. A proper Viscount.'

'Or a sea captain.'

Once inside the library, Fletcher built up the fire.

It wasn't until they were sitting on the couch that she

noticed he was fully dressed. Odd, he had retired long ago, the same time she had.

He took off his coat and set it about her shoulders, then tugged it closed over her nightgown and robe, which, while not sheer, were a little revealing.

'Were you going out?' she asked.

'Not far. There was this itch under my skin, like something was going to happen...like someone was going to go where they should not.'

Someone, who?

'Perhaps I should be offended that you...' Never mind that. She was about to say he did not trust her to do the sensible thing and stay in her chamber. She could not very well say that, could she?

'Were you watching outside my door?'

'At the end of the hallway behind a curtain.' He took her hand, gave it a quick kiss. 'I thought it would be Percy coming to finish what he started this morning.'

'No matter how it came about,' she said. 'It is what he intended.'

'You should not have to be afraid of coming out of your chamber. I will send him away.'

'As wonderful as that would be, I do not think we can. Not with guests arriving tomorrow. We will speak with my parents about it, but I think they will agree that your welcome home party is no time for a scandal.'

'I do not care about a scandal! I care about you.'

'And I care about you, Fletcher.' She wanted to kiss him so badly and tell him that when she said 'care' she meant love. This was exactly the wrong time for it, though. 'You must have a proper welcome which is not overshadowed by Percy.'

* * *

What he must do was protect this woman. Even sending Percy away might not ensure her safety. The moment Fletcher went back to the *Morning Star*, Percy would come slinking back.

There was only one way to keep Eirene safe and that was to marry her.

Only one way to protect Warrenstoke, as far as that went.

The estate had somehow got in his blood. Or it had always been there. For him to feel so strongly about the land and the people? It could not have happened this quickly unless it had been within him all along.

Standing among the books, feeling the warmth of the hearth seep in to his clothes, he made up his mind for good and all. He chose to be Viscount Warrenstoke.

He had to wonder, had his experience as ship's captain been preparing him for the role?

Maybe or maybe not. It really did not matter.

What mattered was keeping Percy away from the place he loved.

Away from the woman he—

Whoa there a minute! Loved? That was not what he meant, it only slipped into his mind unguarded.

He felt friendly towards Eirene, he owed her for what she had done for him at the wheelhouse. He owed her father for taking care of his estate.

'Eirene.' He touched her chin, felt the indentation of the dimple he adored…he could adore it without being in love, surely. 'My cousin is more of a danger to you now than he ever was. There is only one way I know of to keep you safe.'

Her smile was sweet, her expression playful even after what she had just endured. 'Do not say you are going to lock me away in a tower.'

'I need you to hear me. What I am about to say is the only way I have of truly keeping you safe.'

'We cannot sit in the library for ever, naturally.'

'You must marry me.'

She stared at him, looking too stunned to speak. And no wonder. He was stunned, too.

He had not woken with a start this morning because he thought the day would end in a proposal.

'It is the only way,' he insisted.

'It makes sense, I will admit it. But, no, I do not feel I must.'

'What about your dream?' She had gone on quite a bit about it. Seemed so certain of their future.

'I would never have you feel trapped in our marriage. Just because I dreamed it does not mean you have no choice.'

'Forget the damned dream. I do not have a choice and neither do you.' He let his hand fall away from her chin.

'I choose not to be your trap, Fletcher. It is not what one does to someone they love.'

Someone she loved? That could not be. Just because she believed she dreamed she loved him did not make—

Why was his heart somersaulting all over itself? He cared for her. Only Uncle Hal was as dear to him.

He loved his uncle.

'Do you love me? Or is it that you dreamed it and now think so?'

'I love you because you are wonderful. But I am not going to marry you.'

'This makes no sense. Don't women want to marry

men they love? Eirene, you are an amazing woman. I care so much for you...'

He was bumbling, feeling like a cork bobbing on the ocean.

'So...are you saying we are not fated for one another? I thought you believed we were.'

She covered her face with her hands, shook her head. *Please do not let her be crying*.

She sighed, dropped her hands. Oh, she was not crying, but there was moisture in her eyes.

'I do not know what I believe. Only that...' she touched his hair, brushing it away from his face '...I do love you and it is not because of a dream. It is because of who you are, Fletcher. If you stay here or if you leave, I will love you the same. It is why you must have a choice.'

'Very well, I have made my choice.' He turned his face, kissing her fingers where they lingered in his hair. 'I choose to stay here and marry you.'

'And I still choose to say no. I realise that I am going against everything our parents wished for. Against everything that I thought would be. And so—' her voice hitched '—you are free of my dream. It cannot compel you to return my feelings.'

She stood up, handed him his coat and walked out of the library.

He followed her down the corridor, up two flights of stairs and then down the hallway that lead to the wing of the house where his chamber and the Habershoms' chambers were.

At her chamber door, she turned about, went up on her toes and kissed him. Quickly and shyly, it seemed.

If there was one thing she had never been around him, it was shy.

'Goodnight.'

That said, she went into her chamber. He heard the door creak when she must have leaned back against it.

This had very likely been the longest day of his life and it was not over.

He sat on the hallway floor, his back wedged against the door.

His head ached. His heart ached more.

One thing was certain, he was Warrenstoke. This was his place.

Right in the hallway outside Eirene's room, he reaffirmed his decision.

He was home. Regardless of what Eirene chose to do, he belonged here.

Damn it. So did she.

His father knew it. Her father knew it.

Now that he knew it, she had turned him down.

Any future he had ever imagined for himself at Warrenstoke involved her. He must be as blind as a cavefish to have never recognised it before now.

This marriage had been expected of him as much as it had been her.

Now that it was apparently not to be, he felt a proper mess inside. Low and dispirited? Yes, but more than that…heartbroken.

Aw, damn and curse it. How did a man feel those things without being in love?

If it was true and he was in love with her, it was not because he was compelled by a dream.

Eirene leaned against her bedroom door, hand at her throat, trying to force her sobs back down.

She had just been offered everything she wanted. What her dream said would happen.

And at the same time, it was not. In her dream Viscount Warrenstoke loved her. She could possibly accept his proposal…such as it was…and not have that.

It would not be her dream if she did.

Weeping silently, she slid to the floor, pressed her hand on smooth, polished wood where she knew Fletcher sat sentinel on the other side.

Her brave, noble hero whom she wanted so desperately and yet could not have.

Love would find a way, Mother had assured her.

Eirene was certain that accepting his proposal was not the way.

Forced love was not love, she reminded herself.

Which did not make the temptation to open the door, accept his proposal and fall into his arms any less.

She kissed the door, imaging there was no wood between them. She rose, then went to her bed where she finally allowed silent tears to fall.

It took only a moment for her pillow to become damp.

Fletcher rose from the hallway floor when he heard the staff begin to go about their business.

He reached his chamber only moments before his valet came in. Weary to the gills, he was glad for once to have help with his shave and grateful that his clothes for the day were being laid out on the bed.

A bed he would not mind falling face first into.

He hoped that Eirene would sleep late and give Fletcher a few moments alone with her parents at breakfast.

Luck was with him, he discovered as he came into the

breakfast room. There was only Lord and Lady Habershom at the table.

No surprise that Percy was not here.

After greeting them and taking a plate of food from the sideboard, he began the conversation right off with what was on his mind. He did not wish to be interrupted by anyone else coming in.

'There was a problem last night involving Percy.' He tapped his fork on his plate. 'It had to do with your daughter.'

Lord Habershom shot up from his chair. 'I shall kill him this minute.'

'I was of the same mind. But Eirene nearly did it herself.' Fletcher cast a glance at his knee which he was sure Lord Habershom would interpret and understand.

'Oh, marvellous!' Lady Habershom declared, beaming at her husband. 'I was not aware that you taught her that, my dear.'

'I did not.' Lord Habershom arched a brow at Fletcher.

'I hope you do not mind.'

'I'm only glad you did. What was the blackguard's crime?'

Eirene's father sat down when his wife yanked on his sleeve.

'As I understand it, he was making threats against me.'

'Anyone could have told him that was a mistake,' Lady Habershom declared.

'I wish to send him away, but Eirene wants me to get your opinion on it. She thinks it will be a mistake.'

A glanced passed from one Habershom to the other.

'My husband and I believe it would be best if you

do not. For one thing it would take the focus off your homecoming. People will want to celebrate.'

'We also think it would do no good to send him away,' Lord Habershom added. 'He will only do his plotting where we cannot be aware of what he is up to. But as Warrenstoke, this is your decision.'

How did they do that? Tell each other things without saying them aloud.

Just because he was Warrenstoke did not mean he had the last say in what went on here.

He wished to send his cousin away and could not.

He wanted to marry Eirene and could not.

His only hope was that her parents would convince her of the wisdom of them marrying.

'There is something else. I have done things all backward, though.'

'Better just to say what.' Lord Habershom gave him an encouraging nod.

'Last night I asked your daughter to marry me and this morning I am asking you for her hand.'

'Why, that is grand news!' Lord Habershom stood again, thumping him on the back.

Eirene's mother smiled, but Fletcher thought the gesture restrained. 'And what did she say?'

'She turned me down. I explained how there was no way around this situation with Percy but for us to wed. If we are married, he has no reason to pursue her.'

'I assume you intended to remain as Viscount if you proposed marriage,' Lord Habershom said. 'But what will you do now that my daughter has refused you?'

'This is home. I know it now. Lady Habershom, is there nothing you can say to your daughter to convince her to marry me?'

'Not more than I already have. I will tell you the same thing I told her. Love will find a way.'

He would argue that statement. This was not about love, but about safety.

When he would have said so, the breakfast room door burst open and Eirene rushed in.

Breathless, hair undone, and her hand braced on the doorjamb, she gasped, 'Fletcher, I must speak with you immediately.'

Chapter Fourteen

Mother gasped.

Eirene knew she must look a fright, but in a moment such as this it hardly mattered.

How much had Fletcher got around to revealing about last night?

Any of it could be the reason for her father's frown.

All of a sudden anything that happened last night did not loom as large as it had.

Now there was something worse.

Eirene snatched Fletcher's hand, hurried him out of the house across the meadow and towards the hilltop. And all without speaking even though what she had to say was nearly bursting from her mouth with its urgency.

It was foggy this morning and, while not the best of conditions for walking outside, the hilltop was the most private place she knew of.

She flopped down at the base of her customary tree, leaned back against the trunk. Fletcher settled beside her.

'I told your parents that I asked you to marry me and that you turned me down.'

'How did they take it?' She did want to know. One

more moment without bringing up the reason she had rushed him here would not change anything.

'It was hard to know. You dragged me away before I got a feel for it. The last I heard your mother say was something about love finding a way.'

'Oh, that…well, never mind for now. There is something you need to know.'

And how was she to tell him without giving in to panic and sputtering what sounded like nonsense. He was bound to think it was regardless of whether she sputtered or made an elegant speech.

There was simply no easy way to say it.

She took a breath, held it then let it out with a whoosh. 'I've had a dream, Fletcher.'

'Woo-woo? That sort of dream?'

'The sort of dream which must not be dismissed. It was horrible. Do not label it absurd because it is going to happen.'

'I will decide if it is absurd after I hear about it.'

She caught his hand, crushed it to her heart as if somehow it would make him understand how dire a situation they faced.

'This happens on the night of your ball, sometime before midnight. Percy challenges you to a boxing match.'

'I can handle him easily.'

'He kills you!'

Fletcher lifted her hands, kissing them.

'My darlin',' he said.

The endearment sounded so very wonderful. However, this was not the time to feel wonderful.

'You were tired, overwrought by everything that happened yesterday. That's all.'

'That is not all! I know what this sort of dream

means. You must pay attention, even if you do not believe it because I will not lose you this way.'

'You are not going to lose me.' Then he kissed her.

'Do not try to sneak around the problem that way, Fletcher Larkin.'

What she would not give to be able take it back. To never have gone to sleep last night. But, no, she was glad she had so that she could warn him.

'Why are you grinning, Fletcher?'

'Forewarned is forearmed, they do say.'

'I do not know if by knowing what will happen you can change it. It hasn't worked that way in the past. But this time it has to, doesn't it? Or else...'

This was not the time to cry. It was time to fight.

'What happens is that you win the fight, even though your cousin fights dirty. Percy is on the ground appearing to be knocked witless. But then when your back is to him while you are resting on a stool, he rises up. He hits you in the back of the head with a stone.'

'That is quite a nightmare. No wonder it scared you.'

'It should scare you, too.' Her voice emerged strangled, hoarse. She wiped tears from her cheeks with the back of her hand. What was wrong with her? She needed to be strong, not weepy. 'Please tell me it scares you.'

All of a sudden he reached over, gathered her up and set her on his lap. He pressed her head to his shoulder, made soothing, shushing sounds.

'There now, my darlin', no need to cry. It was only a nightmare, I'm sure. But I promise to be careful. Everything will be all right.'

'I wish I knew how.'

She pressed her ear to the hollow between his shoulder and his chest. It was hard and muscular—it also might be the most secure place she had ever laid her head. His heart beat under her palm, comforting and strong. It seemed impossible it could ever stop beating.

Perhaps this was the time a dream of hers would prove wrong.

'You do know how, Eirene. Your mother said it. Love will find a way.'

'It might, but it takes two, I think, for that to be true.'

The way her held her, kissed her hair, then her temple, it felt very much like he did love her. No doubt it was because it was what she wished for so desperately.

He dipped her down into the crook of his arm. The only place to look was up into his eyes.

She had watched many expressions cross his handsome face before, but this was the most tender she had ever seen.

This one robbed her breath because…what did it mean when she imagined she saw her own feelings reflected in them?

'What are you thinking?' She hardly dared to hope, but—

'This.'

And then, with his strong, oh, so manly arm, he drew her shoulders up, smiled…he kissed her.

Somewhere close by a bird stared to sing. Dimly, she wondered if the sun was breaking through the fog.

When he stopped kissing her she opened her eyes, saw sunlight touching his hair with flecks of gold.

'I have changed my mind. I will marry you.'

He kissed the tip of her nose. 'Do you not wish for love to find a way?'

'I am not certain there is time for it, Fletcher.' She

touched his hair trying to catch the sunshine. 'I shall begin along the way and perhaps love shall catch up.'

He shook his head. 'Perhaps love has raced on ahead and is already there to meet you.' He lifted her so they were now eye to eye. 'I love you, Eirene. The wind was a bit slow filling my sails, but now... I love you. We will announce our engagement at the ball.'

'Yes, we will.'

'You needn't look so sad about it,' he said, clearly confused.

It was obvious he had not made the connection. What their confessions of love really meant.

Even after she explained it, he would probably be unwilling to accept the truth it.

'I love you...you love me. We have a love match,' she pointed out.

He grinned, kissed her again. 'Yes, we do.'

'Don't you see? My dream proved to be true. If this one is true then—'

He touched her lips with one finger, shook his head.

'I am not under some hocus-pocus spell. I love you and not because of a dream. And I am not going to die because you dreamed it. I promise I will not.'

It was close to three o'clock when guests began to arrive. Fletcher stood in the grand hall with the Habershoms and Uncle Hal.

Eirene stood between her parents, a vision of everyman's desire.

The sooner the engagement announcement was made, the sooner the young men he was greeting would understand she was his.

More than that, Percy would understand it. Would he accept it? That was what troubled Fletcher.

Neither he nor Eirene had seen him today.

Good thing, too, since Fletcher needed to devote his complete attention to meeting people.

This greeting process was not as harrowing as he had anticipated.

It was as Eirene told him it would be. On the whole his guests were eager to welcome him home. Many of them remembered his father and his brother. Even though their passing was not recent, the guests offered sincere words of condolence.

There was a time when he thought he would not need consoling. Father and Henry had been strangers to him. Not now. They had been within him all along, sleeping in his memory, waiting to be awoken.

Now he found comforting words were truly comforting.

With each welcome he received, he felt his roots growing stronger, expanding into all that was Warrenstoke. As much as he had once fought the idea, this estate was his place in the world.

Even more than belonging to Warrenstoke, he belonged to Eirene. There was no Warrenstoke without her. It was interesting, a wonder more than that, that his father and Lord Habershom had known it on the day she was born.

In the past he would have scoffed at the notion, but now?

Now every time he glanced her way, he had to resist the urge to stride over and boldly kiss her.

He did have to admit, their love did whisper of something akin to fate.

A part of him felt that nothing happening right now was real, but another part? Loving Eirene was more real than anything he had ever known.

There was no mysterious force compelling him to love her. It was the lady herself doing that.

What he would admit was that love, itself, was mysterious.

There was natural magic in whatever made people go from being strangers to being devoted to one another.

One thing was certain: he was not going to die any time soon. He had a great deal to live for, more than he could ever have imagined.

As much as he used to believe he was meant to be a seafaring man, the truth was, that kind of existence made life smaller. It opened the world to be sure, but at the same time, it closed the heart.

A seaman was always saying goodbye. Goodbye to people who lived on shore and goodbye to sailors who took employment on other ships.

But Eirene was his. He was hers. All he wanted was to get her alone, to let the feeling of admitting their love sink into his bones, make a home in his soul.

Given how fast it all came about…all he wanted was to bind her more deeply to him.

Sure couldn't do that with her standing between her parents.

Once the guests were settled in their rooms and resting before tea, he would find a way to get her alone.

He'd kissed her the first day they met, had it on his mind every day since. Now that they were engaged and her father given his blessing, there was no reason for them not to indulge in a kiss or ten.

The weather was with them today. Sunny and warm, it was a good afternoon to be outdoors.

After the last of the guests went upstairs and Eirene's parents had gone to their chamber to rest, Fletcher was finally able to have his lady to himself.

'Shall we take a walk beside the stream?' he suggested.

'That sounds perfect. There is something I need to speak with you about.'

'Talking is not what I had in mind.' He winked to convey what he did have in mind. 'I have never been an engaged man, but I think, if you are willing, kissing is acceptable.'

'Quite acceptable and as far as being willing?' Her smile was soft. It caught his heart. He was not going to die, not when he had finally found love. 'Let's hurry before we encounter someone and are forced to carry on a polite conversation.'

This was the quiet time of day at Warrenstoke and no one was outside.

And then, damn it, there was someone. He had hoped Percy would go away of his own accord. Maybe once the engagement announcement was made tomorrow night, he would.

Since his cousin did not swivel his gaze to look at them, perhaps he had not seen them. Or he had and was hesitant to face Eirene.

At any rate, Percy was walking away from them along the road to the village.

Couldn't blame him, Eirene had proved to be an excellent student.

A smile twined out of his heart, went smack into

a grin. There were many things he looked forward to teaching his excellent student.

As soon as they reached the stream where tree branches on each side of the water touched to form a leafy canopy, he drew her into a long, slow kiss.

In the moment they were a world apart from everything. No guests to impress, no wicked cousin and no bad dream.

Only this woman to kiss and to hold.

'This is where I met you for the first time again,' he murmured close to her ear. A strand of her hair tickled his nose.

'Your mind was on another lady at the time, if you will recall.'

'Ah, the lovely Penny.' He hugged her tight. A chuckle rippled from her chest into his. 'I only ever felt sorry for that lady, being lost and far from home as she was.'

'Even with all her charms.'

'There is only one lady whose charms will ever interest me.' He kissed her again longer, slower. His lady had many charms. He would spend his life appreciating them.

'It's…good…to…be home,' he murmured between taking gentle nips of her bottom lip.

'Yes, but, Fletcher…' She wriggled out of his arms, took a long, halting breath.

She did say there was something she needed to discuss.

Whatever it was could not be worse than that he was going to die…tomorrow.

'What is it, my darlin'?'

'It's only… I think you should go away.'

'That is not going to happen. You may put it from your mind altogether.'

'How can I? It makes complete sense. If you are not here, Percy cannot kill you.'

'I will not be killed by a bilge rat. You can put that from your mind, too.'

'Please.' She clutched his lapels, curling her fingers so tight the tips turned white. 'You must, just for a little while.'

'You had a dream. Nothing more than a nightmare. I will not let it drive me from home or from you. I am Warrenstoke. This is my land and all these people...' he waved his hand in a circle which vaguely encompassed the estate '...I am responsible for them.'

'I will not lose you, Fletcher.'

'No, you will not. Not tomorrow and not to Percy Larkin.' He tipped her chin. 'We came here for a private celebration of our engagement and that is what we will have.'

'How can I just—?'

He kissed her breathless. 'That is how.'

'But—'

'Today is today. As you pointed out, it is the only one we have no matter the circumstances. We are going to celebrate.'

As high as Eirene's hopes had been, which upon reflection had not been all that high, that Percy would not attend the ball, here he was.

The charming Percy arrived dressed in false congeniality. He hid under elegant ball clothes, behind a friendly smile.

His pleasant demeanour would probably not hold

beyond the next five minutes. Father was taking the platform stairs where the orchestra played.

In moments he would announce her engagement to Viscount Warrenstoke.

If only she could rejoice in sharing their good news and accept the good wishes about to come their way.

But the evening was already growing late. Perhaps it was the announcement which would cause Percy to challenge Fletcher to a fight.

'Here we go,' Fletcher said. Lacing his fingers through hers, he gave them a squeeze. 'Do not worry.'

He presented the confidence of a viscount, the boldness of a sea captain, and yet she was afraid.

Viscounts and captains were not immortal beings.

Percy was basking in the attention of a group of ladies when Father began to speak.

'It is with the greatest pleasure that Lady Habershom and I announce the engagement of our daughter Eirene...'

Percy's gaze swung away from his companions and focused sharply on her. In the second it took for him to look away she felt menace creep up her neck like the draw of an icy finger.

'...to Viscount Warrenstoke.'

A great cheer went up.

When she ought to be returning her finance's smile, she was choking down dread.

Percy detached from his companions, walking a straight line towards them.

Fletcher must have felt her grow tense because he whispered, 'Don't be afraid. I'm here.'

She wished he was not here. No matter how she tried to convince him to go away, he would not.

And now, Percy made his way through the crowd, certainly ready to issue a challenge.

'Cousin! Eirene! I would like to be among the first to offer my heartfelt congratulations.' For a man intent on murder he looked the soul of good wishes. 'I know in the past I may not have seemed supportive, but please do accept my good wishes.'

In the past? All three of them knew he still did not. Which did not keep Fletcher from offering his hand along with a smile.

All of their smiles were as fake as some of the jewellery worn tonight.

Anyone looking on would not know the glitter was deceptive.

After the announcement, it was arranged that they, the happily engaged couple, would have the first dance of the evening.

Fletcher was glad of it, if only to take Eirene's attention off his impending demise.

A demise which was supposed to happen before midnight, according to her dream. Three more hours then, until she could relax and know it was not going to happen.

'Show me off, my darlin'.' He held out his hand to lead her to the centre of the ballroom.

With dozens of chandeliers sparkling, happy little lights glinted off everything except his fiancée's eyes.

The orchestra played a short prelude. He held his arms in a proper stance. Eirene stepped into it.

'If you don't smile, people will think that I'm tromping on your toes.'

'Forgive me.' She did mange something of a happy look. 'You will be brilliant.'

He spun her out and about. From the corner of his eye he saw people gazing at them. Some older couples smiled indulgently as if they remembered when. Younger ones as if when would it be for them.

For him, he was happy in the moment, not looking back, not dreaming ahead.

He held his dream in his arms, whirled her about the dance floor feeling…brilliant…grateful and blessed.

What he did not feel was that his next step would be his last.

Another thing he did not feel was his cousin's presence. The man was no longer here.

Percy had not meant a word of his good wishes, but hopefully he had given up on having Eirene and Warrenstoke.

Now that there was nothing for him, perhaps his cousin had gone away.

The dance ended to great applause and genuinely good wishes.

They danced again. With each other and with guests. While he would rather dance only with Eirene, dancing with guests was the proper thing to do, he'd been told.

During a pause in dancing with Eirene, he leaned close and whispered in her ear, 'He's gone. I have not seen him in an hour.'

'An hour and ten minutes.'

'I think he has given up and left Warrenstoke.'

'Maybe he has.' This time her smile flashed bright and happy. This was the smile that had found its way into his heart and led him to where he found himself in the moment.

After another hour and no sign of Percy, Eirene quit glancing worriedly over her shoulder every few minutes. She, too, must feel hopeful that he had left.

Just now she was going into the buffet room with her mother.

His attention was drawn away from thinking how pretty her hair looked curling down the back of her neck by a footman hurrying towards him.

'My lord, there is a stableman asking for a word. I tried to send him away, but he insists it is urgent.'

Ah, well, trouble had no respect for anything but itself. He followed the footman to the hall where an agitated-looking fellow waited.

Fletcher turned to the footman, dismissing him with a nod.

'Is there trouble?' he asked.

'Great trouble, sir. A man has been kicked by a horse in one of the stalls. He looks in sorry shape. Please hurry.'

'Find the butler. Tell him to find Dr Williams. He's among the guests. After that tell him to inform my fiancée that I have gone to the stable and will return as soon as possible.'

He left the house on a run. Damn it, accidents would happen. He only wished there had been time to tell Eirene about it himself so she would not worry unnecessarily.

The stable was dark. The only lamp burning was in the furthest stall on the left.

It must be where the injured man was.

Seemed odd that an injured man would be left alone. Aboard ship, men gathered around a fallen comrade.

Dashing past three horses who watched him over their stall gates, he had no doubt that someone was hurt. Above the normal scents of hay and manure, he caught a coppery whiff of blood.

Rushing inside, he saw the unconscious man in the back of the stall. He lay on his back, blood pooled in the straw under his head.

Fletcher knelt beside him. Touched his neck, feeling for a pulse.

Mathers! What was he doing here?

'Hold on, man. Help is coming.'

Something here was not right. There was no evidence of a horse having been in the stall. No marks in the straw to indicate Mathers had been dragged in, either.

The stableman had sounded certain about him being struck by a hoof.

Rustling straw in the next stall jerked his attention away from Mathers. Prickles of alarm raced over his skin.

A cat leapt on to the low wall, stared down and meowed.

'You make a lot of noise for—'

A blow struck his head from behind. The shock stunned him, knocking him on top of Mathers.

Dizzy, he struggled to rise.

A fist slipped under his chin, slammed up, ploughed into his mouth. Blood from his cut lip dripped on to the front of Mather's shirt.

Before he could gather himself to rise, footsteps ran out of the stable.

Damn it! The fellow had not been attacked by a horse, but by a man. Whoever had attacked Mathers must be the one who just walloped him.

His head was throbbing misery, his mind foggy from the blow. It was an effort to piece together what had happened.

Mathers had made a lot of people angry the other day. This might be retaliation for that. But why in the stable and not the village? It was puzzling that Mathers was beaten this severely so close to the mansion.

Instinct told him to leap up and chase whoever had run out of the stable.

But, no, it wouldn't be right to leave a fallen man alone. Not only was he knocked out cold, but he reeked of alcohol.

Fletcher sent up a quick prayer that the doctor would arrive before Mathers grew worse.

He swiped at his bottom lip. It was bleeding hard and dripping on his white shirt.

'Don't worry,' he said even though Mathers was surely beyond hearing.

Outside, he heard voices, faint in the distance, but growing louder the closer they came.

'Here's help now.'

One voice rose above the din. It sounded angry.

Dozens of people crowded into the stable. Because the lantern only lit the stall, he could not make out their features. It was easy to sense their agitation, though.

'That's him! The man who beat poor Mathers! I saw the whole thing happen and it was wicked cruel.'

What? Fletcher spun about on his knee. Painful flashes stabbed his brain.

The shadow people mumbled. He had no idea who was saying what. Even if he could see them they all spoke over one another and nothing made any sense.

Dr Williams hurried into the stall and then knelt in the straw. 'Is he alive?'

'Yes, but barely, I think.'

The doctor bent low, listened to Mathers's shallow breathing. He opened his eyelids, peered at them for a second then pressed his fingers on Mathers's throat.

'He's passed out from drink as much as the blow. That won't help him pull through this.'

'Tell us what you saw, Mr Green!'

Curse and damn it. Percy had not gone away after all.

His appeal silenced the crowd gathered beyond the stall walls.

'It was like this.' What the blazes story was the liar going to spin? More, why was he going to? 'I came into the stable to…to do a chore.'

'What chore?' A man with a deep voice from the back of the onlookers called.

'I don't rightly recall, after seeing what I saw.'

'Please,' Percy said. 'Tell us exactly what happened. No one here is above facing their due, Viscount or not.'

'I walks in to see poor Mathers on his knees, begging not to be hit with a big stick the Viscount was shaking at his face. Lord Warrenstoke warned him to behave in the village. Then he hit him on the head.'

Dr Williams glanced over his shoulder. 'Sir, had Mr Mathers here made an attempt to defend himself?'

'He only knelt there begging not to get hit.'

'And yet the Viscount has a nasty gash to the back of his head and his lip is cut. Did you see how that happened?'

'Why…well, you see I—'

'We do not need to trouble our witness any longer,' Percy said. 'The man is distraught after seeing someone nearly murdered. We can only imagine how shaken you must have been, sir. And yet, let me know if I am correct in my guess, you wished to protect Mr Mathers. You picked up the stick he had just used and hit the assailant with it. I imagine you must have feared he would turn on you next, isn't that right?'

'Yes, sir, Mr Larkin. That is it exactly.'

The doctor grunted, shaking his head. Fletcher wondered if he believed Percy was putting words in to the false witness's mouth. The question was, did anyone else recognise he was?

The last thing he wished was to bring shame on his new title. If Mathers did not survive the attack, Fletcher might even face a trial and prison sentence.

That would suit his cousin just fine. Warrenstoke might come under his control. Eirene certainly would. He could rise from here and defend himself. If he did, Percy would only have another lying witness step forward.

'I'll have someone make a pallet so that we can take him to the house,' Fletcher said.

As unlikeable as Mathers was, he had been used, set up to make Fletcher look a villain.

'Thank you, Lord Warrenstoke. I shall take a look at your injuries, too.'

Two stablemen carried the pallet towards the house.

Fletcher and the doctor walked on each side of it with the group of onlookers following behind.

People from inside the house spilled out on to the terrace steps.

Eirene was among them. Even by the terrace lanterns he saw the pallor of her face. She must have stood on a chair to see over the crowd because all of a sudden she rose above them.

Anger propelled Fletcher towards the house as much as his legs did. So many people had gone to an incredible amount of work to make this party shine. To present their new Viscount in the best light.

Percy had brought it all to ruin.

And his fiancée, his beautiful, sensitive Eirene who hated even a respectable boxing match…what the blazes was she going to think of him now?

They had only reached the drive in front of the house when Percy shouted.

Those standing on the steps turned to look. The people following from the stable went still.

'You will not get away with this, Warrenstoke! Mr Mathers deserves justice…satisfaction.' Percy shook his fist. 'Since he cannot give it to you, I will. I formally challenge you to a boxing match. If you are not too much a coward to face me.'

Fletcher went utterly cold inside. Everything around him buzzed.

Somehow he heard Eirene gasp…not with his ears, with his heart.

She would want him to refuse, to run away. She had had that blasted dream and would think he was choosing to die.

'When?' What was between him and his cousin had to be settled once and for all time.

No one he loved would be safe until it was.

'Eleven-thirty. At the stable.'

'No!' At Eirene's shout, everyone looked her way. Someone, he was not sure who, gave her a hand down from the chair. People stood aside, letting her rush down the steps.

'You cannot do this. Please, Fletcher. You know what is going to happen.'

'My dear, I am going to show you who your fiancée really is. You will thank me for it.'

Eirene lunged for Percy, her fingers stretched as if she meant to scratch the words out of his throat...at least that was how Fletcher read her mood.

He snagged her by the waist, held her tight to his side.

'Eleven-thirty.' He gave his cousin a hard nod.

Dozens of voices, all of them agitated, followed while he took Eirene inside.

'I forbid you to do this, Fletcher Larkin!'

He did not respond, but rather directed the house-keeper to prepare a place in the library where the doctor could see to Mathers's wound.

Then he turned his attention fully to Eirene.

It was hard to tell from her expression, which changed with every thought flitting through her brain, whether she wanted to kill him herself, or hold him and weep.

What they needed to do was speak of this privately, but the house was buzzing with speculation.

He signalled for a footman to bring their coats.

Lord and Lady Habershom hurried forward, followed closely by Uncle Hal.

'Son,' Uncle Hal and his future father-in-law spoke as one.

Uncle Hal held him by the forearms, his bushy brows cutting low over his eyes. 'You must not do this. You have never fought a man who was not a professional. Percy Larkin will have no scruples.'

'No principles whatsoever,' Eirene's father added.

Eirene stood apart, her expression no longer wavering, but set as if in stone.

Lady Warrenstoke hugged him, whispering in his ear, 'Oh, my dear boy. Please ignore your cousin's challenge. He does not matter and we cannot bear to bury another Larkin. Our hearts will break.'

He heard them all, yet could not do as they urged.

If given the chance, Percy would do great harm to Warrenstoke and to everyone who called it home.

Fletcher was not going to give him that chance. Until his cousin was dealt with, those under his care would never be secure.

'I have no intention of losing this fight.' He reached a hand towards Eirene, only half believing she would take it.

She dug her fingers into her skirt, hesitating. After a moment, she grasped his fingers.

Eirene sat on the hilltop, shoulder to shoulder with Fletcher, feeling numb.

Even having had the prophetic dream, she could not believe this moment was upon them.

'I am not going to die tonight,' he told her for what had to be the eighth time since they left the house.

'It is what you keep saying.'

Looking down the hill, she watched people dashing in and out of the stable. They brought out lanterns, set them in a circle and then lit a dozen or more torches.

This was the spot where Percy intended for everyone to witness him dishonour Fletcher.

Of course it was Percy who would be dishonoured once it was discovered that he attacked his opponent with a stone after losing the fight.

No…she would not look at it. She jerked her gaze up at the sky.

The people of Warrenstoke had come to love their new Viscount and were not going to believe he did what he was accused of. Surely they would not.

'I say it because it is true.'

'You cannot convince me I do not see what is before my eyes. They are getting ready for you to fight and…' She could not say the rest. The words would strangle her.

'I didn't do it, you know. Mathers caused a great deal of trouble in the village and did not take proper care of his child but, still I would never…'

With what she thought to be a muffled curse, he turned away from watching the makeshift boxing ring being assembled. She felt his gaze hard on her so she looked back at him.

Grief shadowed his eyes. His expression broke her heart. She wanted so desperately to hold him while she still could.

But she would not. If she had any chance of changing his mind, of convincing him not to fight, she must appear firm…resolved.

If she withheld her affections, perhaps he would come to his senses.

Or she was simply wasting her last moments with him.

What was she to do? What, what, what? Her brain hurt with wondering. Did she keep him at a distance and pray he changed his mind? Or should she love him with all her might, with every last second, and hope that was what made him change his mind? Or do what she felt like doing and collapse into an inconsolable weeping heap?

The last was what she was closest to. But acting as if she were withholding her affection was what kept her from losing a grip on her emotions. It made her feel as if, somehow, she was in control of what was about to happen when, really, she was in control of nothing.

In the end, she did not believe she would manage to change his mind no matter what she did or did not do.

But he had asked if she believed him. Thinking back to the beginning, since she did not dare to think forward, she had judged him to be an aggressive man. What else was she to think since he made his money as a brawler? She had nearly convinced herself that her dream of her loving him had been wrong since he was clearly unsuitable for her.

But he had not been unsuitable. He had been perfect.

She loved him. Which meant the dream she had of seeing him on the ship was not wrong.

Which meant this dream was not wrong.

'It does not matter if you are innocent or not. Fighting will not convince anyone of the truth.'

'But do you believe it?' He drew a lock of hair away from her cheek, turned her chin so that she had to look at him. It hurt too much seeing his eyes, warm and full of life, knowing that in an hour…how was she to bear this?

She could not. For all that she willed to feel numb inside she could not make her heart feel nothing.

'No one will believe it.'

'As much as you wish it was true, it is not. I'm not asking about them, I am asking what you think.'

'You know I do not believe it.'

Of all the absurd things to do, he gave her a silly grin.

'I am not convinced. I will need a kiss to make me believe you.'

'A kiss? You have lost your wits? No... I will not kiss you and then watch you walk down the hill to your death.' Although the words cut her throat, ripped her heart, she said them. There had to be a way to make him abandon this mad thing he was set on doing. 'I have changed my mind about marrying you. I... I... just cannot.'

Destructive words were her last hope.

'Do you choose me or do you choose...' she pointed to the ring taking ugly, sinister shape below '...that?'

She wanted so desperately to hold him tight, cling to his shirt and cry her grief all over him.

'I do not choose, Eirene. This situation with Percy has chosen me. I cannot run away from it.'

'Even if it kills you?'

'I will not die tonight.'

'There is no reasoning with you!' She leapt up, turning her back on the preparations going on outside the stable.

She walked to the old tree which had grown in this spot for a very long time. She pressed her forehead to the bark. It felt rough, but solid in world that had spun madly out of control.

Hold on to this man, kiss him, love him...was what her inner voice urged. If she listened to it, she would weep and never stop.

Nothing, she feared, was going to keep him from going down and squaring off with Percy.

Fletcher rose slowly from the grass.

'I have to go soon, my darlin'.' He opened his arms wide. 'Come to me. Let us spend this time together. I might be too bruised for hugging when this is over.'

Too bruised? Too dead, more likely.

Why did he refuse to believe her? To trust what she told him? She blinked, pushing back against the tears which would soon drown her.

When she didn't go to him, he lowered his arms.

'We will talk later,' he said, then turned, walking downhill.

'There is no later!' she shouted.

He must have heard, yet his only reaction was to pause, straighten his shoulders and continue down the slope.

She broke. A great bloody crack cleaved her heart.

There was nothing she could do to change an instant of what was happening. She ran after him. He must have heard because he turned and caught her.

Holding tight to each other, they slipped to their knees.

He kissed her hard. His beard stubble caught her tears, smearing them between his cheek and hers.

'I don't have enough time to tell you how much I love you, Fletcher. If I had a hundred years, I still could not—'

'We have now.' He kissed her eyelids, then stroked the line of her brows with his thumb. 'It is all anyone has.'

She looped her hands around his neck, drawing him

back with her to the grass. His weight pressed on her, feeling solid, warm…alive.

Grass tickled her ears. He nuzzled her neck with his nose. She looked past the dark shape of his wide shoulders, watching stars glitter in the deep beyond.

Would he be dancing among them tomorrow night, while she sat here on the hilltop not able to see him through her tears…

Not now, though. She had a few moments.

'There is no death between us, not tonight.' His words filled her up. His kiss wrapped her in love which seemed so hopeful she half believed it. 'I love you. Hold that until I come back up here to get you.'

'I love you, too.' She sniffled. 'And I am going down to watch you beat Percy.'

'No, love. I would be thinking of you when I ought to be thinking of him.'

There was no argument for that. He would need to keep his attention on his cousin and the dirty tricks he would use.

It was not as if she could change the outcome of the fight whether she was here where he asked her to be, or down there where she would distract him.

Her father would be there and so would his uncle. They would watch out for him as best they could.

With one more kiss that might need to last for ever, she held him tight.

Then he rose to his knees, held out a hand and drew her up. 'I have to go now. This should not take long. I will come back for you.'

'I will be right here, in this very spot.'

She watched him go into the darkness between the hill and the stable.

She imagined him crossing the small meadow which led to the stable. Without a moon, she could not see his progress, but she felt it.

She imagined his heart beating hard, felt him fix his resolve on what the next half-hour would bring.

There would be more to face if he survived, with the accusation made against him. Fighting Percy was not going to solve that.

One dire event at a time, she reminded herself. She pressed her hand to her heart, closed her eyes and prayed they would survive this so they could face what came next.

'I forgot to remind you Percy would fight dirty.' With a sob she sat down on the grass where she had promised to wait. 'You know it already, though.'

Although she could not distinguish Fletcher from any of the other shadowy figures below, she knew when he approached the boxing ring.

Voices rose up the hillside louder, more excited than they had been a moment ago.

'This isn't a fight you need to have,' Uncle Hal said. 'No one would think less of you for not stooping to Percy's taunts.'

'It isn't taunts. I could ignore those. What he has made is an accusation. My blustering buffoon of a cousin must think by discrediting me, and in front of my guests, he will get Eirene and Warrenstoke.'

'How will fighting him change any of it?'

'I'm not certain. He made a challenge and I will answer it.'

'Aye, well, after you do there will be more to answer to. The Constable is here asking questions.'

'The Constable? There has not been nearly enough time for him to get here.'

'I suppose we both know how, my boy. Someone sent for him before Mathers was attacked.'

'Percy, curse his black heart. But one thing at a time.'

It was still quarter of an hour before the match was to start. Lord Habershom stood near the stable door, speaking to a few worried-looking guests.

Percy was a distance away from the stable, surrounded by several men from the village.

Fletcher clapped his uncle on the shoulder, squeezing quick and tight. 'Uncle… Eirene is waiting for me on the hill.'

'Yes, I understand.'

His uncle would go to her if the match went wrong.

Twenty minutes later, Lord Habershom entered the hastily constructed ring. He nodded for Percy to enter and then Fletcher.

This was not a professional match by any means. It was a grudge match disguised as one of honour.

Regardless, Viscount Habershom recited the Queensberry Rules.

Fletcher did not need Eirene's dream to tell him Percy would disregard them and fight underhanded.

Going in understanding his opponent, as well as being the more experienced fighter, made Fletcher confident of victory.

Lord Habershom walked out of the ring, head down and muttering.

Moments ago they had spoken of his daughter's dream. A dream Fletcher was about to prove to be false.

Percy did not bother taking a moment to size up his

more experienced opponent. He lunged, swiped his fist and punched air.

Looking flustered, he glanced at Fletcher's belly, a clear indication he was about to deliver a hit below the belt, as dirty a move as there was.

Fletcher sidestepped at the last second which sent his adversary off balance and to his knees without a blow having been landed.

People snickered.

Percy scrambled up, set his stance and pawed the ground with one foot. He looked absurdly like an angry bull. For all that his cousin bragged about his experience, he was proving to be all hot air.

Which made him unpredictable, dangerous.

Percy lunged. He landed an illegal hit to Fletcher's neck. Luckily it was only a glancing blow. Unscrupulous moves such as this one had left men ruined for life, which was no doubt his cousin's intention.

This was not a match to linger over and provide entertainment for bettors of which he dearly hoped there were none.

Given the illegal and dangerous moves his cousin made, it was clear that Percy did mean to kill him, dream notwithstanding.

The sooner he took his cousin down the better. As much as he tried not to be distracted by thinking of Eirene, the knowledge that she was waiting, envisioning the worst, weighed upon him.

Even the brief moment she was on his mind gave Percy an opening. He delivered a hard punch to Fletcher's gut which nearly bent him in half and hurt like bloody blazes.

Had his cousin been fighting in a proper match which

was governed by rules and a referee, he would have been disqualified.

Fletcher delivered a cross punch to Percy's chin. It rocked him back, but he didn't go down. The perfectly legal blow only riled the beast.

Hate, as he had never seen from a proper opponent, flamed in his cousin's eyes.

Using the same hand he had just jabbed with, Fletcher delivered a left hook.

Percy slipped to his knees, then flopped on his belly.

He wasn't unconscious, quite, but too stunned to rise.

Percy must have heard Lord Habershom's announcement that the fight was over and Fletcher was the winner.

Hopefully he would accept the outcome.

Although the fight had not lasted long, it had been intense and wearying.

While people walked away, to the village or back to the ruined party, Fletcher sat on a stool, breathing hard.

His shoulders sagged in relief. It was over. He was alive.

As soon as he caught his breath he would run up the hill and reassure his distraught fiancée.

He could not help smiling. Eirene Smythe was not going to be his fiancée much longer. The shorter their engagement, the better.

A bellow erupted from behind, so close he felt his eardrums quiver. Rage was upon him too fast for him to rise and meet it.

Eirene promised she would wait and so she would. Oh, but everything within her wanted to fly down the hill, dash into the awful, horrid boxing ring and give Percy Larkin a surprise. No one would expect it.

In her mind she pictured it, popping up between the opponents and giving Percy what she had before.

Of course in her mind, it would stay. The reality was, she had been lucky that first time. If she tried to unman him again, it would end badly.

The fantasy was simply an attempt to distract herself from what was going on down below. A way to pretend she could change the outcome of what was happening down there.

She had not attacked Percy in her dream, so maybe if she did, it would change the end of it.

Or be such a ridiculous distraction that Fletcher would be killed some other way.

It hurt to accept the truth. There was nothing she could do but sit here and wait.

This was probably the hardest thing she had ever done in her life. Time slowed down. Her heart sped up. It hurt to even breathe.

And then the first vague sounds of fighting began. Cheers and jeers rose up the hillside.

From where she was she could not see the battle, but she did not need to. She had seen it once before…a dozen times before.

Only this time it was worse. No longer was it a thing to be dreaded. Now it was something she would have to survive.

She ought to be crying, but she could not. Sobs would block the sounds coming from below.

Later she would cry. Now she would cling to a world in which he still lived, his heart still pumped his life's blood and his lungs still gave him breath.

Where their love could still connect on this mortal plane.

She would cry later when she could not connect with his love.

On the day they had buried Henry, there had been an elderly woman at the funeral…a widow. She had come to stand beside Eirene at the gravesite.

She was a round woman with a pretty, wrinkled face and silver-grey hair piled high on her head in a bun.

'Oh, my dear, do not grieve so for your friend.' She patted Eirene's arm softly, as if her fingers were a brush of bird wings. 'Don't you know that love cannot be separated?'

It had proven true. When it came to Henry, she did feel the friendship still connecting them at times.

Excitement seemed to be building at the stable.

Eirene tried to squeeze back her tears, but no longer could. She buried her face between her knees, lifted the fabric of her skirt over her ears so she would not have to hear the fight when it came to an end…and then—

Love could not be separated—she did believe it. But she also wanted to hear Fletcher's voice, feel his kiss and watch his dimples flash when he teased her. She wanted to sail away with him on his ship.

A great roar went up, loud enough to hear with her ears covered.

Percy would be on the ground now. Fletcher would be sitting down on the stool, exhausted.

She dropped the skirt, trying hard to listen now because the next few seconds would tell her if somehow her dream had been wrong. Maybe this one time something had happened to change it.

Something too wonderful to be believed…

But if it had not, Percy would be rising, reaching for a half-buried stone.

She shouted a warning as if Fletcher might, by some miracle, hear her.

Then someone screamed from below. Mingled voices of outrage and horror shot up the hill.

And then she screamed. Screamed with no sound.

She beat her fists on the ground. This could not have happened.

And yet…there was no mistaking what she heard.

Rolling on her side, she curled into a ball, as tight and as small as she could make herself.

If she let everything inside her go still, lay silent and inert, perhaps by some wonder, her heart would connect with his in the moment his soul rose to his Creator.

But, no, in the stillness all she felt was devastated, lost.

Mist drifted in from the ocean. It crept over Warrenstoke and settled over her, damp and cold. Grave-like.

Let it cover her. She did not care.

She could not say how long she lay there, grieving that she did not have a lifetime with the man she loved. She did not even have a fleeting connection with him when he passed, one last precious instant to carry with her.

It may have been moments or hours, it all blended into one horrific wait.

Not that she knew what she was waiting for.

It hardly mattered. Nothing did any more.

The sound of footsteps came to her, muffled in damp grass. Someone must be bearing the news she already knew to be true. Father, probably, or Uncle Hal.

If she did not stir, perhaps they would not see her and

pass by. She would rather stay curled where she was and never hear the words spoken out loud.

A hand touched her hair, brushed it away from her, gently, with utter compassion, she thought.

'I'm not dead.'

Chapter Fifteen

'Not…dead?' She sat up, touched his face, her fingers cold and trembling.

Fletcher caught them, rubbed them between his hands which were still hot from the battle just ended.

'You aren't dead!' She lunged at him, hugging him so tight he could barely breathe. Didn't matter though, he hugged her back as hard.

Finally, she let go, leaned back and blinked as if in disbelief.

'Why aren't you…? I heard screams.'

He kissed her. There would be time enough later to tell what those screams had been about.

'Ah, well… I remembered what you said about the stone. I moved out of the way.'

He sat down behind her, drew her into the lee of his knees and hugged her back against his chest.

Her clothes were damp and her hair dotted with mist. She had to be chilled. He would need to get her back to the house soon.

Also, the Constable would be waiting. He'd won the fight, but there were still accusations to be addressed.

'Do you believe me now about the dream?'

'Hard to say, my darlin'. Your dream didn't happen, did it?'

She turned to look at him with eyes all the bluer for the whites being red. Which was not an easy thing to see in the dark.

'Because you changed it,' she exclaimed. 'I never thought…'

'I am not saying I believe it. But when it came to it, I knew to duck sideways.'

She turned back, snuggled against him. Catching his hand, she gave it a long kiss. Her lips were cold. He needed to get her back to the house.

Damn it if he was ready to share her with anyone quite yet. There was one thing he needed to make clear. As soon as they got back to the house there would not be a private moment. It was not as if the guests simply went home after the upheaval. This was a house party and they would be staying the night.

'I thought I would be able to feel it when you died. That somehow you would be able to connect with me in the passing. I waited so still trying to sense you.' She started to sniffle.

'I promise if I go to glory before you do, I'll take an instant to kiss your soul on the way out.'

'Oh…well.' She hiccupped, sighing deeply. 'I would appreciate that.'

'We need to go back, but there is something I have to make clear first.' He spoke close to her ear, partly so his breath would make her warm, but also to make sure she heard him clearly. 'Maybe there is something to your dreams. After what happened I cannot say positively there is not, but, Eirene, I damned well fell in love with you because I choose to. I am going to marry you because I cannot live without you.'

'I choose to marry you, too. And not because our parents decided I would wed a Warrenstoke. You made me fall in love with you from the first.'

'Which first? Dream first or saving my hide first?'

'Both. But really, it was your dimples that did it.' She touched his cheek, traced the line where they would be had he been grinning. 'Made me go soppy all over.'

She turned again, went up on her knees and hugged him tight around the neck. They really did need to go down and face the Constable. But not quite yet. Once they went back life would get hectic. He could not be sure of what would happen once he stood face to face with the law.

He kissed her for a long time. Hugged her as tight as she hugged him and then kissed her again.

'Did you dream when we would get married?' he whispered. Mist on her hair dampened his mouth.

If she did and it was a lengthy engagement, he would prove her dream wrong again.

'No, but I will put my mind to it after I fall asleep tonight.' It was good to hear her teasing. She had been through more tonight than any woman should. And the night was not over.

'As long as you dream we will wed soon. I will get a special licence tomorrow.' As long as he did not get arrested within the next hour and end up in jail. He really had no way of disproving what Green had accused him of. 'We will be wed aboard the *Morning Star* the week after next.'

'That is the best place I can imagine. But isn't it in the middle of the Atlantic?'

'The ship is due to dock in Margate by then.'

It was time and past to get her inside. He stood, bringing her up with him. 'We must go down. The Constable is here and waiting to question me.'

'Already?'

'Someone called him before Mathers was attacked.'

'I do not need to ask who.' She snuggled into him.

'We need to go and get you warmed.'

'We could pretend we do not know the Constable is waiting. You could warm me here.'

'I will one day. We will make this our special place. Once we are wed I will warm you often, right under the tree behind us.'

She glanced over her shoulder, smiled at the tree and then at him. 'Now that you did not die I will be able to tell you I love you every day.'

'I will hold you to it unless I'm rotting in jail and then I forbid you to come and tell me.'

'You won't rot in jail.'

'I might.'

'You are too innocent to rot.'

'That's all you know…'

And then, in spite of it all, what they had both endured tonight and what they still had to, they laughed.

It was the best feeling he'd ever had.

That night he'd spent the night in the crow's nest with a storm knocking him about, he'd been consumed with the awful turn his life was about to take.

Now he was consumed with how wonderful that turn did take. He had been wrong that night. Eirene's dream had been right. No use in thinking otherwise.

'What happened, though?' she asked, clinging tightly

to his arm while they walked down the hill. 'I heard screaming. Something must have happened.'

'That had to do with Percy. When he went after me from behind, I rolled off the stool and it tipped over. He got tangled in it. His leg was broken in a gruesome way. It's why people were screaming.'

'I don't imagine Dr Williams expected to be working when he accepted the invitation to your party.'

'We will invite him to the wedding to make up for it.'

As long as there was a wedding.

When they were a distance from the house he saw people through the windows, standing in groups. They would be discussing the drama of the evening.

'I wonder if the orchestra is still playing even with no one to dance. They were paid to play until well after midnight.' He did not know why he wondered such a random thing. Must be because it hadn't a damned single thing to do with anything life-threatening.

'After we meet with the Constable, you and I will dance, even if we are the only ones,' she said.

Her confidence that they would do it was grounding. It helped against the worry trying to creep in.

Coming inside, they came face to face with treachery.

Mr Green was in the hall, speaking with the Constable. Half a dozen or more of the staff and several of the guests stood about listening to the man repeat his lies.

Eirene could not let go of Fletcher. She would not!

If the Constable led him away in handcuffs, she would hang on to her fiancé's coat. Even if Fletcher meant to go along peacefully she would drag with all her might.

Death had nearly separated them. She would not let lies do it.

Very well, she would probably not do something so dramatic and useless. However, she was not going to live her life without Fletcher Larkin. That would be as grim as if she were living in one of Mr Poe's tragic tales.

Fletcher stood tall even in the face of Green painting an ugly picture of how brutal, how unprovoked the attack had been.

As Mr Green recounted the story, Viscount Warrenstoke had gone into a screaming rage and then whacked the victim in the head without consideration for his age and frailty.

Perhaps someone who was too weak to bring a cow into the yard was frail…but with drink, not old age.

'And, sir,' Green said to the Constable, 'just look over there in the corner. His poor sweet child is weeping in grief. Have you ever seen anything more pitiful? The Viscount is twice over a criminal.'

Willa was here? The poor child. This was not something she should be witnessing.

'I am afraid there is nothing for it, My Lord,' the Constable said. 'I am afraid you must come with me. The witness is quite clear on what happened and there is no one to dispute him.'

'Please take Willa to the kitchen,' Fletcher said to the housekeeper. 'Give her something to eat and make her comfortable for the night.'

'No, sir.' Willa stepped away from the housekeeper's outstretched hand.

She walked to the Constable, looking up at him through her tears.

'I dispute it.'

'Go to the kitchen, girl. Children have no say in such things.' Green reached for Willa, but Fletcher stayed his hand.

'You must listen to me, sir. I saw what happened.'

'Children are mistaken all the time. They cannot be trusted to know what they think they saw.'

'I was there when Percy Larkin came to visit Papa. I heard it when he offered my father whisky. All he had to do is come to the stable and get it at a certain time. No earlier and no later.'

'That is not true, brat!'

'Step away from the witness, Mr Green,' the Constable ordered. 'Go ahead, Miss Willa. Tell us how you know what happened after that.'

'Many times when Papa is drinking I follow him because he needs help getting home after. So when I heard Mr Green I knew it would be one of those nights. I always keep out of sight because my papa would be angry if he saw me. So I followed him into the stable and hid. Then Mr Percy Larkin came in. He hit my father in the head with a big stick. A minute later the Viscount came in and found Papa. While the Viscount tried to help, Mr Percy stepped out from a stall where he was hiding and hit him, too.'

Mr Green growled in Willa's direction. Willa took a step closer to Fletcher, who put an arm around her shoulder and warned the stable hand off with a severe look.

'What happened after that, my dear?' the Constable asked, gently encouraging.

Willa did not need encouraging, it seemed. She lifted her hand and pointed her finger at Mr Green.

'He came in after both the Viscount and my papa were bleeding on the floor. He shouted to everyone and lied about what happened.'

'She's making it up. There is no one but her and me to say what happened. Who would believe a girl over a man?'

'Go along with Mrs Bower, Willa.' Fletcher placed her hand in the housekeeper's. 'You will be staying here from now on.'

Seconds later, Dr Williams strode out from the corridor and pushed his way through the crowd.

'I will believe her,' the doctor said. 'Mr Mathers has regained consciousness. He says it was Percy Larkin who hit him.'

'Will Mr Mathers recover?' the Constable asked.

'I believe he will.'

'Very well. How long will it be before Percy Larkin can travel?' The Constable snatched Green by the arm when he made a move to slither away between the open-mouthed observers. 'You will come with me.'

'But I didn't do nothin'. It was all Percy… He forced me.'

'Is there somewhere we can lock him away for now, Viscount Warrenstoke?'

Eirene's mind buzzed with all that had happened. Her heart felt a battered mess against her ribs. During the course of the evening life had gone up, crashed down and rolled over on itself several times.

Now, at last, here it was upright.

She was still emotionally a-wobble, but Fletcher's arm came around her waist and made the world stable again. It might not always stay stable, but as long as he was here to hold her against him, all would be well.

'Not sure how I would have made it through all this if not for you,' he whispered in her ear.

'I was just thinking the same thing about you.' She would have gone on, waxing sentimental about how it was the two of them in it for all time and how together they would find strength for whatever came, but people rushed from all over the room to pat Fletcher on the back and shake his hand, vowing they never believed the lies told about him in the first place.

What she wanted to do was tell him how much she loved him, but with all the exclamations crashing around them, she could not. Really, though, there was no need to speak.

She imagined they both felt it simply by standing beside one another, shoulders and souls touching.

While she could not declare her love for him with everyone crowding about, she would as soon as the moment presented.

Leading his guests down the corridor to the ballroom, Fletcher was glad to hear the musicians playing.

While he had imagined a private dance with Eirene, romantic and celebratory, he did have a party to revive.

Both life and the party had gone off track for a few hours.

He meant to reclaim both.

Escorting Eirene to the dance floor where everything glimmered happily, he wondered if his father and his brother had been watching from above, seen all that had happened tonight.

If so, were they pleased with how he handled it all?

Did they feel he was an appropriate viscount even though he had not been raised to it as they had been?

There was no way of knowing something as mysterious as that. He did know that there was more mystery in the world than he had ever known, so maybe...yes, it might be possible.

If Eirene's dream could take an avowed seaman and turn him into an earnest viscount, anything could be true.

'I wonder,' he said, smiling while gliding her in a waltz. 'Now that I'm Viscount, should I cut my hair? Maybe clean up my chin?'

'No, you should not!'

'You don't think I ought to look like the other gentlemen?'

'I think that if you were still wearing a tie, I would take it of your neck and toss it away.'

What had happened to the cursed tie?

It hit him that he looked nothing like he had at the beginning of the evening, no miserable tie, his collar unbuttoned and his shirt ripped. He had lost track of his evening coat a long time ago.

What sort of gentleman wore pants with grass stains on the knees and blood speckling his formerly white shirt? The sort who danced with his fiancée for the pure joy of the moment, not how he looked in it.

'You are the most amazing gentleman here tonight. Seaman and Viscount all at once. All the ladies are envious of me.'

'I will clean up for the wedding, I promise, even if I do strangle on a cursed necktie.'

'I hope you never clean up too much. You were a

sailor the first time I saw you. The first time I knew I loved you.'

'I think the first time I loved you was when you pointed Percy's thug in the wrong direction. Took a while for me to know it, though.' He whirled her off the dance floor to an alcove where there was a bench.

'Easier to talk sitting. Now with the guests back to having fun, we can.'

And then he kissed her…once, twice, three times before he lost count.

'Fletcher Larkin. This is not talking.'

'Sure it is. Just more interesting than using words.'

'Not as informative, though. So, when was the first time you loved me knowing who I am?'

'Can't say there was one, my darlin'. Never had a dream to tell me, it just came to me over time. It's like what happens to the roses in our garden. One day they are tight little buds not aware of anything, and gradually they open up and feel sunshine on their petals… it's like that.'

'Pretty words for man who is only poetic over ocean waves and whales.'

'That is why I am going kiss you instead of speaking.'

They got away with it for a long time before someone found them out and propriety demanded they rejoin the party.

A week or two, as soon as the wedding could be managed, he reminded himself, they would carry on this 'conversation' but in much greater depth.

If there was one thing Fletcher had never imagined happening aboard the *Morning Star*, it was watching

his bride being escorted up the gangplank by her father, a viscount equal in society to himself.

Fletcher never expected to be in society, let alone be equal to anyone in it.

None of that nonsense mattered in the end. They were all people. Family, crew, friends and neighbours, even staff and villagers from Warrenstoke gathered on deck to celebrate his and Eirene's wedding vows.

The only thing more beautiful than the day, with the sun glinting off the waves and the breeze gently snapping the sails, was his bride.

Even had the day been dreary, the gloom could not have stood against her smile.

The wedding march was played by a sailor with a flute and another with the harmonica. This might not be the elegant affair common for a man of his position, but it was what he and his bride wanted.

The coming moment, with vows being spoken, would be both binding and freeing. He thought about that, feeling his heart creep up his throat and his eyes stinging while watching Eirene walk across the deck.

On the one hand they were about to become bound to one another, which was not binding but freeing. As man and wife they were free to spend intimate moments... no, hours, together. Free to spend all sorts of moments together. It was only the intimate ones that were most on his mind at the moment.

Freedom also came in being rid of the threat of Percy Larkin. No one knew how much or how little time he would spend paying for his crime. But this marriage would ensure he would have no reason to harm them again. Not them or anyone who was theirs.

But his cousin did not deserve half a thought in this moment.

Fletcher's eyes filled with the beauty of his bride, his soul overflowed with love for her.

While he was aware of Uncle Hal standing beside him along with his new mother-in-law and father-in-law, it was Eirene, almost Warrenstoke, who captured all of his attention.

At the minister's prompting, he pledged his life to her. Then she pledged her life to him.

When it was announced that Lord and Lady Warrenstoke were one, a new family born, a great cheer went up. The ship's horn blared. It startled a flock of seagulls on the dock, sending them squawking about the masts.

Next there was to be a celebration at a fine restaurant in Margate.

It turned out to be a joyous, but short event. It lasted no longer than it took to lift their glasses in a toast or ten and then eat a meal, which he and his bride managed to accomplish more quickly than the guests.

When an opportune moment presented, he stood. Eirene popped up quickly beside him.

'Good evening to you all.' He took a moment to look about the large dining room, to hold the memory of so many of people of different walks of life gathered as one to wish him and Eirene well.

It was unlikely that a viscount's wedding ever had seamen, villagers and society nobles all gathered together for dinner.

However, he had led two lives and he would have them blended.

'And now my wife and I are off to France. We shall wave to you from the Eiffel Tower.'

To a chorus of laughter and good wishes, and after hugs to the family, he rushed his bride out of the restaurant, then across the dock.

When they reached the gangplank, he scooped her up in his arms and carried her the rest of the way up.

'This is where I first saw you.' Her breath warmed his ear. She pointed to a spot at the rail.

He carried her to the spot and set her down. His heart stretched every which way of blessed.

'I wish I could have been there.'

'Well, Husband, I will admit you took me by surprise. You looked a rough fellow, your lip was bleeding.' She kissed the corner of his mouth. Must be where he had been bleeding. 'You were not at all who I expected you to be.'

'And yet you loved me.'

'How could I not? You grinned at me then the way you are doing now.' She traced the line of one dimple.

'I must admit to feeling cheated. You loved me right here on the deck of the *Morning Star* and I missed it.'

'Whatever will I do about it? I must make it up to you…somehow.'

He caught her hand, kissed it and then led her below deck.

'Let me show you where you may begin.' He opened his cabin door. When she stepped in ahead of him her scent caught him as neatly as a right hook to the heart. However, this right hook delivered pleasure, not pain. 'It will take a while to make such a loss up to me.'

They would sail with the outgoing tide in the morning.

Not that it mattered to him what time they departed. He had no intention of emerging from the cabin.

The ship had a competent captain and crew which left him free to spend every moment with his bride.

'As luck would have it, we do have a while for me to do so. First France and then Spain. And in between we—'

'Will quit speaking with words,' he said.

She nodded, took him by his shirt front and drew him towards his berth.

Eirene had never slept aboard ship before.

She was not sleeping now, in fact.

According to the clock strapped to the wall, it was nearly one in the afternoon. They had probably been docked at the port of Le Havre since mid-morning.

The plan had been to visit the Eiffel Tower today, but it was too late in the afternoon for such an outing.

Tomorrow perhaps…or the day after.

For now she was content to lie beside Fletcher in the bunk and listen to him breathe, to touch his chest and feel his heartbeat slow and strong under her fingers.

There had been a time when she despaired of this moment. She had been certain Percy would kill him.

Fate was not always written in the stars. Sometimes it was decreed by fathers.

Both of those might play a part in getting her where she was in the moment. Far and beyond those reasons, it was because Fletcher Larkin loved her.

He had spent most of the night and part of the morning silently saying just that. She had spent most of the night and part of the morning answering, up until the moment Fletcher took a break in the 'conversation' and fell sleep.

Eirene was getting hungry, food having been the

last thing on her mind since their wedding feast. Admittedly, it had not been uppermost on her mind then, either.

She lay on her back, listening to what sounds she could faintly make out from above deck.

Thumps as if something were being dropped on deck right above them, shouts…answers to shouts. From the open porthole she heard gulls squawking and water lapping the side of the ship.

She understood now, how Fletcher had been content living aboard ship.

'I realise, now, how much you gave up for Warrenstoke,' she whispered to the air.

'Not more than I gained.' He blinked open one blue eye and grinned. 'Besides, I have not given it up. Here I am.'

Half sitting, he braced himself on one elbow. She traced her fingers over the slope of his bare shoulder.

Truly, her husband was a well-formed man.

'It's better now, with you.' He caught the lock of hair falling over her shoulder, wound it around his fingers, stroking the strands with his thumb. Then he bent his head to kiss her.

Her lips, the hollow of her throat, the spot between her breasts where her heart beat. Did he feel it thumping? she wondered.

He lifted his head. She wondered what romantic thing he was about to say because nothing could be more romantic than this cabin in this moment.

'I could eat whale. Are you hungry, my darlin'?'

The endearment would have to do for now and she did adore it when he called her that.

'So hungry I could eat a fish or a crab. And bread.'

'Shall we have it brought down here and eat our meal as bare as jays? Or would you rather eat on deck in the sunshine?'

'We would need to get dressed to go up.' She trailed her finger from his chest to his belly, felt a slight quiver under her fingertips. 'Bare as jays, I say.'

'Later, we will have dinner under the stars.'

'I suppose we will visit the city tomorrow,' she said.

'I suppose. Cover up for a minute while I call for lunch to be delivered.'

He tossed off the sheet, walked naked to the door and opened it a crack.

Her appetite fled. How could a woman think of fish or crabs when a well-muscled man strode bare and bold across the room? Especially when the naked man was hers.

'Patterson!' Fletcher called down the hallway. 'Have Cook deliver lunch!'

Then he closed the door, turned about and strode back to the bunk. Blue eyes glinting, dimples teasing, he was clearly ready for something and it was not lunch.

There was no moon to give light to the meal so a lantern served as well.

Sitting on a blanket spread near the bow of the ship, feeling it gently rocking, Fletcher felt home again.

Half home. Warrenstoke was home as much as the *Morning Star* was.

Yet, neither of those places were home as much as the lady sitting on the deck across from him was.

Warrenstoke? It was Eirene who was home. The *Morning Star*…still Eirene. France or Spain…his bride was home.

He watched her looking at the harbour lights while she nibbled a piece of bread.

'I have never seen anything like it,' she mumbled through crumbs.

'Neither have I.'

'That can't be true. You have seen this sort of thing a hundred times.'

'I was speaking of you, Lady Warrenstoke. I have never seen anything like you.'

He leaned across the blanket, kissed her.

'I love you, Eirene.'

Then picking up a pickle from a plate, he bit into it.

He had not come out here to ravage his bride, but to nourish her so she would have the strength to be ravaged later when they returned to the cabin.

'I love you, too.' She wiped pickle juice from his mouth with her thumb, then kissed him. 'I cannot seem to stop doing that.'

'You do not have to. It is the benefit of being wed. We are no longer forbidden to one another.'

'That is not all the way true. Sometimes we will be in the company of others and then we will need to refrain.'

'We could sail to a deserted island and never be in company.'

'We could, but that would only last until…well, you know.'

'Until another ship arrives with newlyweds?' He knew very well what she meant, but it was fun to tease her.

'Until the children come.'

'How many? Have you dreamed them, too?'

'Not yet. Even if I did dream them, we now know things can change.'

'The first dream, when you sensed we loved each

other. That one will not change. No matter where we find ourselves, that is constant. I hope we end up like your parents.'

'In what way?' She cocked her head at him, curiosity making her eyes bright and playful.

'There is a way they have about them. Sometimes they seem to know what the other is thinking without speaking.'

'Let's try it. You think something and I will guess what it is.'

'Very well.' He closed his eyes, started to think of something to think of.

'No, that is not how it works. You must have your eyes open so I can see your thoughts.'

He shrugged, thought something quite unexpected.

She looked at him this way, then that way. Her eyes narrowed and then quite suddenly widened.

'You wish to go to America.'

He had been reaching for another pickle while he was thinking. He dropped it back on the tray.

'Very well, Mrs Mind-Reader, why do I wish to go there?'

'First, I am not reading your mind, I'm simply feeling your heart. We now have a connection which allows it. You know, bone of my bone, flesh of my flesh and therefore privy to sensing the desires of your heart.'

'What is the desire of my heart?'

'To visit your family in New York.'

Good thing he was sitting otherwise he would have been knocked off his feet.

'How did you know that?'

'I promise it is nothing woo-woo or hocus-pocus. It makes sense that you would be wondering about them. You have most of your life knit together now. You have been able to balance being sailor and viscount and yet a part of you wonders what else you lost when you were young.'

'I have a grandmother living and an aunt.'

'Now you guess what I am thinking, Fletcher.'

The thought was easy to read. He could not say if he saw the answer in her smile or felt it coming from her heart.

What he did know was that he never expected to have this connection to another person. Before Eirene, he'd had no idea there was such a connection.

When their fathers arranged the marriage between their families on the day she was born, they had no way of knowing it was the younger son who would fulfil their wish. Or that it would result in a better outcome than they could have imagined.

He wondered if they knew it now, by some connection between mortal life and eternity. Perhaps if thoughts could connect people here, maybe it was possible for them to continue connect up above.

Ah, but he was wandering from guessing her thought. He was certain he knew what it was. 'You are thinking I should go to America and meet them.'

'Almost. I was thinking we should go to America and meet them. You might as well get used to the idea that wherever you go, I will go, too.'

'Are you finished eating?'

'Yes, after this one more bite of bread.'

When she finished chewing, he removed the tray from the blanket, snuffed out the lantern, then drew her down with him to watch the stars.

She snuggled her head into the crook of his shoulder, sighing.

'You sound content.'

'Quite,' she murmured. 'Will you know how to get us to New York by reading the stars?'

'Aye, love, but we'll have a sextant, too. For the Captain to use. I will be busy doing other things at night.'

The deck rocked as gently as a mother's arms around her child. Water lapped the hull, sounding as sweet as a love song.

It was the stars twinkling down that held his attention most. He thought they kept a million secrets.

One of them must know why he was led to Eirene Smythe Warrenstoke.

All he knew was he would spend his life being grateful.

New York—June 5th, 1876

Stepping down from the carriage in front of a grand house on Fifth Avenue, Eirene felt her nerves stretch and tingle.

It was not that the opulence of the homes on the street made her nervous, no, indeed. As Lady Warrenstoke she was used to opulence upon occasion. Since her marriage she and Fletcher visited London a couple of times when society affairs required it.

She glanced at Fletcher standing beside her. Opulence had not changed him. He was still part-Viscount and part-sea captain. Praise the Good Lord for it.

He was perfectly wonderful as he was.

What he also was, in the moment, was nervous. And no wonder. Who would not be, meeting the family he never knew? One year ago he had not known they existed.

'They are going to love you.' She squeezed his hand. 'And you are going to love your grandmother.'

'How do you know?'

'It's the way life works. Grandmothers and grandchildren adore one another.'

'I was hoping you dreamed it. But I suppose we ought to knock on the door and find out.'

'She's right, Son,' Uncle Hal declared, flanking Fletcher on the other side. 'It's me they are going to dislike, hiding you from them like I did.'

'We all forgave you for it, Hal,' her father said. 'It was not so hard to do.'

'I for one cannot wait to be a grandmother,' her mother said, her brows arched as if hoping to get some happy news right there on Fifth Avenue. 'I am certain the lady will be delighted to meet you at last.'

'What she will want is to know about her daughter. From what the detectives told us, she was distraught at having been kept away from her by my grandfather.' Fletcher squeezed her hand. 'I do not have much to tell her about my mother.'

'It is why we came along, of course,' her father pointed out. 'Mother and I are eager to share our fond memories, aren't we, my dear?'

'I only hope they give your grandmother peace,' her mother said. 'It was a wicked awful thing her husband did to them both. And to you, my boy.'

'Shall we get to it then?' Uncle Hal straightened his shoulders. 'I must make my confession. Standing here waiting to do so is making me feel like crabs are crawling on the back of my neck.'

Fletcher took the first step. Eirene walked beside him, clutching his hand.

The rest of the family followed.

They had not got halfway up the stairs before the front door opened.

A slender woman rushed past the doorman and out on to the terrace.

Fletcher's throat tightened. Something about the slender older lady seemed familiar. Odd, since he had never met his grandmother.

'Viscount Warrenstoke?' she asked, her hand playing nervously with the cameo at her collar.

'Fletcher Larkin,' he clarified. He was not a title to family.

The lady did not try to smother a happy screech. She hurried down the stairway to embrace him. The top of her head did not reach his chin.

She was strong for a little bird of a woman. When she released him, he said, 'May I present my wife? Eirene Larkin.'

'Oh, my dears! I am your Auntie Gracie. Your grandmother's sister…younger sister.' She hugged Eirene. 'Oh, my dear girl, I cannot tell you how pleased we are to have a daughter in the house again.'

The vice that had been constricting his belly for the past hour gradually relaxed. He had yet to meet his grandmother, but hopefully she bore resemblance to her sister.

Fletcher introduced his uncle and Eirene's parents.

'Let's go inside and meet your grandmother, my dear boy. She did not sleep a wink last night. But no one did, we were all so anxious to meet you.'

Going inside, Uncle Hal walked next to Auntie Gracie.

'Your niece greatly resembled you,' he heard his uncle say.

That would explain why his aunt looked familiar.

'We had that bond, among others. But Fletcher must resemble his father.'

'He does,' Lord Habershom declared. 'As did his older brother, Henry.'

They were ushered into a cosy parlour with a fire simmering in the hearth even though it was late spring and rather warm outside.

A woman sat in a wheelchair with blankets tucked around her. Her eyes were bright blue with moisture standing in the corners.

He could not say what overcame him in the moment, but he hurried across the room, knelt in front of her chair and gave her a hug.

She returned his embrace. It seemed stronger than her small frame would account for.

They were strangers, but it did not feel like they were.

'Oh, my dear boy. It is something of a miracle seeing you with my own eyes. I never dared hope to.' She took his face in her beautiful delicately lined hands. 'Now let me look closer at you.'

She smiled while looking at him more deeply than anyone ever had. Except for his wife, but those were looks of another kind.

'You are wrong, sir. So are you, Gracie. The boy looks just like his mother.'

He did not, but no one was going to dispute what his grandmother saw within her memory.

'In the crinkle of his eyes, perhaps,' Lord Habershom said.

'She is the image of me, Emily. How many times have we said so?'

'You do have a lot to say, Gracie.' His grandmother sent her sister a pointed frown. 'I suppose my sister made a great point of saying she was the younger sister. She always does, you know. Ten months only, which hardly qualifies as younger.'

'I am sprier than you.'

He glanced back and forth between the sisters, relieved to see it was friendly sparring going on between them.

'Of body, perhaps, but I am sprier of mind. Now, shall we all sit? Gracie, with your spry younger body, will you ring for tea?'

Uncle Hal looked as nervous as Fletcher had ever seen him. Better get this done with, then.

They all took seats with Emily Sterling at the centre of the cosy circle around the fireplace. Fletcher sat in the chair next to her.

'Grandmother, my uncle has something to say to you.'

Uncle Hal stood, clasping his hands and looking down at his feet.

'You knew my daughter well, I have been told.'

'I suppose you were informed of my part in all this.' His uncle looked up. Fletcher figured it took all he had to face the lady he had wronged. 'So, yes, I did know your Anna. The truth is, I loved her as if she were my own child.'

'Which she was not.' His grandmother sighed, pressing her lips tight.

'No, she was not. I was wrong to keep her and Fletcher from you. I am forever sorry for it.'

'But you mustn't be, sir,' Gracie said, nodding at his chair beside her as an indication he should sit.

'I cannot imagine why not.' Uncle Hal sat down, his expression confused. 'I kept Anna and Fletcher from you. You must think me as black-hearted as they come.'

'I am grateful to you, sir,' his grandmother said. 'You loved my child when her own father did not. It is he who was the black-hearted one.' His grandmother turned her attention away from Uncle Hal and settled it on Fletcher. 'Had Anna managed to come home her father would have made her life miserable and yours, too, I suspect.'

No one spoke. It was as if his grandmother walked in the past for a moment.

Then with a smile, she looked at Uncle Hal. 'Oh, I did miss her with every breath, but I prayed that she would not come under her father's control again. You, Mr Holloway, did me the greatest kindness.'

'It is true, sir.' Gracie smiled warmly at Uncle Hal. 'Were it not for you caring for them, they would have had no one. My brother-in-law's soul was taken by greed. A millionaire who was willing to turn his own child and grandchild away at the door…well, he was not a nice man.'

'You are our hero. I can say so now, seeing how wonderfully you raised our boy.' She squeezed Fletcher's hand.

It stunned him to hear it. Not about them calling his uncle a hero, but that his grandmother had referred to him as their boy. He had grown up not knowing they existed and yet all that time they had held him close to their hearts.

Second by second he felt a bond growing with these ladies he had only just met.

They were family. His bond with them was the same

as it had been with his father and his brother. They shared blood, if not history.

Only a year ago it had been just him and Uncle Hal. Now his family had grown in ways he had never expected.

A servant rolled in the tea cart, then went out of the room. Gracie poured tea. She filled Uncle Hal's dainty teacup, giving him a smile.

Wait! What sort of smile was that?

Eirene must have noticed it, too. She slid a sidelong glance at him, then winked.

Good, then, she had noticed. He had not got it wrong.

This silent communication between them was becoming second nature. In the moment, surrounded by love of every kind, he felt complete.

Uncle Hal might not, though. If he developed deep feelings for Auntie Gracie while they were in New York, it would be difficult for him to leave for home.

The seven of them spent the next two hours talking about his mother, mostly.

His mother-in-law and father-in-law told the ladies things that made them laugh and cry in turns.

When Uncle Hal told the story of how Anna learned to swab a deck and sing like a sailor doing it, his grandmother and his aunt laughed until they had to grab their sides.

His grandmother and his aunt also told him about his mother. At the end of it, he felt he knew her...not only shadowed parts he recalled of feeling loved by her.

Another thing he knew was that it was going to be gut-wrenching to say good bye to his American family.

He was not nearly ready to. He had only begun to love them.

'How long will it be before your ship leaves New York?' Auntie Gracie asked, the question directed at his uncle.

'A week.' Uncle Hal appeared as sorry as Fletcher was.

'What do you think, Gracie? Can we be packed in time?' Grandmother asked.

'Since we started two weeks ago, I think it can be managed.'

What? They meant to—

'You are coming to Warrenstoke?'

'But of course. Auntie Gracie and I have missed enough of your life as it is. When the great-grandchildren begin to arrive, we do not wish to miss it.'

'We will not lose another second.' His aunt was looking at his uncle when she said so.

Warrenstoke—September 1st, 1876

'They look happy,' Eirene said, thinking that Fletcher's grin might split his face.

In her opinion there was nothing better than seeing the joy on the faces of a bride and groom in the second after the minister pronounced them man and wife.

She remembered when it happened to her and Fletcher. A kiss and a new family born.

Lord and Lady Warrenstoke.

Fletcher...rather like a dream come true.

She would remind him of it when she had the chance. For now it was all about the bride and groom.

'I've never seen my uncle kiss a woman before.'

'He's doing a splendid job, I would say.'

He shook his head. 'It's odd.'

'It is not odd. It is wonderful.'

'For us it was.' Fletcher did not seem convinced the same should be true for his uncle and Aunt Gracie.

'For them, too. Don't you remember how special the first married kiss was?'

He slid his gaze away from the newlyweds, let it settle on her in the look which invited her to rush upstairs to their chamber.

'I remember it. What I was thinking about was...' his voice went deep, like the deep rumbling purr of huge cat '...what would come later on.'

One would think she would get used to feeling like soppy inside, but she had not. Nor did she ever wish to.

'Look at them. They are in love. I hope they have every blessing that we do.'

'Well, you are right. I wish everyone that. Its only thinking of my uncle that way seems wrong.'

She gave him a jab in the ribs with her elbow and laughed.

'Do not think of him, then. Think of us.'

There went his dimple. There went her heart.

His hand snatched hers.

'Where are we going?'

'To the hill. Do remember what I said? What we would do up there after we were wed?'

'Have long conversations?'

He patted her bustle. Frowned at layers of fabric which was in the way of what she knew was on his mind.

With everyone involved in the reception for Uncle Hal and Auntie Gracie they were sure not to be interrupted in what they had to 'say' to one another.

'I'm trying to sort out what sort of relative Gracie is to you now. There are different ways of seeing it,' she said while they crossed the meadow.

Reaching the top of the hill, they sat and watched at the celebration.

The vows had taken place on the front steps of Warrenstoke in a small but joyful ceremony.

From up here she saw her mother walking down the steps without having to hold her father's arm for support. She had gone up on her own, too.

Eirene no longer read to her mother in the mornings because she, Auntie Gracie and Grandmother were now fast friends who enjoyed spending time in the garden each morning.

'What shall we talk about?' Fletcher asked.

He lay back in the grass, drawing her down on top of him.

I have wanted to do this for the longest time, his smile said.

She looked at his mouth, traced his bottom lip with the tip if one finger. 'So have I.'

He grabbed a handful of her skirt, 'You have too many clothes on.'

She reached down and took off a shoe. She arched a brow and he grinned.

Not for long, was what she took his groan to mean.

He rolled and took her with him. Then he plucked a long blade of grass, tickled her nose with it, then drew it slowly down her throat.

Life with you is fun, his dimple said.

She clasped her arms around the back of his neck, drawing him down for a kiss. 'You are my dream come true.'

She had no doubt he would read the message in her eyes. They had become so attuned with one another that words were not always necessary.

'And you dreamed me here to a life I never would have expected, my darlin'.' His breath skimmed her mouth. 'Plucked me right off the deck of my ship and me not even aware of it happening.'

'Ha! You only half believe it. The choice was yours.'

His fingers worked at the buttons at the neck of her dress.

'I would choose your dream again, a thousand times over.'

* * * * *

If you enjoyed this story, make sure to read
Carol Arens's The Rivenhall Weddings trilogy

Inherited as the Gentleman's Bride
In Search of a Viscountess
A Family for the Reclusive Baron

And why not check out one of her other great stories?

To Wed a Wallflower
'A Kiss Under the Mistletoe'
in A Victorian Family Christmas
The Viscount's Christmas Proposal

COMING NEXT MONTH FROM

(H) HARLEQUIN
HISTORICAL

All available in print and ebook via Reader Service and online

A ROGUE FOR THE DUTIFUL DUCHESS (Regency)
by Louise Allen

Sophie will do anything to protect her son and his inheritance. Even ask distractingly handsome rogue Lord Nicholas to retrieve her late husband's diaries before their contents bring down the monarchy!

HIS RUNAWAY MARCHIONESS RETURNS (Victorian)
by Marguerite Kaye

Oliver, Marquess of Rashfield, is society's most eligible bachelor. Except he's already married! Conveniently wed years ago, he and Lily have built separate lives. Only now she's returned...

SECRETS OF THE VISCOUNT'S BRIDE (Regency)
by Elizabeth Beacon

When her sister begs for help stopping her arranged marriage, Martha pretends to be Viscount Elderwood's bride-to-be. She soon discovers there's more to the viscount than she'd been led to believe...

A MANHATTAN HEIRESS IN PARIS (1920s)
by Amanda McCabe

New York darling Elizabeth Van Hoeven has everything...except freedom. But now Eliza's traveling to study piano in Paris and falling for jazz prodigy Jack Coleman in the process!

BOUND TO THE WARRIOR KNIGHT (Medieval)
The King's Knights • by Ella Matthews

As the new wife to stoic knight Benedictus, Adela finds herself in a whole new world. Their union is one of convenience, though her feelings for the warrior are anything but...

GAME OF COURTSHIP WITH THE EARL (Victorian)
by Paulia Belgado

American heiress Maddie enlists Cameron, Earl of Balfour, in a game of pretend courtship to win suitors. But now Cameron—who has sworn off love—is the only man she craves.

YOU CAN FIND MORE INFORMATION ON UPCOMING HARLEQUIN TITLES, FREE EXCERPTS AND MORE AT HARLEQUIN.COM.

HHCNM0223

HARLEQUIN
PLUS

Try the best multimedia subscription service for romance readers like you!

Read, Watch and Play.

Experience the easiest way to get the romance content you crave.

Start your **FREE TRIAL** at
<u>www.harlequinplus.com/freetrial</u>.